THE INFINITE INFINITE

BOOK 1 OF THE FEMININA SERIES

M.K. Williams

Copyright © 2019 by Mary K. Williams

All rights reserved. This book or any portion thereof may not be reproduced or used in any manner whatsoever without the express written permission of the publisher except for the use of brief quotations in a book review. The use of any of my works in AI learning or NFT is prohibited.

Printed in the United States of America

Publisher: MK Williams Publishing, LLC
Library of Congress Control Number: 2019911184

ISBN-13:
978-1-7333929-0-7 (Paperback)
978-1-7333929-1-4 (Hardcover)

Mary K. Williams
2333 Feather Sound Drive, A607
Clearwater, FL 33762
1mkwilliams.com

Cover Image Credit: Adobe Stock

All Persons Fictitious Disclaimer:

This book is a work of fiction. Any similarity between the characters and situations within its pages and places or persons, living or dead, is unintentional and co-incidental. Any names used that happen to match the name of a real person is either coincidental or intended as a compliment.

Interior design by FormattedBooks

Other Works by MK Williams

FICTION
The Feminina Series
The Alpha-Nina

The Project Collusion Series
Nailbiters
Architects

Other Fiction
The Games You Cannot Win
Enemies of Peace

NON-FICTION
Self-Publishing for the First-Time Author
Book Marketing for the First-Time Author
How to Write Your First Novel: A Guide for Aspiring Fiction Authors

Dedication

To Jason – You are my constant

Table of Contents

For those accustomed to a linear story told in only one universe, below you'll find a linear table of contents. For those aware that you can be in two places at once and can accept that each of these events occurred at the same time, there is a non-linear table of contents.

The order of how things happened:

Table of Contents

PART 1

I've come to find that traveling the multiverse produces the same effect as a gnarly hangover induced by tequila, very distinct from one brought on by wine or whiskey. I have some experience with the former, more with the latter.

The first time I crossed the Plain, I didn't even know that I had made such a significant leap. I woke up in the bed that I had shared with Parker. Only it wasn't the bed that we had shared, at least not the one I was familiar with. For the annals of science, I have been meticulously documenting my experiences. This is how it began:

A

August 8, 2018

This isn't my bed. Those words appeared inside Nina's skull almost instantly as her eyes opened and the consciousness of the day settled upon her. The sheets were bright white and felt fresh on her skin, not the ones that she had fallen into the previous evening. No, she was sure that she had crashed onto the pink paisley sheets that were the last remnant from her college days. Parker had teased her about them at first, but he got used to them and she doubted he would have excused himself from their evening activities because of them. Last night was no different.

What had happened last night? A healthy meal, maybe. Definitely too much to drink. The bright daylight poured in through the half-opened blinds in the most unforgiving manner. Her hand flew up to her head to shield her sensitive eyes, bullied by a splitting headache and alcohol-induced dehydration. Or so she assumed.

"Hey there, sleepyhead," Parker cooed as he entered the room. He had a glass of water in one hand, the other folded over; she guessed there was a painkiller in there for her.

Nina groaned in response.

"I figured as much," he said sweetly and handed her the medicine. She gulped down all of the water selfishly. *Did Parker have a hangover; did he want any water?* Nina didn't ask because at that moment she genuinely didn't care. Anything to stop the pounding in her head.

She was also coming to realize that while she did not wake up in her own bed, she didn't wake up in Parker's either. He decorated his bachelor pad in deep dark blues and greens with some trekkie movie posters taped to the wall. This sleek and elegant room with clean lines and a king mattress with a pillow top was comfortable beyond anything Nina had ever experienced. Although, perhaps the leftovers of her intoxication were simply trying to compel her body to sleep in.

It wasn't a hotel room. In spite of the plush bedding, she was sure of it. The bedframe pushed up against the window, the harsh light unimpeded as it headed for her eye line. Every hotel she'd ever stayed in had blackout curtains and the beds solidly against the wall. That practice never made any sense to Nina; people could still hear the happenings in the adjoining room.

Nina sat up slowly. Parker continued to dress; he didn't seem to be as groggy and hungover as Nina. A bit of memory trickled into her mind. They had gone out to dinner and then to the new tapas bar around the corner from their subway stop last night. She couldn't recall why they had been out celebrating, or how much they had, or when they got… not home, *here* she guessed. She wanted to ask questions, but she also wanted silence.

Parker had been jovial the previous evening, excited as though he was on the edge of something. Nina had been worried that he planned to propose, as though his grand plan to end their new pattern of bickering was marriage. And then he was sweet and caring this morning. She tried to not be bitter and sarcastic, even in her internal thoughts. She knew that caustic material would seep out in her words and given how kind he had been, she didn't want to appear ungrateful. They had gone a full two weeks without fighting and she didn't want to be the one to spoil it because of a wretched hangover. Nina knew herself; she already felt grouchy and irritable because of the headache. Her stomach turned; she was hungry in the meanest sort of way.

"I'm going to shower," Nina announced. Parker was more interested in the buttons on his shirt than anything that she had to say at the moment. She hoped that the water would help her head, both the ache and her splotchy memory, all inconsistent and irritated from whatever alcohol she had consumed.

"Go for it, Sweetie. You're already a little late as is, so you might as well enjoy the morning." Parker pecked her on the cheek as he strolled out of the bedroom, adjusting his tie along the way. He was very chipper and unusually non-verbal, almost intentionally brief. *What, no diatribe that my behavior today would become a pattern of tardiness that would lead to fewer raises and therefore one-day cause me to become a penniless beggar or some other doomsday scenario?*

Ack, that putrid cynicism. She had to push it back. The mental processes were working painfully slow that morning and had finally caught up and pushed the vitriol to the side.

"Wait! I'm late, what time is it!?" Suddenly every cell in her body was awake. She glanced at the clock on the bedside table. An artsy analog clock with four hashes on the 15s and nothing in between. Clearly, this was something that neither she nor Parker would have selected. Parker had a binary clock in his apartment and he always got a chuckle when Nina would try for a full sixty seconds to decode it before giving up and just checking her phone. Nina had a digital clock, because for all the benefits bestowed upon her by the parochial schools she attended, some rudimentary skills had been omitted in favor of new technologies like personal computers and typing. Granted, the latter had benefited her greatly in her career. But she felt like a complete dolt for not being able to read an analog clock as though it were a second language. She always had to double check in her head a few times that she read it correctly and even then, she would peek at her phone to check.

Nina's brain was in no state to try and decipher this minimalist art piece masquerading as a clock. She lunged for her phone, quietly charging on the nightstand. It felt thinner in her palm, as though she had to squeeze it a bit tighter to keep it from sliding out. She swiped across the screen to unlock it and saw the time. 7:45

"Crap!"

It was Wednesday. She had a weekly staff meeting every Wednesday morning at 8:00 sharp. Nina opened her texts to the most recent messages, ignoring the other alerts and reminders that scrolled along the top of her phone. The first text message in her history was from Carol, her cube-mate. "You coming in today?" Nina pinged her to let Carol know she would be tardy and asked if she could cover for her in the meeting.

Nina quickly undressed while she listened to Parker moving about downstairs, water running on and off, cabinets sliding open and closed.

"Hey Parker!" she called out, hoping to catch him before he strolled out for the day.

Nina's phone buzzed.

"Of course! Happy to!" Carol responded. Nina could always count on her. Nina smiled as she pushed the notification away and headed into the bathroom, conveniently located off the bedroom. It was an intuitive location for it to be, but it still shocked her that she had located it so effortlessly.

"Yes?" Parker asked from behind her. She spun around to see him perched at the doorframe.

"Where are we?" Nina asked in a mild tone. She didn't want it to sound like she had forgotten whatever romantic gesture had brought them to this location. "I definitely drank too much last night; can you help with the details?"

He smiled and approached her. As she stood half-naked in this strange room, the act of his peck on the forehead reassured her. "It's okay. We're good," he said with a wink before he turned to leave the room.

Uh oh. She must have said something horrible or spurned his advances the night before. All Nina had learned from that brief exchange was that she had to start working at fixing things between them before he ran out of steam. She had noticed his increased efforts to make things better two weeks earlier when he arrived home with a bouquet of scarlet roses and his usual churlish remarks had ceased. *Could two weeks erase months of bickering? Wasn't there something once said about love not keeping a scorecard?*

Her brain worked rapidly to try and sort every piece of information coming in, all while battling a nasty headache. Essential activities won out for the moment and she focused on getting cleaned up.

The impeccable design carried into this room with neutral tones, carefully positioned succulents, and heated floor tiles. She fiddled with the knobs for a moment or two trying to figure out if up or down meant on and which one turned the distinct jets from a drought to a torrent. The shower was hot and steady. The separate jets that hit her upper and lower back were soothing, enough so that she almost forgot that she was in a strange bathroom. Almost.

She found the bottle of shampoo, conditioner, and body wash were all high quality. She assumed this was another one of the benefits of staying in a gig-economy rental, the logical conclusion she had reached as she pieced together the few clues she had to work with. If only she could remember what happened last night. *A naughty staycation night at an upscale apartment to escape our usual routine, perhaps?* An unusual idea, but at least Parker tried something new.

She emerged from the shower; yesterday's dirt cleaned away. Annoyingly, the hot water and steam did little to assuage her headache. Nina moved to put her clothes back on. She would have to go home and change. Parker sat waiting for her in the bedroom when she got out of the shower. "Feeling any better?" His face was as hopeful as his question. His large brown eyes looking up at her, puppy-dog eyes if there ever were a pair. His brown hair swept to the side, hair gel holding it in place, for now; it usually fell across his forehead into his eyes by the end of the day. The stubble that played with the idea of banding together into a beard had been cleared away; Parker's scruff from the day before shaved clean.

"Slightly," Nina shrugged as she started to turn the clothes that she had strewn on the floor right-side out.

"You could always skip out today. Go back to bed, rest, relax. You work too hard anyway," he stood as he said this and opened the closet on the far side of the room. He grabbed a set of polished black shoes. It was at this moment she noticed that Parker had dressed much nicer than usual. His days were spent in a theoretical physics lab. Jeans, Converse sneakers, and a black tee with some scientists-only joke printed on it was his standard uniform. *Did he have a presentation today? Should she have remembered that?*

"That would be nice," she answered as though she were some artificial intelligence, having found the appropriate response that required no custom linguistic flare or personalization. That would be nice, something any person or robot could spit out on command.

"I could stay with you," he looked up at her with a hopeful suggestion in his eyebrows.

"I wouldn't want you to skip out on work today; you've got important things going on." *Wow, said like a genuinely supportive girlfriend.* Nina amazed herself at her ability to be compassionate in response to his kindness. To mirror his sweetness with her own. Is that how couples were able to stay together for so long, following the path that their partner laid for them? I smile, you smile. I scream, you scream. A self-fulfilling prophecy either way.

She noticed as Parker donned his 'fancy' shoes, that the closet was indeed well stocked. Parker had helped himself to the shoes. *Had he stored them there last night?* She must have looked like she had a seizure after eyeing the clothes for too long.

"A closet full of nothing to wear again?" he asked in a mocking tone.

"What? No. I like my clothes," she answered in a playful tone, being mock-defensive of his jibe.

"Well, get dressed then. I don't think the dress code has changed in your office," he gestured with his open hand to the closet.

The fabrics were familiar in spite of their novelty. The colors were pleasing to her eye, as though she had already curated this selection. At that point in the morning, Nina had accepted that she was in the throes of an extremely vivid and uncharacteristically lifelike dream. This was the only logical conclusion that her brain could arrive at. What else could explain everything?

Her dreams were usually flashes of macabre scenes between infinite darkness. The images in her mind were always dark at the edges, blurred, not quite clear. While she would occasionally find herself in a familiar place or with a familiar person in a dream, the absurd would always spill in. Perhaps whatever drinks were still working their way through her liver and kidneys were delighting her thalamus and cortex with this cinematic fantasy.

A good day with Parker, although that happened more often now, an expertly designed apartment with plush and luxurious trappings, a full closet of clothes that would make her look more polished than she could ever pull off. This must be a dream.

Sure. Let's indulge.

She dressed and twirled, savoring each additional minute of her tardiness. This was dreamland after all. Parker approved and they waltzed downstairs together.

It was a good thing Nina had accepted that she was dreaming or the myriad of framed professional photos of their faces on the walls would have alarmed her. Photographs she had no memory of ever posing for.

The décor fit neither of their tastes, further confirmation that this was not their home. They didn't even live together technically, although they spent most nights at her place. The subject had been broached months earlier but hadn't resurfaced. Perhaps his recent changes sparked some hope in her unconscious mind that they would move in together and that unspoken wish manifested into this very dynamic dream.

She gathered her tailored satchel and a set of keys to this dream house. Standing on the front steps, Nina recognized where they were immediately. They were on 28th Street NW, a brief walk for Parker to get to work and a significantly reduced commute for herself as well. Her apartment, in the waking world, was in the City Center and required a metro ride between two decent walks in the rain, sleet, snow, or heat.

Happy to stay in this dream for a bit longer, they parted peacefully and she went on her way. It was only as she crossed into her office building that Nina realized that she had left her phone behind. Oh well, as long as her hyper-realistic dream continued, she wouldn't fret.

Nina wound her way through the cube maze after she exited the elevator. Without her phone, she wasn't sure of the hour, but assumed that the morning meeting had already ended. Better to miss the whole thing than come in at the end. She found Carol at her desk working diligently. Her posture perfect, her clothes demure and stylish, her hair sleek and pretty. Her small hands were making quick movements across the keyboard, converting the keystrokes into intelligible commands at a speed that seemed improbable.

Nina plopped down in the rolling chair at her cube, the one directly across from Carol's. "I made it," she said in an exasperated gasp, letting the weight of her body push the chair back slightly. Carol spun around to greet her, as was their routine.

"Hey, glad you made it in. Are you feeling okay?" Nothing seemed out of place here, except Nina might have expected some jibe about being late or sleeping in. But, as long as she was in the dream world, she could let a few things slide.

"Yes," Nina replied automatically. Her headache surged at that moment as if it were insulted that it didn't warrant consideration. "Well no," she elaborated. "I have a rough headache, but I'm hoping it will pass."

"Oh no," Carol offered. Their usual banter felt stifled, cut short. Something was off. Nina expected the dream to break up with the appearance of a 20-foot squid or some other Lovecraftian monster. Instead,

Sonali, one of the team's new designers, interrupted them. She appeared at the cube wall with a mug of hot coffee.

"Hi, Nina!" Sonali said with a cheerful smile, her thick and shiny hair framing her face and accentuating her grin. Sonali's sweet greeting was a little too loud for Nina's head to handle. But Sonali couldn't have known that and Nina didn't want to take that out on her.

"Hi, Sonali!" Nina mirrored her.

"Do you need anything else, Nina?" Carol asked, a concerned look on her face.

"No, I'll just get to work." Nina spun the chair around slowly, she figured it would be best to let the two of them have their conversation. *Had she somehow offended Carol and didn't remember it?* That might account for her polite but cool interaction. With this being a dream, perhaps her unconscious needed to warn her about potentially harming her friendship with Carol.

As Nina faced the desk, she quickly became aware that nothing was the same as it had been when she left the previous evening. The set-up was off, the frames contained unfamiliar photos of a family, an Indian family. This was Sonali's desk and Nina had been looking at it for too long to pretend that this was all a joke, playing at using someone else's desk. She got up and headed towards the hallway. Nina forced herself to walk slowly, ambling past the cubicles so that she might catch her name tag or a familiar photo as she passed. For a dream this felt tedious. The minutiae were never this pronounced in any dream she had ever experienced before.

Finally, Nina found her name. It wasn't on her right where the rows and rows of cubicles lined up. It was on the left, affixed to the door of an office. Nina peered in and found a photo of her and Parker, a copy of one that hung on the wall of the apartment she had seen earlier in the dream. The décor felt muted, calm. There was an array of post-it notes threatening to lose their spot on the computer monitor, throwing the entire milieu into disarray, or perhaps giving it some life.

In this dream, she was an executive. This direction of the dream took an interesting turn, perhaps this would be a very nice dream; it fed all of her ambitions. A happy, healthy relationship. A successful career. Her dreams were never so linear or direct, never so pronounced. They had always been oblique, requiring further introspection. Most dreams were to be avoided, forgotten at all costs.

She settled into the desk and went through the motions of starting the computer, sorting files, all the while waiting for an oversized bee to walk into the office and demand a report on honey. Or something, dream-like. Nightmare-like.

Carol popped into the office and asked if she wanted a recap on the morning meeting. Nina acquiesced and Carol detailed some of the latest projects. "There's been a lot piling up for the past few days, but I told the team it was a family matter. I'm hoping everyone will be too polite to say anything. If you need something, just let me know." Carol expressed her compassion through her words, although they were undercut by a mild touch of irritation. So, Nina was returning from an extended period away from the office. Carol likely needed to cover for her with no notice. A family matter, perhaps this little detail would turn the dream into a nightmare. Some horrible loss.

Nina's mind flashed on a memory, distant, not as exacting as it used to be. Perhaps this was about to morph into her previous nightmare, the one that had hunted her down and stolen her rest for years. But that didn't happen. Instead, Carol left with the promise that she would continue to fend off questions about her time out of the office. Nina looked at the neatly piled stack of form envelopes on the far side of the desk.

In the orderly desk tray of small supplies, she found a thick-handled letter opener. Nina always viewed this as the butter knife of the office. She was used to ripping letters open with her fingers. Her clean and pristine dream world was not about that. She decided to use her usual method, the waking-Nina method.

The first letter appeared to be a direct mail appeal from a database vendor that had been after their corporate business. She inserted her index finger into the gap and slid.

And then she felt it. The exacting edge drawing across the delicate skin of her finger. A sharp and thin cut left a bright red line on the knuckle. She winced and immediately, reflexively touched it to her mouth to stem any blood.

She had a pain reflex. She tasted the copper of the cut, the small bit of blood that leaked from the surface. She bent the knuckle and felt the sting.

Wake up, wake up, wake up.

She forced her eyelids closed and tried to come out of this dream. She knew that her brain could do many things, but the pain, the taste, all of it shouldn't have been possible. She stood up and headed for the bathroom, something the waking Nina would have done right away to fetch a bandage.

On her way out of the office, she crashed into Derek, who in her waking world had been a top-level director, but here he seemed to be moving to his cubicle. The jolt sent her falling to the ground.

That should have woken me up. Without fail, every time she fell in a dream, she woke immediately. *There was a term for that, right? A hypnic spasm? Or is that when you are falling asleep?* She couldn't remember clearly because of the panic starting to set in. There she was, still on the thin and poorly patterned carpet of the office. Derek stood over her, apologizing profusely and extending his hand to help her up. The headache, the paper cut, the tumble.

This wasn't a dream. This was somehow real. The first of over a thousand questions began to flood her mind.

1

2 Weeks Earlier

The lights flickered for a moment, but Nina didn't even blink. She finished organizing the random files that accumulated on her desktop over several years with the agency. An image for a client here, a CSV file of some report there. Her desktop background had been a sunrise view of the Grand Canyon. It had been one of her favorite photos of the monument, taken by a professional, of course. The reds in the sky at dawn shot out in all directions and highlighted the sandstone just beginning to awaken for the day, ready to continue the slow and arduous process of eroding into the Colorado River.

Her errant files had formed a grid pattern of icons to cover the entire image across both monitors. The files were nice and orderly until she realized that the one in the top left corner actually contained a pile of files on top of files. It was 4:50 pm that afternoon when she noticed this issue.

"I'll be a little late this evening. A big project just came up." She shot off a text to Parker and started to identify the files and put them into obliquely labeled folders. "Personal" for insurance documents and memos from HR on annual PTO allotments. "Images" for the array of graphics that she had used at one time or another over the past several years in various campaigns. "Reports" for everything from traffic and attribution metrics to basic accounting of the one work trip she took to a conference the previous year. As she pulled icons from the top, they all started to dance, realigning to make room for the icons that had been stacked on each other. By 5:30 they stopped adjusting, meaning that she had almost reached the end of her task. After another 30 minutes, she was done. Now only those three folders sat in the corner of the screen, leaving her view of the Grand Canyon unobstructed.

She meandered to the metro station and heard the train approaching as she scanned her card. The man behind her nearly knocked her over as he ran to catch it before the doors closed. He made it. Nina watched with apathy as the train rolled away, content to wait for the next to come along.

She checked her phone, no message from Parker.

Figures. As if the universe dared her to be frustrated, the lights went out. *It could get worse.* The metro station was black as pitch, none of the ambient light that she would have expected to come in from the above ground streetlights snuck in. There had been the occasional summer brown-out from the energy grid being overloaded with excess A/C usage. But this one felt different, more menacing. As though a poltergeist or rogue monster had devised this blackout to trap her, terrify her, kidnap her.

She tried to look from left to right, but it was all black. She didn't dare rise up from the bench for fear of tripping and falling on the tracks.

Nina hadn't realized how quiet it was without any power on until it came whirring back to life. The fluorescent lights blinkered and thankfully, the walls had the same graffiti as usual. No new menacing messages scrawled out on the tiled walls to warn or taunt her. No horror movie like scenarios, just the DC metro.

She was about to get up and leave the station, opting to walk home and waste her train fare when she felt a buzz in her hand. As if he could sense her frustration, Parker had sent her a message.

"Hey, are you okay? Getting late, text me to let me know you're okay."

Nina double-checked the number to make sure it was Parker. Wow, this was a first. Not that he hadn't expressed concern over her working late before, but usually it stemmed from his own inconvenience of having to wait to eat dinner or his annoyance at having prepared a meal that went cold by the time she got home.

Nina had campaigned hard for a promotion, arriving early and leaving late for eight months. During that time, she received perfect responses from client surveys and brought in two six-figure accounts. When her boss resigned, she thought she was a shoo-in for the replacement. Nina prepared her resume so that she could apply for the internal posting, though she secretly hoped that she would just be awarded the position. When her new boss was announced in a staff meeting without any job being posted, Nina was crushed. She hadn't worked late since that happened a few months earlier. It was around this same time, she started avoiding Parker. She had finally stepped up and put herself out there, she really tried for it, but she failed. She didn't want to hear Parker tell her that she needed to go back and finish her degree or that she needed to apply herself. Nina didn't want to be the loser girlfriend anymore, she felt that she was meant for more.

Perhaps it was that they had both settled into the routine of her leaving work at 5 on the dot. Perhaps it was the lazy way that they had both defaulted to dining and sleeping at her place because it was closer to the University for Parker. Perhaps it was the feeling that she would be locked in her current position forever, doomed to be a mid-level manager in a mid-level relationship for all time. Nina had used up her goodwill with the world when she had-

She stopped herself from going there. The train arrived, noisily pulling into the station, the rails below starting to hum. She shot a quick auto-text to Parker. "On the train."

It was perfunctory and it was true. She wasn't even sure if the message would get through the thick steel and concrete above her.

Nina spent the minutes on the metro trying to get her head right. She felt grumpy, dissatisfied, and maybe she had been fooling herself that she was happy for a long time. Nina either needed to commit to the role of happy girlfriend or split. In light of that dilemma, she couldn't see herself continuing to smile through Parker's paternalistic lectures on what she should be doing with her life, or his condescending man-splaining of things she already knew about, or his quick dismissal that she wouldn't be able to understand his work. Hadn't he been attracted to her ability to keep up with him?

This was it; this was the moment Nina had been avoiding because she didn't want to be on her own again. But she wasn't afraid of being alone anymore. She was afraid of being stuck in her current reality: crappy job, crappy boyfriend, crappy mood.

The doors opened and she marched off the metro car, up the stairs, and out of the station. She had to do this while she still had the nerve. Nina rehearsed in her mind what she would say to Parker the second she got in the door. No 'hello', no 'how was work', no chit chat. She needed to dive right into the fact that she wasn't happy anymore, and she suspected that he wasn't either.

Nina had plotted her words and the anticipated first responses as she approached the door to her apartment. The key went into the lock, the door opened and so did her mouth. She needed to get it out right now, the words felt like bile looking to escape her body.

But she choked them back down. She looked at the number on the door again, a metallic "8" screwed on above the peephole. This was the right apartment; the door unlocked with the key on her chain. The view in front of her didn't align with what she had grown accustomed to over the past few years.

For starters, the lights were off and there were several clusters of white candles lit on the kitchen counter and then on the dining room table. And there sat a bucket of sparkling wine chilling between two perfectly polished place settings. Hiding in the shadows that the candles cast, the petals of red roses invited her fingertips to reach out and touch them.

This was new, this was a surprise. Parker closed the door behind her, Nina hadn't noticed that he had moved closer. When the door latched, she jumped a little, startled by the sound. "Welcome home honey!" he cooed in her ear. All of her gumption evaporated. She couldn't break up with him when he just put together this romantic display. She convinced herself this was the start of a new era for them. Not seeing it for what it really was, the final implosion before they would be repelled from each other with a great violent force.

B

August 8, 2018

Nina burst out of the elevator and ran for the front entrance of the building in swift and inelegant motions. She couldn't think straight. If this wasn't a dream, then where was she? The people and most of the places were familiar. If she wasn't asleep, then perhaps this was an elaborately orchestrated prank. But to what end? *What was the punchline here?*

It was on her way out of the office and over to Parker's lab that she started to take notice of all the things around her. Different in subtle ways, almost imperceptible if the adrenaline and fear were not drawing every fine detail into sharp focus.

Every street was litter free. A surprise and a welcome reprieve from the usual hopscotch of dodge the crushed beer cans and sidestep the overflowing garbage that she usually had to handle, a part of routine city life.

And there were no homeless people on the sidewalks, shuffling their belongings as they passed the painful hours. Nina crossed clusters of homeless on her way to and from work each day, avoiding eye contact. She always observed when they were there, but there they weren't. And she noticed it.

The streets weren't lined with parked vehicles, and the street traffic was light except for bicycles on the wider than usual bike-lane. The advertisements on the few buses and taxis she saw, the billboards in the distance, had all changed overnight. Instead of glamorous models, they all featured products with a solid color background. No beautiful eyes to watch her as she passed along, silently casting their judgment on her fashion choices. This wouldn't have caught her attention before, but now everything caught it.

It seemed like a steady stream of pedestrians were all intently focused on their smartphones, the blue light illuminating their faces in a ghoulish manner. No different from normal, except that these phones all had perfectly round circles on the back of them. This struck Nina as odd, where was the ubiquitous apple?

She walked briskly and crossed over Wisconsin Avenue, only it wasn't Wisconsin Avenue. Nina stopped once she reached the other corner and stared at the sign for a while. "E Roosevelt Avenue" the green and white sign proclaimed, perched atop the metal pole.

"East Roosevelt?" she mumbled aloud. *Am I even heading in the right direction?*

A man approached her, hovering in her periphery without her notice. Maybe it was only for a second, but she jumped when she realized that he was there. "Sorry to startle you, ma'am. Are you lost?"

He kept a respectable distance. His facial expression: knitted eyebrows, seeking eyes, mouth slightly open without any obvious smirk or grimace. He was genuinely trying to help her.

"I think I might be," she tried to play it cool. "I'm heading towards the University?" It sounded like a question when it came out, the usual up-speak that had always allowed her to put her defenses aside and accept help from a man.

"Yes, keep heading down this street here, O Street and you'll hit it in a few blocks," his arm signaled that she should continue down the road, continuing the route that had seemed intuitive before she stopped to question it.

"Okay, thank you," her hand went to her forehead, a sign that she felt bewildered, and a chance for her to try to keep her mind from spinning around the same frantic circle of problems.

"Of course, happy to help," the man, as forgettable as he was, started to head down Wisconsin Avenue, only the sign said Roosevelt.

"Excuse me, sir," she caught his attention before he stepped off the curb.

"O Street runs East-West, that's why taking this will get me right to the University, right?"

He nodded.

"Then why is the cross street East Roosevelt?" she pointed up at the sign. Not trying to suggest that he was wrong or anything, she was genuinely stumped. And in the span of time that she had realized that she was not dreaming, this detail momentarily became the object of her fixation. Not the bed she woke up in, or the office where she cut her finger. This street sign, her mind was hung up on it. It had to be important, right?

"Huh, you know I never thought about those tripping people up before. I guess most people see T Roosevelt or F Roosevelt and they know the initial isn't a direction."

"Ah," she nodded along. "So, E is for Eleanor then?"

"Yes, of course! Who did you think it was?" The man chuckled at her seemingly absurd question.

"No one, I thought it was East," she shrugged her shoulders feeling painfully dimwitted for not catching it sooner.

"Yep, all three Presidential Roosevelts are now memorialized with Avenues that run North-South throughout the city."

"Well, thank you for your help. I'll head this way down O Street."

He nodded and looked both ways before crossing the street and heading on his way. He was about his day when she started off down O Street. Three steps in and his words finally processed in her brain. *Three Presidential Roosevelts.*

"Wait, Eleanor Roosevelt wasn't ever President of the United States!" she wanted to call out to the stranger, but he was long out of hearing distance.

C

Nina tried to walk, but there was something about the still quiet of the long hallway to the lab that always made her want to break into a jog. Maybe it was the urge she always felt to barge in at the moment of an immense discovery, to become part of the story. *"And then, out of nowhere, Nina burst into the lab just as we discovered the Higgs-Boson!"* Although, she knew enough about what Parker studied to know that had already been discovered and he had nothing to do with it.

But, on this day, she wanted to break into a run because she had to find Parker. Even though they had hit a rough patch over the past couple of months, she still loved him. She still relied on his guidance, especially after everything she had seen already that day, she needed him. She needed to feel his arms around her and the gentle "it'll be okay" of his smoky voice filtering into her ears.

Nina willed her legs to move slower. She began to count in her head to force her footfalls to match that pace, a mental metronome. The hallway was usually bright white, the walls, the lights, the flooring all clinically free of any color. But the fluorescent bulbs in the middle of the corridor were always acting up, blinking out within a few weeks of being changed. Parker informed her of the running joke on the team to see how long they would last after each replacement. Eventually, they just stopped putting in maintenance requests.

Nina passed through "the dark spot", it always unnerved her, how quickly the illuminated hallways would be plunged into darkness with just a few bulbs out. As she cleared that portion of the hall, the lights flickered, giving her a strange sense of unease.

She finally reached the door to Parker's office. It was a small and stuffy room that he almost never used, most of his time was spent in the lab. Her eyes quickly confirmed that he wasn't there with the door closed and no light coming out of the gap at the bottom. She secretly enjoyed seeing his title on the door: Dr. Parker Lovett. She was so proud of him, which is what she said out loud. But what it really meant was that she was proud of herself for being worthy of his time. This genius of a man had deemed her worthy and thus she was satisfied with herself.

Next, she passed the closed office of his boss, Dr. Norman Thurston. His staff called him "Thirsty." Nina was sure there were other lewder nicknames that he had been afforded, but those were never officially mentioned to her.

During one of the dinners she and Parker had with Dr. Thurston and his wife, Nina caught him looking at her chest. And not that it would have been excused if they had been bigger, but she barely filled an A-cup. *What was he even looking for? And his wife was right there!* But he didn't leer or make any comments, he never tried to break the touch barrier by offering a hug at the end of the evening, so she shook it off. He's harmless. A man who can't help the impulse to look, but otherwise harmless.

Parker had been working with Dr. Thurston for the past seven years on something that Nina didn't quite understand. Parker had explained most of it on their second date. Over time she began to understand his work, but she needed a little help with the finer details. So, for the past three years, she told everyone she was dating a theoretical physicist and left it at that.

Nina pushed open the lazily hanging doors, so light and easy on their hinges, and moved into the lab. She could immediately sense that something was off. Dr. Thurston had leaned back against one of the long lab tables, his army green sweater slouched against the folds of his stomach, the fabric as loose and worn as the expression on his face.

Of the times that she had visited Parker in the past she had often encountered Dean Winchester in the hallways, or in the lab, or leaving Dr. Thurston's office. She was everyone's boss in her role as the Dean of the College of Arts and Sciences. As physics is a science, their team was nestled under her command. Dean Winchester was striking, she had piercing brown eyes and dark-as-night skin. She had enough fortune to be attractive, it was a fine line for a woman in science. Not pretty enough and she would be ignored, too pretty and she would have been disregarded. Dean Winchester had just the right balance of looks and brains. Her steely grey hair usually pinned back and her suits were well tailored and coordinated, but today her locks were twisted into thick braids covering her head. Her usual attire eschewed for a more business casual look. Nina never aspired to that kind of job, but she secretly hoped to age like her. Fine but not unattractive smile lines, a good mix of grey, white, and black hair, not too pronounced, dignified in a way.

Nina certainly noticed the tone that the men of science would use when they mentioned Dean Winchester. Their god-complexes were on full display as they complained about having to explain their research to someone who didn't even know the difference between quartz and a quark. Nina would always nod quietly when Parker would go on one of those rants. It was clear that he had more knowledge in the world of physics, but Dean Winchester had the business sense to find ways to keep the lab running, something that Parker never acknowledged. Nina even looked her up once, and discovered that she had led groundbreaking research on the use of chemical compounds in advancing psychiatric treatments. *Not too shabby.*

Nina sensed the tense mood in the lab as she walked in. Dean Winchester stood tall, her energy towering over Dr. Thurston. His posture hunched and uncertain, she had never seen the man who measured six foot six inches look so short next to the five-foot-eight inch woman.

The doors slapped shut behind her, they continued their noisy pattern until their energy expended and finally settled into stillness. Nina's presence elicited annoyed stares from Dean Winchester and Dr. Thurston. Parker, with his own posture hunched as he sat on one of the swiveling metallic stools that reminded Nina of high school chemistry class, leaned over to look past Dr. Thurston's paunch to see who had arrived.

"Feminina," Dean Winchester addressed her with a forced smile.

"Hello," she barely managed to choke out. No one ever called her by her full name.

Nina had hoped to catch Parker alone in the lab to make some sense out of everything her brain had failed to process. But she seemed to have stumbled into another riddle, she was in the thick of this new problem while still in disarray.

"Dr. Thurston, let's continue this conversation in my office," Dean Winchester didn't offer this as much as she commanded it. She turned on her heels and stalked past Nina on her way out. The doors swished loudly, back into the swing of things again. Dr. Thurston followed, moving his feet imperceptibly, trying to forestall what would surely be a rough conversation. But he had to face it, he was clearly in the middle of a grave 'talking-to.' Nina would feel bad for him if he hadn't so regularly second-guessed the Dean. She guessed Winchester had finally grown a spine and decided to put her foot down on some insane expenditure or delayed publication request.

After Nina heard the door flap once more, she checked behind her before rushing to Parker. He was taller than her, but his overly lean build made her feel like she could snap him whenever they hugged. She secretly thought this was the mark of a genius, his brain requiring so much additional energy and substance that his muscles could never develop beyond their basic functions. He wasn't scrawny, but he most certainly was not strong. Which is why Nina was so shocked to feel that his arms were heavier around her shoulders. They felt, *muscular. Had Parker started working out without telling her?*

"Hey there," he murmured as his hand caressed her back. Her thoughts on his arms evaporated. She didn't want to let go. She felt scared, and her headache continued to pound against her skull, and for all the times she had been too proud to let him care for her, she needed comfort.

"Parker, today has been absolutely crazy, and you know how when you are dreaming you can have these intense and very lucid dreams, but no matter what if you fall you wake up? Like no matter what happens in your dream, if you fall you have to wake up," she repeated. Her words were tumbling over each other, clamoring to get out, to cross that oral finish line before the next one. "Well I fell this morning and I didn't wake up, but I have to be dreaming because so many things are off. And I forgot my phone, so I couldn't just call and I'm sorry to barge in but I'm freaking out!" It all ran together like one word.

He nodded and his hand gently rubbed her shoulder. He took a deep breath and she mimed his action. Nina felt slightly calmer to just have him standing next to her.

"I'm surprised it took you this long to get here. I thought I was going to have to explain everything before my morning coffee."

Her face must have exhausted all of the emotion she had to offer, her vocal chords were paralyzed under the strain of the contortions she could feel on her forehead and cheeks. That was not the response she had expected. *There is an explanation for this?*

He eyed his surroundings; the lab was empty except for the computers and a large machine in the corner that had been in pieces the last time she had visited eleven months earlier. There was another section of the lab beyond the large plastic flaps that extended across the far wall. They reminded her of a warehouse backroom or the entryway to the kill floor of a meat-processing plant. Nina realized she was staring off, visually drifting away from the live-action of that moment with Parker.

"Come on, let's head home and we can talk there."

D

The tumbler clunked as the lock released and the front door opened with a whine. The tell-tale sign of a haunted house in decades of films, but it hadn't seemed haunted to Nina. If anything, it seemed to be elegant and chic.

Nina and Parker returned to the home she had awoken to that morning, having walked there in total silence. This was a conversation to have behind closed doors. The entire walk had been an exercise in self-control for Nina. Her mind played through every horrible scenario, she braced herself for the worst. Had she been in a coma and lost all of her memories? Did she have a tumor that pushed on some part of her brain, giving her a dazzling display of what reality could be?

Parker moved about the kitchen as he brewed a fresh pot of coffee and assembled a snack. Apparently, whatever explanation he had to deliver, it necessitated food and caffeine. Nina hadn't repeated her concerns as they made their way silently from the University. Do not pass go. Do not collect any contextual clues. Do not risk a scene in public.

The phone that she had forgotten to bring to work remained sitting on the white marbled counter, abandoned in her hurry to get out the door that morning. She saw the faint blue light at the top corner blinking. There were some missed calls and messages. They would have to wait a bit longer.

She scanned the kitchen and dining area. There were warm touches and decorative items delicately placed in each corner. The dark wood kitchen table was clear, no sign of bills or receipts or other scraps of paper that inevitably pile up. There was a spot on the far wall that looked slightly brighter than the rest around it, as though a picture had recently been taken down.

When the mugs were set down and Parker joined her at the breakfast counter, he began to speak.

"So, you know all about my work, right?" He reached down to touch her knee as he spoke. A subtle and effective technique for persuasion that she had read or heard about at one point or another.

"Yes," Nina defaulted. She knew it was theoretical physics. "Something to do with a guy named Nabokov."

"Novikov," he corrected. His words were curt; she should have known this by now. Nina should know this inside-out and backwards and forwards. She pushed her lips together, willing them to squeeze shut so tight that she could rewind a few seconds and really think on the name before blurting out the wrong one.

"So, that's been the latest focus with Thurston over the past few months. We think we proved one of his principles wrong. Or invalidated it to be exact, but for all intents and purposes, he was wrong." His face lit up; his shoulders began to pull back a bit. Nina could see it in his eyes that he was about to go into professor-mode, her name for when he would go on a very specific, very scientific tangent.

"I've proven that his self-consistency principle is unnecessary." His statement was so short and his look was so expectant. His eyebrows raised, his rueful grin, his head leaning towards her as though he was waiting for her to respond with a delighted jump.

"Awesome," Nina replied but her forced smile was too strained.

"Have I not explained this to you before?" This was a genuine question, not one of the usual sarcastic ones he would throw her way when she didn't follow along with his scientific commentary. Usually he would subtly criticize her for not being able to understand these principles, assuming they would go way over her head. Then if she ever didn't catch on, she would be given no opportunity for questions, just vacant nodding as Parker strayed further and further into the brambles of science that nicked and scraped at her limited knowledge.

"No, you haven't. At least not in any way that I could join in and have a conversation with you." Nina couldn't look at him as she said it. She knew this would ruin the goodwill that had been accumulating between them over the past few weeks. Calling him out like that.

"Hey," he waited for her eyes to meet his before he continued. "I'm sorry."

It seemed like it had been a long time since they had last locked eyes like this, their vulnerabilities laid bare. At that moment, it was like she was really seeing him for the first time. Nina wanted to hug him and say that she was sorry too. Nina was sorry that she had always compared him in her mind to someone he would never be. She suppressed it though, she didn't want to delay his explanation any further.

"Let me start from the beginning as best as I can. Have you heard about the theory where each decision that you are faced with, you actually choose?"

She searched her mind for something familiar. He must have noticed the blank look that she usually put on her face when she wasn't sure of an answer.

He gestured to the coffee cups next to them on the counter. "So, you have a choice every morning. Coffee, or no coffee."

"That's not a choice." Nina often tried humor to cover for her confusion. Parker chuckled. *He actually acknowledged one of her puns!* She tried to contain her self-satisfied smile as best as she could.

"Very true, but in general. Say tomorrow morning you decided to cut caffeine completely and only drank water. Your day starts sluggish and you are a little irritable from the caffeine withdrawal. You make some silly mistakes because of this and you come home at the end of the day grumpy."

"Okay, that makes sense." She sipped on the coffee in front of her, a reflex. Perhaps her tongue worried that it might never taste the bitter elixir again.

"But you also pick the coffee. You have a normal day with your usual energy and pep." Parker smiled in his 'ready for the lecture circuit' manner. It was rehearsed; he would practice social cues and niceties. It had helped him a lot, but his smile was still just a touch too smug at times.

"How can I pick both?" Nina asked, expecting that this was the correct follow-up question.

"This is one of several theories of the multiverse." His arms slowly spread to illustrate the vast size and possibilities of the term.

"The what?"

"So, we have this universe, this reality. But if our reality exists, then so could others. There are several running explanations for this. Of those articulated by Brian Greene —"

"That name is slightly more familiar, -" their conversational pattern of interjecting had commenced.

"Yeah, I've watched some of his Ted talks a million times. Of the potential multiverse theories that Greene has articulated, Thurston and I have been working on the quantum model. So, your morning decision of coffee or no coffee didn't take place in this universe. In this one you picked coffee. And in another one, you pick no coffee. The two don't interact. Hence, a paradox could not be created. And therefore, Novikov's principle is useless."

"This sounds like the plot to *Sliding Doors*." Nina blurted out.

"What?" Unfamiliar with not knowing something, Parker's face puckered with a question. The need for information souring his expression.

"The movie, with Gwyneth Paltrow. We watched this together." She tried to jog his memory; it had been a while since they had seen the film.

"Who?" Again, the indignant expression.

She reached for her phone to do a quick search for the actor's image. Only the results came up with a few newspaper articles from a local paper in Connecticut and a business magazine feature of up and coming CEOs. She switched over to images and the pictures matched, but there was only a handful of her. No movie posters, no red-carpet images, no iconic pink gown at the Oscars. "What?" she checked her spelling and Parker continued to elaborate.

"She isn't famous?" he seemed to be more scientifically curious than concerned about that lack of information.

"I don't get it. This isn't right." Nina wanted to slam the phone down on the counter, but it was marble and she had never lived in a home with such a surface and didn't know if it would shatter the screen. *And come to think of it,* "This isn't my phone either."

"No, that's your phone." Parker didn't blink as he said this, his spine straightened and he nodded his head like an obedient dog.

"No, it's not. It doesn't fit in my palm the right way. I thought it felt off this morning, but now I realize that was because it's not my phone. It's a little too narrow. And the icon on the back is a circle, not an apple."

She pointed to this small disc affixed to the phone, as though that would make her point self-evident.

Parker let out a deep sigh and reached for her hand. "You aren't in your reality, Nina. You are in a parallel universe to the one that you know. That's why things are similar enough. Same handsome boyfriend," he smirked, trying to get her to laugh. "Same city, the same company that you work for. But this one is much nicer for you. A better job, better home."

She opened her mouth to speak, but Parker wasn't done selling her on this place. "And a much better society. From what I observed in your reality; women are still maybe a century away from the parity that they experience here. That's why you are the director at your company here, and not a lowly analyst like you were back in that universe."

Nina looked around the room very slowly. This wasn't her home. She was in some other universe; she was an alien in this system. *Shouldn't this reality be fighting against me, as though I were a parasite?* Nina thought. Where were the white blood cells of this universe that would attack her and expel her from the system? Nina stood up, unsure of whether she needed to pace the kitchen or run down the street, but she needed to move. When she did, the blood and adrenaline in her system interacted and she actually, embarrassingly, fainted.

2

August 10, 2008

The pain in her skull was the first sensation that made Nina aware that she was awake. The thick smell was next. Heavy with cleanliness, the air stuffed with particles of solvents and solutions, dense with recycled ambient gases. The pillow that her head rested on felt dull and deflated. It was inadequate for the task, like the ones handed out on airplanes or in:

HOSPITALS

In the fraction of a second that it took her eyes to open, she recalled the last few moments of her memory. A replay on a VHS player, scrambled and whining, Nina saw these things fly through her consciousness:

Smash
Click
Punch
Scream
Kick
Darkness

The ceiling tiles above her were standard issue with white and grey flecks. Nina tried to move her head, to adjust it a bit, but her neck didn't move. Nina began to panic. She urged her limbs to flail.

Please don't let me be paralyzed, she thought.

"Hey, hey," the soothing and reassuring voice of her father called from out of her line of sight. "Nina, you're going to be okay."

Apparently, her efforts had resulted in some movement. His face appeared above hers, his white hair a mess and the usual stubble on his chin grown out into the beginnings of a beard. Seeing his face calmed her down. Maybe this was a bad dream and she would wake up back in her childhood bed, able to sneak into the kitchen for a late-night bowl of ice cream with her obliging father who never seemed to sleep.

Graciously, he adjusted the controls on the side of the bed and Nina found herself sitting upright. Her neck still immobilized, but Nina could see her feet wiggle beneath the thin sheets.

"They have your neck in a brace and a contraption keeping your head perfectly still against the bed." He read her mind, the way a good parent can, one that is in touch with their children. "It's a precaution," he stopped himself from elaborating further.

A man entered the room with his white coat, beaten down eyes, and bright orange-red hair and beard to deliver his prognosis. He gave a perfunctory physical assessment; her father provided no additional details, but said that the police would be visiting soon.

Nina followed the doctor's finger with her eyes; she looked directly at the thin light on the end of his ballpoint pen. She moved her arms and legs as instructed. She answered basic questions. *Who is the President?* Bush. *What year is it?* 2008. *What is your name?* Nina. *What is your father's name?* Xander Marks. *What city are you in?* Washington DC.

Then it was Nina's turn to ask. She regretted her question immediately. *What happened?* How basic and pathetic her voice sounded as she spoke those words. The answers were unstoppable and relentless. The information had been relayed quickly. She couldn't get them to stop or slow down. Just like the liquids being streamed into her veins through the connection in her hand.

Stuck in and taped to her skin, Nina couldn't stop that blend of medicine. It was already in her, just as the knowledge of the worst memory she would never recover was being forced into her ears. She couldn't stop it. She couldn't hold her hands to her ears to cover it, not with the cords and wires plugged into her. She couldn't ask them to stop talking when all she could do was listen, it was the only thing that she understood at that moment. Language, words. Nina's brain could convert those sounds into neural impulses and from there into concepts that she could register.

She had more questions, but her father said that he couldn't say any more until the police spoke to her. She didn't understand why, *had she done something*? Other than crumble under the force asserted upon her by a stranger's boot, she had no idea what the questions could be. Perhaps her father worried that his version would color her own narration.

Without asking for clarification, Nina understood that Hank was gone. The doctor had said that "you were both attacked," but he continued with "you were lucky to survive" implying that her companion, her best friend, her boyfriend (if a word as pedestrian as that could ever be applied to a soul mate), had not been so fortunate. The doctor, or a faceless nurse, or some mastermind behind the scenes at the charge desk, must have upped her pain killers because she felt a warm tingling across her face and chest as the pain in her head receded. It also pulled back the tears that were starting to wash into her eyes, like the tide being pulled back before the tsunami. The tears would indeed come, but at that moment, they were gone, now to become part of the torrent that would flood her eyesight, impair her judgment, and stain her face in the days and weeks to come.

The police were apparently already there, or they had arrived very quickly, waiting outside of her hospital room. Nina's father refused to leave her side. Neither her guardian nor legal counsel, he didn't have to be there, but she was glad that he stayed. They asked her for all that she could recall.

Nina told the story quickly. She and Hank had gone out to dinner at a new restaurant his coworker had recommended. It was out of their normal neighborhood so they decided to walk home and enjoy a stroll past storefronts and buildings that were foreign to them. It seemed to be a better option than poorly lit and sour-smelling metro cars.

They passed in front of a wide alley, more like a vacant lot. The space between buildings had been cast into the impenetrable darkness that often haunts such places.

Nina heard a bottle smash before she realized that someone had hit Hank across the head.

This person, unknown to them, a stranger, waved the sharp glass edge at them. He lunged at them quickly.

Nina felt a punch land in her gut.

"I thought we were being mugged, so I screamed to catch the attention of anyone within hearing range," she explained.

Doubled-over from the pain in her stomach, she felt a boot connect with her head and then nothing.

That was it; that was all she could remember. The police confirmed the particulars. Yes, Nina and Hank lived together. She squirmed a little under the hospital sheets. This was something that her father already knew, but to have two strange males inquire about it in front of him, it seemed wrong.

The men took their notes and told her that if she remembered anything else that she should reach out to them. They would be in touch in the coming weeks. One of them offered her a business card. After a fraction of a second, the officer directed it to her father. At least they made the gesture to offer it to her first.

They left and then her father told her what happened. They were attacked, Nina and Hank. The attack was interrupted by a group of men mid-stop on a bar crawl. Thankfully they were just drunk enough to be brave, but not too inebriated to be ineffective.

Nina wanted to ask for confirmation, but she couldn't form the words. "Is?" That was the best that she could muster.

"He cut 'em good. They did everything they could, honey," she saw his ancient and wise eyes water and it turned them from a stone-gray to a bright Caribbean ocean blue. Two things that Nina inherited from her father, the ability to offer platitudes in horrible situations and eyes that would experience drastic color changes. She remembered seeing his eyes get that way when she was little, when he would look at her mom's picture. But he must have stopped looking at it, or moved on, or he just did it in private now because she hadn't seen that color in a long time.

"How long?" She fought past the pain in her throat, the squeezing tension that made every second of this conversation excruciating.

He understood what she meant. How long had it been since it had happened? "A day, he hit your head really bad. That's why the doctors don't want you to move it just yet." The room felt confining, stuffy. He looked uncomfortable in the standard issue hospital chair. Nina thought the bulk frame was likely to cause spinal problems for anyone who sat in it. He reached forward in the chair, his hips at a horribly acute angle, but he did it to hold her hand. His calloused hands were gruff and reassuring. They had been that way as long as she could remember.

Nina found out a week later that the man who had murdered Hank and attacked her had tried to escape, and the group of men who stopped him literally sat on him until the police arrived. She found out at the same time that this man had been remanded to a psych ward, ranting and raving. She also found out his name, Gus Blanity.

Nina found out three months later that the prosecution would not call her to the stand to testify. They told her it was because she had blacked-out and therefore all of her testimony would be easy to discredit.

She found out nine months later, at the beginning of the trial, that the defense planned to argue that Nina had attacked Hank of her own volition and that Mr. Blanity was only trying to stop her. Thankfully, the men who came to their defense were able to testify to the contrary.

She found out a year later that her heart was still broken even after "justice had been served" to Mr. Blanity, because Hank was still gone. No amount of time on Blanity's sentence would ever bring Hank back to her.

She found out 14 months later that her dad had cancer and they were both back in the same hospital, two floors higher on the oncology ward, and she held his hand as he received his aggressive but ultimately futile chemotherapy treatments.

She found out 10 years later, what it was all for.

E

August 8, 2018

Nina laid on the chaise lounge in the formal sitting room of the townhome, she couldn't think of it as theirs yet. A piece of furniture she never would have considered, but yet there it was. The upholstered fabric taut and clean beneath her body, comforting her spine as she laid the ice pack over her eyes.

"I couldn't just come out and tell you this morning. I hated lying, I'm sure you noticed how jittery I was and trying to not make eye contact. I knew if I told you that you wouldn't react well. You needed to experience it before I could give you the explanation. Otherwise, the pieces would never fit together in your mind." Parker paced a few feet away; she could hear his footsteps on the hardwood floor as they went back and forth.

"How did you get me here?" Her voice sounded like a groggy and scratched thing, something she didn't even recognize. Add it to the list of things that didn't match up that day.

"Sedative and a sleeping bag," he muttered as he turned his back to her, she could tell because his voice sounded ever so slightly further away. He seemed so matter-of-fact about it. As though that were the obvious method for inter-dimensional kidnapping. The truth of it sounded violent. Like some kind of date-rape alliteration that would be whispered around college campuses, a warning for women, a calling card for lotharios. But, according to Parker, that kind of thing didn't exist in this reality, until he used it to bring her here.

She asked more questions. How long had he been in her reality? (Two weeks, observing and learning). How did he know things were better here? (Trust him, he said. They are). When did Eleanor Roosevelt become President? (She was sworn in within hours of her husband's death. She ushered in an era of peace and prosperity). Was there another version of her in this reality? (Yes, but as a matter of paradox, they couldn't exist in the same place at the same time. He went on about some other dead scientists that she couldn't follow). What about the Parker that she lived with in her reality, wouldn't he notice that she was gone? (Same mumbo-jumbo, it made her headache flare up).

Parker excused himself to let Nina rest, she heard him running the faucet in the kitchen before she moved the ice pack further up on her forehead. She felt like she was in the middle of a Michael Crichton novel, she needed to know more about this reality to ground her to something. She grabbed her foreign phone and turned to the internet for more answers.

With the early onset of modern feminism, the timeline for equality had been pushed up by about two decades. Parker estimated that by the year 2040 many of the social ills that plagued the society that Nina had left would have been resolved. They were just loud and noisy on their way out. According to the internet, the 1980s in this universe had been a time of turbulence. There had been societal discord and the violence had peaked before it imploded, much like a dying star, screaming out as it collapsed onto itself.

Nina didn't hear him when he walked back into the room. "Don't tell Thurston." Parker eyed her sheepishly. "I was supposed to arrive at the lab, introduce myself and return immediately. We could tell that your universe had the machine built but hadn't yet found the power source needed to turn it on. When we activated on our end it would fire up and give me enough juice to go back across the Plain."

She listened intently. How scary to be the first to do something so drastic, how brave. She wanted to bestow that compliment on him, but didn't dare to interrupt. This man, the first traveler of the multiverse, how much more did he have the potential to achieve?

"But, when I arrived," he laughed at this memory. "No one was in the lab. Looks like the average workday in your reality is a bit more relaxed than the one we have here." Nina wanted to tell him that the Parker and Dr. Thurston she knew were loath to follow arbitrary rules such as standard workdays, dress codes, or anything else that the administration might request. She wanted to tell him that his alter-ego had a raging God-complex. Her-Parker felt that if he put in four hours of honest work in a day that he had done humanity a favor while the rest of the world could toil for twenty hours a day and still not match his greatness. She bit her tongue.

"I was only meant to travel to a parallel universe and arrive at the same exact date and time. 12:30 am, August 8, 2018. But the Portal dropped me off on July 25th, 2018 at 6:00 pm." He threw his hands in the air, as though this error was something goofy, trivial. It was unlike Parker to ever make a mistake. She listened as he continued.

"So, I wasn't supposed to leave the lab. But no one was there. This auspicious moment in history had happened, and no one knew it, but me." He stared at his feet as he spoke, and it occurred to her that this was the first time he'd been able to tell the story, the real story, to anyone. If he didn't want her to tell Thurston, that meant he hadn't been able to share this with him either. *How terribly alone he must feel,* she thought. The compassion and empathy that she had felt for him early in their relationship started to seep back in. *The relationship she had with her Parker,* she reminded herself.

She waited for him to continue his story. He looked into her eyes as though he was debating how much more to tell. *Should I encourage him?* she wondered.

"Why did Thurston pick you to go through? I'm surprised he didn't want to save that honor for himself." This was the most pressing question on her mind.

"Well, there is a reward for being the first to cross the Plain, eternal glory. But it could also result in total failure. To him the risks outweighed the benefits, I felt the opposite way."

"Makes sense, so you arrive and no one is there to greet you. What did you do next?" She moved her legs so that he could join her on the lounge. Still in shock about his revelations, her brain processed each new bit of information. But she leaned into his words, this was, after all, an exciting story.

"I looked around the lab. At first, I thought I had just walked right back into our lab. I wasn't sure that I had gone anywhere. I ventured out into the hall. I saw my office and Thurston's office. Same, same. I opened the door to my office and noticed a few differences. I knew for sure that I had made it when I opened my day-planner. In the front, I have my name and home address listed. It was different from our address. I knew I had done it."

Nina smiled at his ingenuity. If her Parker, the one she had been dating for the past three years, had told this story there would have been much more bravado. Maybe this man, this version of Parker was right. This reality would be better for her. She could pick up where she'd left off with Parker and have a better job, a better relationship, a better life here. She felt a nagging worry in the back of her mind though, that while he looked and spoke the same as the man that she knew, the person sitting next to her, was, in fact, a stranger. And one who had technically kidnapped her. Her mental justifications began to roll in.

"I saw a smartphone on the desk and it unlocked with my thumbprint. I read a text from you." The way he said it, so carefully and tenderly, that ubiquitous word "you", he seemed to have really cherished that moment. "I wasn't sure if we were together in that reality," he reached for her hand as he spoke. "So, it was a relief to see that you were there too. It's silly, but," he waited for her to meet his gaze. "It's like you're my constant. We're supposed to be together in this universe, and in the next."

Parker felt the warmth of Nina's hands in his. His fingertips sensing her pulse, ever so faint. He tried to find a flicker of affection or relief on her face. He had a habit of being too direct, or just doing something before explaining himself. Logically, he knew he would have to explain this decision to Nina, but he hadn't planned out exactly what to say. *Would she stay with him? Could he keep her here, even if she wanted to stay?*

Winchester had asked for a full report on that morning's first test. *Was it only this morning?* He had lived an entire two weeks in another universe, it felt like a lifetime ago. Thurston expected a briefing on what had happened and had downloaded the logs to add to the record. His great historical record of a successful transfer across the Plain. Parker had an explanation for everything, but he couldn't mask the power signature. There had been additional power surges in the milliseconds between his departure and return.

They would figure it out soon enough, and when they did, he would have a lot more explaining to do.

3

August 20, 2011

It was the time in-between. Because this part had to come to an end. Nina was in-between losing Hank and finding new love. She was in-between the woeful mourning from her lost father and the time when she would just smile in a bittersweet manner when she thought of him. Those eventualities were yet to manifest, but they had to. Right?

After the worst three years of her life, she set out to fix herself. She chose the anniversary of the attack as the day that she would finally call to schedule an appointment with a psychiatrist. August 8th.

Nina had decided to do this a few weeks beforehand, but it felt symbolic to make the call that day. She had inferred that she wouldn't be able to get an appointment on the actual day of the anniversary and didn't want that potential setback to throw her off course. So, she set herself up for success. Surely, one of the three shrinks in the area that were covered on her work's health plan would pick up the phone. If they were all mysteriously out of business or out to lunch then she would have taken that as a sign from the cosmos that she was not meant to heal through this method.

The receptionist at Dr. Syvilak's office answered after one ring. Syvilak's was the first name returned on the health care provider website. "0.6 miles from your current location" the results spat out, as though the proximity should have been the deciding factor. As though Nina wouldn't have made it the extra 0.2 miles to the next doctor on the list. But on a list of indistinguishable names, the distance was the deciding factor. It was easy. Perhaps Nina's easy-going attitude was a sign that she had already started to make a change. She didn't retreat, didn't shy away. She was moving forward.

Nina spent the evening celebrating the dismal holiday in her favorite way, a full bottle of wine and a digital binge of all the photos she had on her computer with Hank. She followed that up with more than a single serving of ice cream and bawling until her sockets were dehydrated, watching their favorite old film, *The Shoppe Around the Corner*. But she had made progress that day, she allowed herself some sorrow for a bit longer. That is, until she paid the doctor a visit and would emerge immediately cured. At least that was her assumption.

The day of the appointment arrived. Nina was a nervous wreck. She hadn't been able to sleep the night before anticipating every probing question that could come her way. *What was she willing to share? How should she tell the story of how the world, the universe, had invariably pursued her and eviscerated her chances of happiness?*

That morning Nina felt exhausted and on-edge at work, more jumpy than usual. Carol sent her a message on the inter-office system. "You okay?"

Carol sat only three feet away, but Nina appreciated her asking this question silently, digitally. "I'm just nervous about an appointment I have this afternoon."

Carol knew that she had planned to finally 'see someone' to talk through 'her issues.' The euphemisms made it moderately easier to discuss. Nina still hated admitting that she needed help. Carol had been incredibly supportive, but Nina knew she couldn't use her as a pseudo-therapist for much longer. It was a parasitic dynamic and Nina wanted to keep Carol as a friend. Besides, Carol had plenty of other options for friends; Nina, on the other hand, didn't.

"Good luck!" The exclamation point at the end of Carol's message confused her. But Nina took it as an enthusiastic amount of luck coming her way, not Carol being happy about her needing help.

Clearly, Nina's neuroses needed diagnosis given the level of self-shaming and paranoia she had resorted to.

The time came to depart for the appointment. Nina arrived at the office on a pleasant and surprisingly mild August afternoon. The humidity had broken after a brief morning sun-shower. The short walk, all 0.6 miles of it, was easy. In spite of this, her hand started shaking uncontrollably as she reached for the handle on the large Victorian door. It was painted black with a lacquered finish; the embedded glass etched with an infinite loop of scrolls.

The row of pristine houses, perfectly preserved and artfully architected could have been the choice location for anyone to be. Except for Nina. Her body started to fight back against this plan, every molecule within her scared, afraid to let go of the pain. The handle rattled in her palm, but she forced her thumb down, releasing the latch, willing herself through the doorway.

On the other side, she felt a surge of adrenaline. Nina had literally stepped over the doorway. She stood inside now; she had committed. She could have run away, back to the safe confines of her cubicle and eaten her soggy tuna salad sandwich at her desk. She could have continued to waste away, a black hole inside her body eating at her matter until she had been completely consumed. But she stayed.

The receptionist desk was positioned several feet back from the entryway. It looked like a home, not a doctor's office. Smiling, polite, the receptionist gestured for Nina to wait a moment in a plush chair just inside an ante-room. Nina wondered at the dynamic. The banister that led to the second floor was polished and smooth, inviting her eyes to follow it up and up and up as she waited. She wondered about whether the receptionist's desk stayed in that position all the time, just off the stairs. Wouldn't it get in the way on weekends? Or perhaps the doctor liked to have a physical barrier between her work and living space. She didn't have long to think of the dynamic.

"Marks," the receptionist called out. Nina turned slowly to face her.

"She'll see you now," her smile was kind, inviting. As Nina walked to the door, she tried to continue to distract herself with errant thoughts. *Did the receptionist have to smile calmly at everyone? If she was curt would she trigger an anxiety attack in a particularly prickly patient? Had another patient left and Nina missed them? Perhaps there was a back exit? Or perhaps the doctor was just eating a quick lunch before she was ready to see her?*

Nina turned the knob of this door much easier. The distractions had helped. But then she walked inside the room and saw the doctor. She looked nice, someone who Nina could have met at a yoga class or at a networking mixer. They might have been friends in other circumstances. But now this woman was her doctor.

"Welcome, Nina," she stood and extended her arm, offering a handshake. Her hands were smooth and cold; it's the cold handshakes that always make the biggest impression. Not the firmness or duration, but the shock of the icy skin.

"Hello," Nina sat timidly.

Syvilak assessed Nina as she shifted on the couch, finding the exact right position for her hips and thighs and aligning her shoulders and knees just so. Patiently, Dr. Syvilak waited. It wasn't until Nina made eye contact that she spoke.

"So, why are you here today, Nina?" No pen in hand, no notepad. Maybe the doctor recorded her sessions. *Had she signed off on the session being recorded when she mailed in the new-patient paperwork?*

Nina went back over the past three years. Her perfect relationship with Hank and how he was stolen from her in one violent evening. The painful and drawn out manner of her father's demise. His promise to help her get better, only to be diagnosed and then rely on her to care for him. Nina said that she felt empty, cheated, that everyone that ever mattered to her was now gone and that she knew she couldn't go on like this.

The doctor asked her to elaborate on what "this" was. Nina detailed her solitary lifestyle. The friends that had faded away because of her perpetually gloomy demeanor. The anxiety she barely kept at bay and the anger that Nina always misdirected at the people around her.

"And do you think you would feel better if you could direct that anger to the people responsible?"

The question caught Nina off guard. "How do you mean?"

"I mean if you could beat up the man who killed Hank? If you could torture him? Or the head-honchos at the cigarette companies that laughed at the success of their campaigns that enticed and addicted your father? Do you think if you could take your anger out on them – get even – would that help?"

Nina had pictured the former. But not for some time, that was early on before his sentencing. And she had never considered the latter. Genuinely, earnestly, she replied, "No. I don't think that would help."

"So, what do you think would help?"

Nina was struck dumb. *Was the doctor asking her for this answer? Wasn't she supposed to help Nina figure that out?* She could barely form a clarifying question in response.

"We're almost out of time, and we'll continue on this. But for today, what I want to hear from you is what you think would make you feel better." Nina hadn't realized how long it had taken her to go through the details of her history with the doctor. The time had flown by, slipped away without permission.

She nodded, accepting the assignment and felt like a child called on in class and she had no idea what answer the teacher wanted to hear.

The doctor prompted Nina one more time. "Complete this phrase for me. I could be happy, if I just had – blank."

Nina could be happy if she had Hank back. If she had her dad back. If the large pieces of her that had been lost when they died could be returned and replaced, all would be set right. So, the answer popped out easily. She didn't mean to sound insolent in her response, and she didn't genuinely think she would ever have one. The only answer that she could foresee giving her any happiness seemed comically out of reach, an impossibility, a farce.

Just before the gentle tinkling of the alarm sounded, Nina looked Dr. Syvilak in the eye and said, "A time machine."

F

August 8, 2018

It probably would have been for the best to stay inside for the rest of the day and sleep off her headache. Nina should have spent more time writing down each of her questions and asking Parker for answers. She should have figured out an explanation she could give at work for her erratic behavior and leaving so suddenly. Although that would only matter if she stayed.

Instead, she asked that Parker take her back to the lab. She wanted to know how it had worked. She had caught bits and pieces over the years from Parker, or rather her-Parker, not this new one. But she never knew enough to really grasp it, to have a tangible understanding, something she could toy with in her hands.

Parker convinced her that they should wait until Thurston had left for his midday lecture; he might get suspicious if he saw Nina in the lab twice in one day. "Won't he find it suspicious that I rushed over this morning and then we both left?" Nina didn't know what she hoped to discover with this question, but his responses began to worry her.

"No, I uh," his eyes could not find anywhere to rest as he spoke. He looked at everything in the room except for her. "I had to come up with a story. I told Thurston there was a family emergency, I kept it vague. So, if he sees you with me again, he probably won't want to pry to be polite."

"Oh, I guess that makes sense." Nina nodded as she waited for him to settle. He must have anticipated her next question. "What did I say about your absence?"

"What do you mean? I was with you for those two weeks." Parker crossed the room, turning right to head into the kitchen.

"No, not me-me. I mean the 'me' that was living here," Nina called after him, hoping he heard her as he left.

But he returned just as quickly, a glass of water in his hand. "Your alter-ego?" he confirmed.

"Yes, what did the Nina who lived with you here have to say about you disappearing for two weeks?" He stayed silent for a moment too long. *Was he debating if Nina could handle the truth, or was he creating a story?* She couldn't tell.

"I honestly didn't think to tell her. It was two weeks for me, but it was only a few moments here." He shrugged his shoulders.

"Then how did Thurston and Winchester not see me come back with you when you returned-"

He cut her off. "I've spent a lifetime theorizing and speculating on multi-dimensional travel. And the main thing I learned from the past two weeks, or I guess the last 12 hours, is that there is so much that is still unknown. I don't know why Thurston wasn't waiting for me when I returned this morning. I don't know what Nina," he clarified, "my-Nina would have said. And now I can't ask her because you're here. The two of you can't exist in the same place at the same time." It seemed that some aspects of Parker were indeed the same no matter what. That harsh retort was something Nina had grown accustomed to and it was the root of her displeasure in their relationship. But not everyone could be as perfect for her as Hank had been, so she couldn't expect perfection from Parker.

"So, is she now in my reality, or-?" Nina let the question sit in the air. Did her presence here mean that she was dead or that she didn't exist? *Did she slip from reality? Was she suspended between universes waiting for Nina to leave?*

"That is still something that we'll need to figure out, it's all still a mystery." Nina wasn't sure why, but she felt responsible for her. *Where was she now?* Lost to the void or otherwise, Nina struggled with this change and at least she had someone here to explain it to her. If their roles were reversed, if she were in her position, their position, the other Nina's position, she would be scared. If Nina stayed, would she condemn her alter-ego to a non-existence, to death?

Unsatisfied, Nina let her questions simmer. She had never probed Parker so much about his work. The knowledge she gained that morning alone had astonished her and also terrified her.

Parker glanced at his wristwatch and suggested that they grab something to eat. An easy enough way to pass the time, everyone has to eat, right? They headed out, back into the strange but familiar world. As they walked along the street, she recognized it. She had been there before. In another world, another life, she went to see someone for help on that very street. *"Complete this phrase for me. I could be happy, if I just had – blank"*

She pushed that memory aside as she tried to take everything in with her eyes. So much looked the same, she still couldn't believe that she was anywhere different. The trees still lined the road in the same manner, thick and full after a long summer of growth. The people of the city hustled by with their attention on their smartphones. They crammed work into every possible second they could before arriving at their destination. The same smells wafted out of food carts. So much of the city was familiar.

Parker took her to their favorite place, a diner not far from campus. Only he had to tell Nina it was their favorite place; she had never been there before. At least, not as a diner. Nina recognized the cross street, but this had been a laundromat in her reality. The mailbox on the corner looked the same, the accountant's office on the opposite corner too. The slow-moving traffic waiting in the intersection crawled by just as she expected, except for the lines of bicycles rolling by. But the building before her was different.

The diner itself looked like any other. Swivel stools lined the counter where single diners could eat by themselves. Couples and groups stuffed into booths covered with outdated plastic. Customers slurped on coffee, waitresses brushed by with large platters of food, a grease-cook hollering out orders from the kitchen. Parker directed them to a corner seat with a view of the entire intersection.

She wondered at the things that were different. How had these differences manifested? All from Eleanor Roosevelt being President, or were there other changes that she would never be able to pinpoint? There was so much that she didn't know about the history of the world. How could she tell what was or wasn't out of place? And how could she presume that something was out of place, perhaps this was the primary universe and her own home universe was some perverse derivation?

Nina's headache had finally abated, her eyes safe behind the tinted windows of the diner. Able to focus on something other than her head pain, her hunger surged. A waitress appeared to take their order, breaking Nina's distracted focus. She had been looking out the window, taking in all the people who walked past.

"Earth to Nina," Parker commented as he snapped his fingers. She looked over quickly at the expectant woman. She looked like any woman might. Medium height, medium brown colored hair pulled back in a bun, moderately good looking although she looked neither happy nor unhappy. She appeared to be plain, tired from a long shift working a minimum-wage job. For a second, Nina wondered if she worked as a waitress back in her home universe as well.

"Oh sorry," Nina blushed as she requested a bacon cheeseburger. She caught that the woman's name was Tracy. *Would she remember to go to a University diner when she got home to see if Tracy was there? Would she ever go back to her home?*

Nina salivated over the savory aroma of hot fries that passed by until finally, their order came up. "Nina never would have ordered that," Parker said as Tracy placed the thick-cut bacon cheeseburger in front of her.

"No?" She wondered at the statement as she placed a paper napkin in her lap. It was as though she was being compared to her predecessor, the annoying way men would comment on how their previous girlfriend would do this or not do that. But that wasn't the case here. Parker was just comparing one version of her to the other. Nina had some trouble drawing the necessary distinctions herself, she tried to empathize with Parker's point of view as well. She looked just like his girlfriend, they had the same name, so much was similar. From the photos on the wall, they were identical. But Nina knew they were completely unique people.

"No," he shook his head as he dug into his pile of chicken wings. "She usually gets the chicken strip salad. 'It's the greenest thing on the menu,' she always says."

Nina smiled at the thought that some version of her somewhere was able to easily make healthy food choices in addition to being endlessly chic and stylish. She balanced a large glob of ketchup on a french fry, about to satisfy her desire when it occurred to her that this foreign food may not sit well with her stomach. "Can I eat this? Will there be some foreign substance that I'm not supposed to have?"

"From what I can tell, our universes are similar enough that you should be fine. I was starving for my first two days with you, but then I gave in because I was just so dang hungry." Nina recalled that the candlelight dinner he prepared had indeed been delicious, although he barely touched his plate. It all fit now.

"My stomach hasn't thrown a fit since," Parker dismissed her concern. Nina was happy to hear his response and accepted it gladly. With his blessing, she devoured the food before her. She worried that she looked like a ferocious animal, only stopping between bites so that she could take a sip of her water to help get more food down.

Parker didn't seem to mind; he focused on his plate as well. She wondered if he had a headache too and if he was equally famished. She didn't ask, she just focused on her task at hand: demolish the cheeseburger.

Once they were both finished, their plates clean except for the errant streaks of ketchup that didn't get scooped up by their fries, Parker excused himself to pay the check. Nina let her eyes idly fall on the street as she waited for him to return. College students filtered past; the older ones tended to live further from campus in an attempt to pay lower rent. Professionals rushed by, on their way to catch the metro. The sky was a perfect blue, the color it should be. A gentle breeze rustled the trees along the sidewalk, the leaves moving on the limbs, casting shadows on the ground, giving the illusion that they were dancing.

And then her heart stopped beating for just a moment.

His hair looked longer than she remembered, the full curls spilling over his ears and the collar of his shirt, the first traces of gray starting to highlight his hairline. His shoulders were slightly hunched as he marched forward, his cell phone pressed to his ear. He appeared to be listening intently to the person on the other end. He looked frustrated; his forehead creased into deep lines of confusion. Or, perhaps given the years since she had last seen him, it was just age that had marked his skin.

No, I'm clearly seeing things. Her rational brain tried to shut down her excitement. She tried to drink in more of the details, but he had already rounded the corner and continued away from the diner. Without noticing it, she stood up and craned her neck to continue looking at him for as long as she could. If she hadn't been so distracted, and if her phone hadn't been set to silent, she might have noticed that it had been ringing.

"It's not possible," she breathed as her head and her heart tried to make sense of the visual details that her eyes had relayed. It couldn't be. There was no way that the changes in this universe would bring this about, there was no way. *Don't be a fool*, she chided herself. But she couldn't bring herself to look away, even after he was long gone from view.

"Everything okay?" she heard Parker ask as he returned to the table.

"Yep, just ready to go," she replied too quickly; the lie too easy. Nina wasn't about to tell him what she saw or what she thought she saw. This was something that had been locked up deep in her heart long ago, and while Nina had let her Parker in very briefly on a few occasions, she wasn't about to lead them on a wild goose chase that she had to convince herself would be fruitless. Nina needed other answers first, but what she wanted, what she longed for was potentially heading away from her on foot.

She tried to stay calm as she and Parker walked to the University. *What if it was him*, and that was all she would ever see of him again? Something so big, someone so important to her. No, it couldn't be anything as inconsequential as just watching him walk by. *If it was really him – no, it simply wasn't him.* She needed to accept that or she would spiral back into the darkness that she had receded into so long ago.

"Pick up, pick up, pick up," he muttered as he walked back to his apartment. As though his idle pleas would somehow quiet the ringing on the other line that never seemed to end.

"Hey, this is Nina. I'm not available-" he hung up before the recorded message could finish giving its instruction. In his frustration, he pictured throwing his phone, but he knew that wouldn't help. It would feel good, it would make him feel powerful, but it would solve nothing. She was missing. That's what it had to be. That she was missing, but in that case, then he needed to find her. People don't just go missing. *They get disappeared.* Hank recalled a sinister line from one of the detective shows he watched on Tuesday nights.

He scrolled through his call log, a long row of the same name repeated over and over. He tried her number again.

Today of all days, Nina? He thought as the line rang once more.

He had only another block to go before he got home. But he didn't want to be there, not alone. Not feeling like this. Again.

He knew that if he went home, he would pull out their photos, he would start to wallow, he would drink, he would cry, he would call again and again. Had he been foolish to believe her?

The heavy feeling that settled into his gut had now morphed into dread. Ever since the previous Friday night when he first thought that she stood him up, he had been fighting off that nervous worry. Maybe it wasn't a change of heart. Even on their worst days, even though she had fallen for that pompous jerk, she never ignored him on this day. They needed each other on this day. Anna's day.

He looked down at his phone and navigated to the recent call log. He clicked on her name one more time and the phone started to ring again.

Nina's head swam with questions and impossible desires as they walked back to the lab. The hallway abandoned, much as it had been earlier, only it now felt hollow. She could sense the emptiness, the lack of people about.

They passed the lab table where she had found Parker earlier, walking past the computers and models that were humming and past the thick flaps of plastic that functioned as a partition to a large warehouse portion of the lab. The team had hosted a guest lecturer there last year and it looked the same, or at least this event had happened in Nina's home universe.

Open valleys of exposed concrete and corners of boxes and metal shelving dotted this side of the lab. Everything was the same, except for the sizable machine in the center of the room. It looked like an airport body scanner retrofit on a line of track that extended out to the left and right of it. The scanner, the doorway, whatever you want to call it, stood dead-center in the middle of the track.

"This is how we can travel to other universes," Parker said reverently, as though they had just entered a sanctuary, as though it was hallowed ground.

"The theory of the multiverse has existed for some time now, but it has only ever been a theory. One of the main tenets of the theory was that it would, in fact, be possible to travel to parallel universes. Some of our contemporaries put their energies into theories about singularities and wormholes. Thurston and I focused on a mechanism that could be controlled or harnessed."

"So, you can use this contraption to get to a parallel universe?" Nina stepped ahead of him wanting to examine it closer. The materials didn't seem to be remarkable. Steel, aluminum, plastic fittings on the edges, bolts, screws, and wingnuts. Put together one way they could have been a table or a car, but these had been constructed to create a passage to another dimension.

"Yes, actually we can use it to get to most of them. The trick is, going to one where you can get back. There are only a handful of other parallel universes where the Portal," he gestured to the machine, "or something like it has been developed."

"So, have other people traveled here?" Nina whipped around quickly, excited and terrified by the idea.

"Not that we can tell. Thurston built a non-functional prototype about twelve years ago. We built this model last year; we just needed a consistent power source. We don't think the other universes have found it yet. But once they do, this could become a super highway." He advanced past her and placed his hand on the frame, caressing the smooth metal, petting it.

As if anticipating her next question, he continued: "There are no laws around this kind of thing. Some moral and ethical quandaries, but nothing else. It's the wild-wild west."

"Wow," Nina's head spun with the ramifications. *What would this mean for our species, for our existence?* Based on the humanity she had experienced, there would be resistance, strong resistance here. She tried to process all of the new information coming into her brain. So, she settled for a basic question next, thinking that she would have more time to probe Parker's mind.

"So, what did you call this? A Portal?"

"That's a simple name for it. But the official name that everyone will identify it as, is a time machine."

G

lthough it had no magnetic properties, the Portal lured Nina in. She was a starship locked in a tractor-beam; she had seen that in a movie once. That is what it felt like; she was compelled to draw closer to it. She took in the entire device, not just the doorway that led to other dimensions. The console to the left of the track would have been unremarkable if she didn't know what it was capable of. The desk was loaded with monitors and computers. There were no knobs or dials as popular science fiction movies may have had her believe. No, it was a clean desk with a massive set of screens. There were large bundles of wires snaking across the floor of the warehouse, leading to components unknown. There was a printer off to the left that appeared to be spitting out a read-out of some chart; it looked like those seismic scale machines that measure earthquakes. "What is this for?"

"That lets us know if one of the other universes is about to engage with ours." Parker picked up the scroll and pointed to the massive spike. "This is when we came back early this morning," the chart did seem to get much more frenzied at that spot compared to the rest. "We only did our first tests in July. We found a pattern of quantum jitters and realized we would have to time the jumps to coincide with the jitters. The readout on our quantum computer showed us that the jitters would start to happen with more regularity up until today, the 8th, and then settle back down over the next month or so."

"Okay, the quantum computer you've-" she paused to correct herself, "Parker mentioned to me before," Nina started.

"We need a lot of power to calculate all of the probability wave lengths. We have this," he held up a thick metal block with a USB connector on the end of it. As wide as his palm, but as thin as his thumb, it looked like a weighty item. "This is our quantum drive. It's like an external hard drive but for the quantum computer. It allows us to save known frequencies and locations so we can access them later. No way to do that with a standard laptop and USB, even if it is high end."

Nina continued, unphased by Parker's interruption. "But what is a quantum jitter?"

Parker set the printout back down, letting it continue to print and spool in an ever-curving pile leading from the console to the floor. "Um," he looked around for a moment, scanning the room for any object he could find. A faded world map was tacked up on the far wall of the warehouse, the corners peeling away in a weak escape. He beckoned her to follow him.

"Okay, so this would be better if I had a globe. But you know about the polar lights?"

"Yes, the aurora borealis and the aurora australis," Nina responded, immediately.

"Wow," Parker eyed Nina suspiciously.

"We were planning to take a round the world trip when you did your sabbatical to try and see both," Nina stated.

"That's a great idea," Parker remarked, as though he had never thought of it before. And really, he hadn't, the other Parker had.

"So, what about them?" Nina asked.

"Right. They're caused by-" Parker started.

"Electromagnetic radiation from the sun." Nina finished for him. It was rare that she knew exactly what he was about to say and she relished the opportunity to show that she could also be smart.

"Right. So, electromagnetism is what I wanted us to get to, but you already know about it. So, these items are just out there in space, they exist in fields." Parker ran his hands over an imaginary smooth surface in the air, as though his fingers were skirting an actual field.

"Yep, got it," Nina nodded.

"There are electrical fields, magnetic fields, electro-magnetic fields," Parker began to tick them off. Nina nodded along to show that she followed his explanation. "Okay, so there are also gravitational fields." Parker pointed to the floor, "and when we think about where we are in space, and where we are in time, we actually need to think of it as spacetime. The two are fixed together." Parker brought his two index fingers to a point.

"Okay, I follow you," Nina waited for further elaboration. Perhaps her alter-ego hadn't attended as many of his guest seminars over the years. Nina hadn't just been arranging the snacks and taking video. She had been paying attention.

"Our gravitational field dictates the curvature of spacetime. If we understand the field, we can understand how spacetime moves. These are all things we can calculate with the quantum computer." Parker gestured back to the console. Nina understood what he had said.

"Okay, so we know that there are always irregularities in any system. Glitches, imperfections. A jitter in an electrical field might result in a short loss of power," Parker elaborated. Nina's mind flashed back to the subway station two weeks earlier. The flickering lights in the office that night. A jitter. "Any field can experience a jitter. Now a jitter in spacetime is a quantum jitter, because it doesn't make the lights go off; it can cause a bit of a mess. But for us, we use it to take our jumps. It creates just enough of a disturbance that we can slip through," Parker slid his right arm under his left, as a rudimentary demonstration.

"So, how do you know when they are going to happen?" Nina wondered at how simple Parker had made it sound. Simple, but not easy.

"We were able to notice a few on the system a couple of weeks ago, but we only caught them when they happened. We looked at the patterns and used the quantum computer to run a regression and saw that today, August 8th would see a high volume of them throughout the day. It's like the perfect storm of quantum jitters."

"Why August 8th?" Nina asked reflexively.

"Thurston and I haven't solved for that one, we know it is one day past the halfway mark between the June solstice and the September equinox. But the numbers consistently point to August 8th."

"And that's why you had to bring me here today," Nina wondered at the significance of the date. A day she had marveled at on the calendar as a little girl, a day turned into a black spot on her calendar years earlier. This day. Of all the possible days, it was this day.

Nina heard the gentle slap of the plastic behind them and turned quickly. "I knew it!" Thurston called out as he pointed a finger at Parker.

Nina shifted her gaze back to Parker, unsure of how he could explain things. From what she could tell so far, she wasn't supposed to be here. Parker wasn't authorized to bring her across with him, and if Thurston had heard what Parker had just said, he would be caught.

"I can explain," was all that Parker could muster.

"My office, now!" Bellowed Thurston, his face red with frustration. His salt and pepper hair, his glasses, his Rolex watch all seemed ridiculous next to the flush of his anger, as though everything was for show and his anger didn't go with any of these added features.

Parker looked at Nina quickly. "Don't touch anything, okay?"

She watched him slink away, his thin frame hunched over, marching with heavy feet behind his boss. Nina turned back and walked closer to the console. Leaning in, her hands carefully wrapped behind her back she assessed the symbols and patterns on the screens in front of her. Most of it looked vaguely familiar in a way, sure she had seen each of these elements on a sci-fi show or in some documentary that Parker had insisted on watching. Her eyes kept slipping back to the actual structure of the Portal.

Nina quickly looked over her shoulder and confirmed that she was completely alone in the lab. Hesitantly, as though the very act of standing and taking a few steps closer would cause the device to explode or smother her in radiation, Nina approached the Portal.

"A time machine," she breathed as she held up her hand. Hadn't this been something she had once named as the solution to her problems? It had been her pessimistic answer to what seemed unsolvable. But looking at it with her eyes, feeling the hair on her forearm rise as she crossed closer to it, it felt silly that she had once thought it so unrealistic. Maybe somewhere in her mind, the dark unconscious that she never could have articulated, that had been what had truly drawn her to Parker. She only somewhat understood what Parker worked on, and yet, she managed to find the person who made her outlandish demand a reality. She always told herself it was all "above her head," but she had followed Parker's explanation easily enough.

Nina stretched her hand out to touch the steel frame. She had a premonition that it would shock her with some kind of static electricity, but not exactly that. A chill ran through her fingers and up her arm. The cold sensation of the metal was almost too much to handle, she withdrew her fingers quickly, putting them in her pockets.

Another memory unfolded quickly, like a tattered piece of lined paper. "This is a two pocket-store" her dad would say when she was a child. That was the scale he used when he needed to run errands and couldn't find a sitter. The most common stores were zero-pockets, which meant her hands were free to roam across the endless varieties of cereal boxes in the grocery store or the patterned band-aids at the pharmacy. The hardware store was a one-pocket store, one hand in her pocket, the other one in her father's hand to ensure she didn't get into any tools that she could inadvertently maim herself with. And the two-pocket stores were rare, but they did exist. Both hands in her pockets the entire time she was in the store. All of the items in easy reach were breakable and expensive. As Nina stalked the Portal, examining it from different angles, she clenched her hands into fists in the pockets of her dress.

She hadn't thought about her father and his inventive wisdom in a long time, at least not to any level of conscious awareness. So much of him was intertwined with the person that she had become, but she hadn't pulled out any memories in a long time. She hadn't heard his voice in her mind since she buried the pain of losing him and Hank deep within her soul. She speculated that it was the proximity to the machine that caused these flare-ups, these time-trips in her own mind.

As this thought made its final lap through her mind, she sensed something. Not anything visible or tactile, an energy of some kind. She pulled the cell phone out of her left front pocket. Still a little too small to be hers. There was an inbound call coming through, but the screen announced that the number had been blocked. Without a second thought, she declined the call, an instinct that had carried over from her own home world. She scanned the notification bar at the top of the phone, quite a few items that had been neglected. Nina swiped the work emails and junk emails to the side. There were some inane social media notifications, "so and so liked your photo" and "you have memories with so and so today." Easy to ignore for now until she got her mind around where she was and what would happen next. *Could I go back, should I?*

Nina swiped that thought away as she noticed 12 unread text messages, and 57 missed calls. The texts were from Carol and were mostly from the previous Friday. She inquired about why Nina wasn't at work yet, would she be coming in, was she okay, and then finally a longer one that was broken up into several shorter messages expressing her condolences. Nina marveled at the fact that she hadn't noticed them that morning, but she was fighting a pounding headache so perhaps that explained it.

The rest were from an account "II" which had her stumped. Who was II? Two resolute hash marks? Was it code for something?

Nina opened the texts and they started out much like Carol's but instead of eventually trickling off, they only became more and more intense. "Please, just let me know that you're okay," and "if you have changed your mind then okay, but please just respond so I know that you are alright." Without any context to be able to make an educated guess about who the mysterious sender was, Nina moved over to the call log. All of the calls were from a blocked number. She assumed they were all the same blocked number. The frequency appeared erratic, some of the calls first thing in the morning, others late at night. Potentially not a robo-caller or telemarketer. Nina saw that there were no voicemails, and figured that the caller must not have been that committed to getting in touch with her when she remembered that calls from blocked numbers can't leave a message.

As though the person who had been trying to reach her could sense that the phone was in her palm, it rang again. Nina jumped back just a bit. The call was from the blocked number. Nina hesitated over the "cancel" button and moved her thumb to the other side of the screen. With maybe a couple rings to spare, she accepted the call.

"Hello?" Nina tried to keep her voice steady. Her palms felt swollen and moist, and the skin on the back of her neck started to tingle.

"Nina?!" the voice on the other end nearly shouted. She heard a man's voice, deep and smooth. He must have been outside because she could hear the background noise of people chatting and a motorbike zipping past.

"Yes," she didn't know how else to respond.

"Oh, thank goodness," she could hear the air being let out, as though they had been holding it since they had started calling her days earlier. Nina heard something in the voice that kept her from replying. It was trying to place the familiar gravel and pronunciation. Before she had realized it, her mouth had already found the necessary response. She hadn't been hallucinating earlier. It was him.

"Hank?"

4

August 1, 2018

She hadn't realized it, but in a way, she had been holding her breath ever since she came home to candle-light and roses. Nina hadn't actually been holding her breath, she didn't have the lung capacity for that whatsoever. After a week of pleasant interactions and not one bickering match, she told herself to be more optimistic, but she was just waiting for the grace-period to end. Something felt off. Nina tried to tell herself that unhappiness had become her new normal and that she felt out of place when that emotion was counteracted with anything positive.

It was August 1st, the alarm clock on the nightstand had announced that it was a new day and she was the only one watching it. For a second, she was the only one who knew that it was a new day, a new month. Nina dreaded August. Nothing good ever came from it, and the following months weren't much to look forward to either.

She heard Parker rustling next to her. He had always been such a sound sleeper; whatever he set out to do, he did it with his undivided attention. It fit that sleep would be the same, but he had been restless for the past week. Nina had always been a light sleeper. She wasn't getting a good night rest anymore with Parker's tossing and turning. He told her that their research project had made some major advances so she understood why he would be up all night. But she didn't want to have to sacrifice her own sleep as well.

Out of nowhere, he broke the silence. "If Hank were still alive, would you prefer to be with him now?" She continued to stare at the clock, debating if she should answer or ignore his question.

It caught her off guard. She had spent so many years keeping his name out of her mind for fear that she would say it aloud and the painful reality of his loss would wash over her anew. She had told Parker about Hank once and only once.

On one of their early dates, he inquired about her last relationship. She couldn't lie, so she told him that it had been a long relationship with Hank. He was the boy who she grew up with until one day they weren't playing anymore, they were in love. Parker asked how it ended. "Violently" was all that she could offer in return. It was true, Gus Blanity killed Hank in a violent manner and his very sudden loss was so traumatic to Nina that it could only be classified as such.

She knew that Parker had looked it up because one day she got out of the shower and walked out into the apartment dripping wet, all of the towels were in the basket, clean and waiting to be folded. Nina caught him looking at an old online article, one that she had spent months looking at herself. "Good Samaritans Save Local Woman" read the headline, very unlike the news media to not lead with the blood. The men who had stopped Gus Blanity were photographed, each of them smiling. They had done their good deed. Nina had thanked each of them in her blind stupor of that first year. But what she really wanted to do was yell at each of them. *Where had they been five minutes earlier? Why hadn't they saved Hank?* She could see the corner of the photograph over Parker's shoulder. A quick glimpse was all it took to recognize the article. He clicked away as soon as he sensed her presence, an admission of guilt.

Nina had been silent for too long in the dark. Parker had to know she was still awake, and each second that passed without an answer would only fuel his unease. What did it matter? Hank was gone, Parker's question seemed foolish and she didn't like the unreasonable seed of hope that it planted deep within her soul.

"What does it matter?" She could only answer his question with another, stalling, putting off the truth. Deep down in the happy part of her unconsciousness, it was Hank who she visited each evening. Hank who would be waiting at home at the end of a long day to comfort her. Hank who would have filled the dull places of her life with happiness.

"It matters to me; I don't want to think that you're settling for me." His voice sounded much further away than it really was. Nina could feel the weight of his body next to her, but those inches that separated them felt like vast valleys, glacial plains that were flooded over and over again in the spring.

She had to respond. She had to say the right thing, because it was already tomorrow and they both needed to sleep. And maybe, she needed to hear the words out loud to force her heart to fully let go. "We probably would have grown apart by now, we wouldn't have lasted."

Nina heard him let out a sigh. Of relief or frustration, she couldn't tell. Her eyes were wide open, fixed on the shadow of the night side table as she lay on her side. She thought he had fallen asleep when she felt him roll closer to her, resting his hand on her arm. Possessing her. She had said the right thing; had comforted Parker and made him feel like he wasn't her second choice. But, everything in this life was a second choice to living with Hank. She disgusted herself, felt the tears brimming on her eyes but she refused to let them fall. She hadn't cried over Hank in years, hadn't cried over anything in years and she wasn't about to start now.

Figures she would be upset, it was August. A few minutes into the month and Nina already felt miserable.

PART 2

Just as there is a forecast that instructs pilots of when to fly, there is one for those who travel the multiverse as well. You wouldn't take off in a lightning storm. You wouldn't paddle out in a squall. You wouldn't plant your crops at the wrong time if a reliable almanac told you not to. But this multiverse forecast isn't necessarily the most scientific, if you can believe that. For all of the advanced formulas that were required to construct the Portal and then solve for the necessary energy source to allow people to travel across the Plain, the best date to take off is August 8th.

8/8. The Infinite-Infinite. The people who are most likely to make the trip have a special connection to the date. Their birthday, a special anniversary, a major life event, an early affinity for symbols and the recognition of the double infinity signs will do. It doesn't mean that you absolutely will make it, just like a clear forecast doesn't guarantee a smooth trip, but it certainly makes it more likely.

"Men are afraid that women will laugh at them, women are afraid that men will kill them." – Margaret Atwood

H

August 8, 2018

The universe had just been upended. All of the pieces and places, the people and the particles, slid off a grand checkerboard and crashed into the ground, scattershot.

"Yes, of course, it's me," he breathed, irritated by the question. "I've been trying to get in touch with you for days. I was worried sick." The last words were strained, raw with panic.

Nina didn't know what to say. In all the years that she had spent missing him and the dreams that she had of reuniting with him, she had never planned out what that first sentence would be. *What do you say to the love of your life after you've lost them?*

"I'm so sorry, Hank," was all that she could muster, responding to his expressed worry.

"Where are you?" His voice was set, her ears seemed to prickle at the vibrations of his sound. Happy to hear them again, regardless of the words being spoken.

"I'm-" Nina paused before continuing.

"It's okay if you changed your mind," she could hear his mood deflating. "I just had to know that you were alright."

"I'm fine, I am just having the craziest day right now." Without meaning to she had wandered over to the rolling chair in front of the monitors and slid into it.

"Okay," his resigned words sounded final. Nina couldn't let this be it, the last conversation that she would ever have with him. She would not allow this to be it.

"Can I see you?" What Nina really wanted to ask was, *can I hold you, can I never let go, can I get back the years I lived without you, can I keep you forever?*

"Of course. I'm near campus, but I can meet you wherever you would like." She closed her eyes and pictured the man she had seen through the diner window. Hurried, walking with purpose. That is who she would meet, not the young man that she lost years earlier.

"How about the green by Healy Circle?" Nina hoped that the name hadn't changed between universes.

"Perfect, I'll be there in 15 minutes," she could hear him moving quickly.

"I'll see you soon," she could feel the smile on her face pushing her cheeks so far up that it hurt her eyes. Maybe this was the moment she had been waiting for, all those years floating through, feeling as though something was off. This was it. This was her chance at happiness. It wasn't crazy to think she could have everything that she wanted. It was here, he was here. All along, Hank had been alive out in the multiverse and they had been brought together again.

But how would Parker feel about this? Should she even tell him that she was popping out to meet up with another man? She didn't hear anyone on the other side of the lab and time was of the essence. She slipped quietly towards the back corner of the lab. Nina ducked out using the back exit, the gray door that nearly blended into the concrete wall. She hadn't meant to sneak away from Parker, it just happened to be the closest way out. Not passing him or having to explain where she was heading was a pleasant benefit of her snap decision.

I

Nina's lungs burned as she dashed across campus, indifferent to any side-glances or judgments from co-eds with their overly relaxed gaits that she sped past. She marveled at the fact that she still knew her way around so well. For all that might have been different in this reality, the campus remained very similar. Her orange dress made her appear like a flame cutting a line along the sidewalks. And she was indeed on fire. She made her way across campus and on the green. Impatiently, she waited at the crosswalk, not daring to cross against the light for fear that she might perish before being able to see him again.

In the few moments that Nina had to wait, her thoughts flickered between excitement and worry. What if he looked different and she didn't even recognize him? What if she didn't feel anything when she saw him? What if he was mowed down by a bus just as he was walking towards her? All of the things she had never imagined in her dream reunions with Hank were now percolating up, all of the gritty realities that this universe would present her with had not ever existed in her wildest imagination. Being with Hank again? Yes. Sarcastically replying to a psychiatrist that the only thing that could make her happy was a time machine? Yes. The steps that would need to happen to make those things a reality? Never.

She paced by an empty bench, conveniently shaded by a rustling birch tree. Nina scanned the path from right to left, looking for him, turned and walked in the other direction checking there as well. Nina's fingers were in her mouth, her nails the unlucky target of her anxiety.

She heard his feet first, pounding against the sidewalk as he ran towards her. Nina turned to see him approaching, his hair long enough to bounce along with the rhythm of his half run, half walk manner of reaching her. It would seem that she hadn't been imagining things in the diner earlier, the man she had seen walking away from her, down the block, had been Hank. Without warning, tears threatened to cut loose across her cheeks. She choked back a scream; of what emotion she couldn't tell. She felt everything all at once: joy, despair, anger, fear, excitement, love. All of it coursing through her at that moment.

He didn't slow down as he approached. He kept moving until he was right on her, his arms thrown around her so quickly she couldn't even catch a good look at his face.

"I'm so happy that you're okay," he breathed in her ear. His hands were supporting her back and her neck, the heat of his touch reminded her that this was real. And if it did turn out to be a dream, she knew that she never wanted to wake up from it. It was as though they had picked up right where they had left off. They were attacked and now Hank looked relieved to see that she was okay. Could it be that her Hank had been sent here, not to heaven or some other state of being, but to this universe instead?

Hank pushed himself away as quickly as he had enveloped her, breaking Nina's train of thought.

"I just had to know that you were okay," the skin around his eyes straining, pulling tightly, as though he were trying to draw her likeness into focus.

"I – I – I," all Nina could do was stammer. Only a few seconds into their reunion and it appeared that it was already starting to sour.

"I put myself out there, all on the line, Nina. I won't do this again." Her joy ripped away; he seemed disappointed with her. He sounded unhappy with himself. How could he not feel the importance of this moment? Was he not in tune to the cosmic significance?

"Hank," Nina breathed out his name. Where her own thoughts and words were beginning to fail her, she picked up an old and faded song lyric that drifted to the top of her consciousness at the right time. "I'd rather live in your world, than without you in mine." She gripped his hand as she said it, trying to push the force of her emotions, communicate all the pain and relief from the past decade to that very moment to him.

She said it with every bit of strength she had in her, almost sang it out, but her flat voice would not have helped her case. Whether he recognized the song or not, whether Gladys Knight and her Pips were known in this universe or not, those words did seem to soothe his ire.

"What happened then? I've been worried sick about you," he gestured to the bench.

"I don't know. Hank, this day has been crazy. You won't believe me if I told you," Nina started to worry that if she told him the explanation that Parker had given her, then Hank would question her sanity. She wasn't even sure if she totally believed it herself. But there was Hank, aged and older but still the same. *So, it had to be real.*

"Try me," he held the tips of his fingers pressed together. Nina had seen his father do that a few times; she memorized that stance during the hours of the trial where Gus Blanity asserted his mental incompetence. She couldn't focus on the court proceedings, so she had memorized how everyone in their row passed the hours, their little ticks. The thought of the courtroom and the reality of Hank's death swept over her again, a wave of tears flooded her face before she could keep it at bay, as futile as any attempt to control the churning sea.

His arms folded around her once again, comforting her. Nina wanted to tell him everything, but her throat had swollen shut. It hurt to try to breathe, to try to speak. People were passing by as she made a scene. Her sense of decorum, her ability to be embarrassed must have been left behind in her home reality because she took far longer than was appropriate to get herself together.

Finally, with her sobbing under control, her cheeks red from her hands wiping away tears, Hank spoke. "Was it Parker?"

The magnitude of the question dawned on her. In this reality, her alter-ego still had some connection to Hank, an affectionate one at that, if not romantic. But she, her alter-ego that is, was also living with Parker and their framed professional photos lining the hallway.

"What? I am having one of those days where nothing makes sense. Can you jog my memory?" Nina tried to act as though that was a totally normal request. Hank's expression appeared incredulous at best.

"Are you feeling okay?" Hank had resumed his original tone of concern.

"Please, today has been a lot already," Nina could feel the remnants of the dreadful headache she had woken with making a final scream on its way out. Instinctively she rubbed her forehead, trying to keep the pain at bay.

"I had everything ready, cleared out half the closest. I got your text that you would be over with your suitcases, I waited and you never showed. After an hour, I got nervous, after three I was beyond concerned. I kept calling and texting but you weren't responding. I thought you had changed your mind. Again." He added the last word with emphasis. Apparently, Nina's alter-ego planned to leave Parker for Hank, and she hadn't shown up. And this hadn't been the first time she had let Hank down in this regard.

"I took these out," he pulled two rings from his pocket. "I didn't think you would start to wear it again right away, but-" he trailed off, the pain of his open-faced honesty apparent. So, they had been married in this reality, but somehow it had ended. As much as things didn't seem to make sense earlier, now Nina knew that something was wrong. How could she ever end things with Hank? He was the pinnacle; he was the paragon and their relationship had been perfect before it was stolen from her. Or at least that was the narrative she had lived by. She had never imagined that they would have ever been apart or unhappy. Or broken. Even if she had said things like that to appease Parker, she didn't believe it. But now the proof was right in front of her.

Nina took the thin gold band from his hand and slipped it onto her finger, it fit perfectly. Of course, it did. Her wildest dreams had come true, but it still felt all wrong.

"How long have you been trying to get in touch with me?" Nina asked as she inspected the gold band, smooth and polished to a shine.

"It's been a few days, Nina! I knew you couldn't ignore me today though. Not today!" Her brain skipped past his latter statement and focused on the former.

"A few days," she muttered. She had been missing for a few days. Carol had said the same thing, and all of her worried texts had started around the same time as well. She could feel the small semblance of understanding that she had about that universe start to shift, slide, slip away.

J

The stench of fresh vomit and everyday detritus pushed into Nina's nostrils. The pungent odor clung to her hair even as she pulled her head out of the waste bin conveniently located next to the bench. Her entire lunch, french fries and all, which had been so eagerly devoured, now lined the trash bag. Hank had run off to the hot dog cart not twenty feet away and returned with a bottle of water.

She sat on the park bench, too focused on piecing together the information colliding in her brain to notice Hank's hand rubbing her back.

"You said I was missing for a few days?" She finally muttered after drinking most of the water bottle in one long swallow. Nina had a theory forming in her mind. The muddled timeline that had brought her to this universe started to take shape and it didn't give her any comfort.

"Yeah, I was really worried. But I knew you wouldn't ignore me today. Never that. You wouldn't do that." His face looked grim. "I just had to know that you were okay, Nina."

She wanted to tell him that she was more than okay, that seeing him was a miracle and it would be a continuous source of joy for her. She felt like a love sick girl all over again. But she was still so confused and didn't know how much to share with him.

"Hank," Nina turned to face him now, not caring if her breath smelled abominable or her face looked messy from getting sick. "I've been having the craziest time, but if you will still have me, I'll pack up and leave with you today."

He let out a deep sigh and turned his face from her. "I can't keep doing this, I don't-"

"Please," Nina could feel the heat on her face, the sensation of water brimming in her eyes. She couldn't lose him again. Nina knew some version of her could have eventually made peace with his being happy without her, so long as he was alive. But the version of Nina sitting on that bench wouldn't survive losing him again. She reached for his hand and squeezed it as hard as she could until she felt him squeeze back.

"We're not finished here, Parker!" Thurston hollered as he followed his protégé out of his office. Students passing by in the hallway stopped to see the spectacle. Two professors arguing with each other, loud and in the open. They were fascinated by the drama of it all.

Parker stormed down the hallway towards the lab. He was apoplectic, he felt too mad to speak, to even think. How dare Thurston try to hold him back? How dare he try to say Parker was somehow to blame or in trouble for what he did? The old man might be content to just wait for someone else to be the first to cross the Plain. But Parker was a man of action, he wouldn't just be the welcoming committee for the first traveler. No, his name would be in the history books. He had figured out how to stretch an hour into two weeks. He had been able to find the additional resources to continue his explorations. He had lived a lifetime in the past 12 hours and now Thurston wanted to ground him? To keep him from ever using the machine again?

"Parker!" Thurston had followed him into the lab. "We have to answer some very serious questions today or we will be shut down. Please see reason here," the old man pleaded.

Parker stopped just before he reached the partition between the classroom and warehouse sections of the lab, turning quickly on his heels. "I have seen reason. I have seen it and I have waited. I will not apologize for making our machine a functional device. For seeing the multiverse first hand." Parker had been taking meticulous steps closer to Thurston. He had his index finger extended, as though pointing at the man would somehow turn the tide.

"But, Nina-" Thurston started as he stood his ground. Even as Parker continued to advance, Thurston didn't budge, didn't take one half-step back.

"Let me worry about that, you tell Winchester to keep her nose out of things she doesn't understand," Parker sneered as he turned back to head into the warehouse section.

"Parker, what has happened to you?" Thurston continued his questioning as he followed Parker into the warehouse. He stopped short before crashing into Parker who stood just inside the entry. Getting no answer, Thurston pressed on. "You were supposed to walk around, take in a few observations, and leave. Surely a fifteen-minute cursory stroll would have provided you with enough insight to fill volumes. Instead, you took a two-week vacation. I knew that you were upset when she asked you to le-"

Parker cut his mentor off as he shouted, "Nina?!"

Parker stood stock-still, his muscles tense, his hands slowly forming into fists. The warehouse appeared exactly as he had left it a few moments earlier. Except for one critical detail: Nina was not there.

"What is it?" Thurston asked, seeming to take advantage of Parker's stillness.

"Nina, she was just here!" Parker barely contained a scream. He was quickly losing control of the situation. He told her to stay there and not touch anything and she had run off. Probably with him, Parker's inner voice added, feeding his ire. He started off towards the console, then switched back, unsure of his next step. He paced back and forth in perfect rhythm. A human metronome sliding from one potential path to the next. Parker lifted his hands to his temples, as though he were just trying to massage a headache. Thurston spotted an ever so subtle tremor in his hand, a shaking that Parker was trying to quell, to keep it from reverberating out.

"We need to find her, she needs to go back to her universe," Thurston continued to plead with the back of Parker's head, unable to have an actual conversation with the young scientist.

Parker stormed past Thurston nearly knocking him over. "I'll find her," Parker yelled back over his shoulder, the echoes of Thurston's pleas quickly fading as he continued down the corridor and out of the building.

∞

It poured back into Nina's brain quickly, the fine details crawling out of the folds in her grey matter and carrying on as though they had never gone into hiding. She did still know him. She missed the last ten years of Hank's life, of this life, but she still knew who he was, and within a few moments, there was no doubt in her mind that this was the definition of a miracle. The impossible thing, the thing that she never let herself hope for had occurred very quickly. Or really, it had been happening all along in this world.

They walked hand in hand on their way to the house that she had only recently left with Parker. Parker, what had he been up to? The mismatched pieces of information were battling in her brain. Parker had been in her reality for two weeks, but she had been missing in this one for only a few days. It couldn't be a coincidence, but it didn't align. Something seemed to connect here, Nina just wasn't sure what. And then, like a lightning bolt, she remembered something germane to this entire situation.

It was August 8th. How could she forget? It was exactly ten years from the day that she lost Hank. He had been killed late that evening as they walked off their dinner. She had marked the passing of that day every year with a somber remembrance. Even with the extenuating circumstances of inter-dimensional travel, how could she ever forgive herself for forgetting? How did she not realize it until halfway through the day? Perhaps she could excuse herself given the multiverse-related funk she found herself in. But how lovely that it also happened to be the exact day that she got him back. Nina gave his hand a squeeze as they walked on, realizing that they had been silent, unspeaking, for several minutes.

"What was that for?" he asked with a smirk.

"I just like being able to hold your hand," she could explain that basic surface level feeling. Nina would have to find a way to tell him everything one day, but for now, this would suffice. She couldn't say what she was really thinking, because it could have come out like the ravings of a madwoman. *Oh, you know, I lived for the past decade in a reality where you were dead and now, I get to see you again.* Even if she had said the more poetic words that were in her heart they might not have sounded completely right. *You're like the tide, you keep coming back to me. And each time you do you bring fresh salt spilling and gurgling into my wounds and you take away the ground that I stand on, leaving me to wonder when I'll fall again.*

At that moment, that perfect moment, she wondered if Hank felt that this was as perfect as she did. Nina hadn't seen him in a decade, her feelings at that moment were based on another reality. *How was Hank feeling, what was he thinking?* She knew him as a young man, but now, who was he? Did he sense all that could have been?

With all of the things that she could or could not have said at that moment, the one question that slipped out was, "Does today's date, August 8th, mean anything to you?" Her voice sounded tentative, nervous. If he said no and asked why she would need to think of a reason, and explanation.

He stopped abruptly, their hands untangling as she continued to walk. Nina stopped and turned back to look at him. Oh no, had she killed him? Had her mere hint at the existence of another reality caused him to die here too? She looked up to see his eyes staring down at her. He waited for her to look at him.

He took a deep breath and started to speak. "Of course, it does," his voice trembled. She could see a dark pool starting to fill his lower eyelids, waiting to spill over. He looked away, across the street. Not wanting her to see him cry, but averting his own eyes instead of covering hers.

Had they been attacked in this reality too? Had he run for help, but returned too late? Did he blame himself?

"She would have been eight this year," he whispered. Nina felt the motion of all the planets and satellites in the known universes stop.

This was it. This was why they weren't together anymore. Nina moved quickly to hold him, to kiss him, to make some sort of physical apology for her words, her stupid words. She had no clue what she would uncover and now that she did, Nina wanted to bury it once more. *Give me back that perfect moment,* she thought. But Hank didn't let her hold him. He continued walking, slightly ahead of her, leaving Nina to think through all that she had just learned.

In this universe, maybe they had never been attacked. Hank hadn't been murdered. If Nina's math served her correctly, they would have had a daughter roughly 2 years later. But she was gone. Nina wanted to know more about her. What was she like? Did she favor Hank's features or Nina's? How long did they have with her? How did it happen? But she didn't dare to ask. She imagined Hank's suspicions would be even more acute, how could a mother not know those things?

They rounded the corner onto 28th Street and Nina felt grateful to almost be at their destination. She could fill the strained silence with logistical directions. *Yes, grab those shoes. No, we can leave that.* She didn't even know what she would want to take from this alien home.

Hank remained silent. What Nina really wanted to do was apologize for bringing it up, because what kind of a stupid mother would she be to bring up the child that they lost in that manner? Instead, she held him quickly and whispered, "I love you," before they headed inside. Nina wasn't sure if Hank and her alter-ago had returned to the stage of exchanging "I love yous" in this reality, but she felt it in her heart and it couldn't go unsaid anymore. His arms were tense and then relaxed, she felt a gentle kiss on the crown of her head before they let go.

They entered the home and with her head clear for the first time, Nina noticed something that she hadn't earlier in the day. A thick fragrance permeated the air, flowery and artificial. Hank must have noticed it too because his nose wrinkled for a second, a micro-expression come and gone on his face.

With the front door latched behind them, Nina made her way up the stairs to the bedroom so that she could pack. The smell didn't carry all the way up the stairs, thankfully.

Nina hoped that in removing and un-organizing all of her alter-ego's things that she would learn more about her and the life she had built here. Nina tried to move quickly, instructing Hank to take all of the items on hangers and put them into a suitcase. The first one that she grabbed was already half-full. A few pairs of high-heels, a make-up bag, and a framed photo. It was a picture that Nina recognized. The one with her Dad, their Dad, hers and the other-Nina's. He had been caught off guard at Nina's high school graduation as one of her classmates snapped a candid photo of the two of them laughing. He never smiled for photos, to see him laughing in this one made him still feel alive to her.

Why was this packed away? Had her alter-ego already tried to pack some things up? Where had she been for a few days? According to Parker, she wouldn't have disappeared from this reality until Nina had crossed over herself.

Parker. Right. Just then, Nina became nervous that Parker would return at any moment. He might have already realized that she had left the lab. She had lost track of time, how long had it been since she had answered Hank's phone call.

Nina wanted to avoid confrontation. She developed an eerie sense that the Parker in this reality wasn't like the one in her own reality, not in the fundamental ways that made up a person. The same name, look, profession. But underneath something was different. Nina's Parker was removed and above it all, above everyone, but this Parker seemed too invested, too intense, too much of the wrong things.

Nina knelt by the bed as she tried to unplug the phone charger, quickly. She yanked at the cord and bumped her head on the underside of the nightstand. That was when she heard heavy footsteps behind her.

K

Hank had two duffel bags stuffed to bursting in his hands. "You okay?" he asked as Nina rubbed her head and placed a power cord in her purse.

"Yeah, it's not a good day for my head," she said, trying to make light of her own predicament. Hank was baffled by her vague references, but he decided to let it slide until they were out of this house. Seeing the sugary-sweet photos of Nina with Parker on their way in was just enough to make him roll his eyes and gag. What had stopped her a few days ago? This question gnawed at him; Nina was never one to flip-flop on her decisions. But she seemed intent now as he watched her fill a bag with shoes.

He helped her pack another bag, but he knew that a life's worth of belongings wouldn't fit into four bags. With no moving truck, they would be bound by the limits of what they could carry. Nina had settled on clothes for a few days. With a few quick sentences, they had decided to come back later for more things: the big boxes stored in the basement, the knick-knacks that meant something to her, the crystal glasses handed down from her grandmother -

"The basement!" Nina called out, turning to leave the bedroom before Hank could stop her. Hank grabbed the two small bags and followed Nina down the hall. He considered that there could be some heavy-duty luggage in the basement. The kind with wheels and handles made for easy carrying. It would certainly make this process easier, but he started to feel the time pressure. He didn't want to find out what would happen if Parker came home to discover them packing Nina's things. The image started to form in his mind, *what if he had interrupted her a few days earlier?*

Nina marched downstairs and opened the door to the basement. Hank followed, leaving the already packed bags in the foyer. He must have sensed the odor first because he called out from the top of the steps, "Nina!" But she already reached the final step, grasping in the air for a chain to turn on the light. He watched her slowly take the final step into the basement in the dark as he continued down the stairs behind her. Hank hoped she would find the light before either of them could knock into something. He could hear Nina's feet shuffling against the basement floor, the sound soft and grainy.

As he continued down the steps, he ran his hand along the wall, looking for the light switch. *Odd, shouldn't Nina know where the switch is?* He wasn't a heavy man, but he was certainly heavier than Nina. The boards groaned and squeaked, announcing his approach. His hand landed on the switch; he flicked it quickly. The basement filled with yellow light. Just in time too, Hank had reached the final step.

Nina turned around to see Hank standing on the bottom stair, the plastic switch next to his outstretched arm. She opened her mouth to speak, but Hank didn't notice. He was fixed on the image before him. His nostrils were flared and his forehead creased, as he tried to discern what he was smelling. His jaw slackened, at first, it looked like he might yawn, but his mouth formed a perfect agape "o" instead. The color on his face drained, as though a plug had been pulled. The stark light cast off shadows across his face as his neurons put together the details. He was in shock, in horror. Nina must have read it on his face because she spun back around to see what he was looking at.

On the floor, in front of a box labeled "decorations," they saw a broken picture frame. It must have been a beautiful decoration when it had been on the wall, ornate carvings on the wood, a distressed glaze around the border. The glass had been cleared away, leaving only a wrinkled photo in the middle. It looked to belong to the set that decorated the rest of the house, posed photos of Nina and Parker. But they couldn't tell for sure. A burgundy stain covered the center of the image.

Next to the frame lay the focus of Hank's attention. A thick plastic tarp wrapped around an object. He heard Nina gasp; she covered her mouth quickly. That plastic tarp was thick and mostly opaque. But he could still see just enough. Wrapped in plastic, he could see the face of a woman, her face pressed against the outermost layer. Her features were blunted, but her eyes were dark, her lips were pale but full, strands of her black hair were trapped in lines criss-crossing her face. Nina's face. Hank's eyes darted between the two women in front of him: one standing, in shock, the other lying dead on the floor.

They had found the "other" Nina, but Hank didn't know yet that there was another Nina to be discovered.

5

August 31, 2015

They met in a bar; nothing could have been more basic and unremarkable as that. Nina was out with Carol, her closest friend who did not know it, but at the time, she was her only friend. After years of closing everyone out, Nina had only herself to blame.

Nina found that as long as she was able to keep Carol talking about herself, she was content to hang out. Besides, if Carol had asked Nina anything, she wouldn't have had much to say. Carol had created a rotation of happy hours at the bars within walking distance from the office. She wanted to be out and about, looking for love in all the places that movies and television shows had told her it would be hiding. She would often look over Nina's shoulder or crane her neck to see which men might be milling around.

So, it surprised Nina that Parker managed to sneak up on them without Carol having first spotted him. Parker seemed very clever, perhaps he was just lucky and slipped in when Carol was distracted. His slight frame might have led her gaze to pass over him even if she had spotted him. It was an easy comparison to draw in her mind right away, Parker being so thin when Hank had been so tall and broad-shouldered. Hank had a physical presence that would have dwarfed Parker. But Parker had a cerebral presence, his brain put out a kind of mental energy that was palpable.

That evening, he approached their table fueled by bravado and bourbon. Parker was with another egghead from the University. A shy and lanky aerospace engineer whose name was Woody, or at least that is what

79

everyone called him. Woody impressed Carol with his awkward silence as she chatted to him about her family, her gaggle of sisters, and her cat.

Parker used this opportunity to romance Nina. This surprised them both, she later found out as they reminisced on that first night many months later. Parker, used to being woefully smarter than everyone in the room, seemed impressed by her intelligence and ability to keep up with his banter. Or so he told her. She softened when she learned that he was a scientist. This made her think of her dad, the chemistry teacher, and in an unexpected moment of honesty, she told him that right away. It seemed that her honesty had endeared him at that moment. The cycle of softening and melting, massaging the walls they both possessed had begun that evening. Like a stick of butter, she started to collapse in the microwaves of Parker.

Woody left when he got a text from his roommate who had managed to get locked-out of their apartment. Parker offered to buy another round for both Nina and Carol, but Carol sensed that she had become the third wheel and declined his offer. After Carol left, Parker and Nina continued to talk and sip on their drinks until the bar closed. She couldn't even remember all of the things they discussed that night, but she did remember thinking to herself that it was the first time she had spoken that much in years.

Parker walked Nina to her doorstep and asked for her phone number. She hesitated for a moment. All of their talking had occurred so naturally, it hadn't really processed that she was flirting with a man who wasn't Hank. The thought caught her by surprise, it had been 7 years since he had been killed. At that moment, it felt like her life with Hank had been in another lifetime, he was as far away as another galaxy.

And so, Parker and Nina began their relationship. They became stitched together like scar tissue, so new, so fresh. Shiny and taut, no one could pull them apart. But Nina had never seen a scar swallowed by the unblemished skin around it. It never assimilates, never belongs. And in the end, it is just a violent reminder of what put it there in the first place.

L

"What is going on?" Hank roared as he lunged past Nina towards the body in the plastic sheet.

"I have no idea!" she said earnestly. Of all the places that she thought her alter-ego might be while she was in this universe, dead in the basement was not one of them.

"Nina, who is this?" Hank demanded. She couldn't tell if he was asking her or pleading with the corpse of his Nina, the real-Nina to him.

Her thoughts were slippery, like wet clothes she couldn't quite get a hold of them. She couldn't faint again; her head had been hit several times and she wasn't some antebellum debutant bound up in corsets and petticoats. Nina still found it hard to breathe as the facts began to swim in her mind.

Hank said Nina stopped returning his calls a few days earlier. Parker visited her universe that morning, but had stayed there for two weeks and lived there with her until very early that morning when he brought her back here.

What happened before Parker left for her universe could be the key to figuring this all out. Maybe the Nina here had been robbed while Parker was gone and the burglar hid her body down here. Maybe she slipped and fell when she came down here looking for luggage, but then that doesn't explain her being wrapped in plastic.

The theory that had been looming in the back of Nina's mind finally came to the forefront. Parker did this. A few days ago, when Nina, the other Nina, said she was leaving him. He killed her, hid her body, and then crossed the multiverse to find another Nina, brought her back here, and no one would have been the wiser. Except she wasn't that Nina. The other

Nina's body still laid in the basement. So, he would still have to come back home and move it. Nina worried about when he would do that.

The electrical currents of these thoughts swirled in her mind, finally coalescing into a single terrifying word. "Parker."

Hank turned around and met her gaze, the other Nina still cradled in his arms. "We have to go now!"

Without hesitation, they ascended the stairs, grabbed the few items at the front door, and headed back out into a hot summer afternoon. They walked briskly, nearly running until they were around the corner and down the street. "We need to call the p-" Hank started to say between exasperated breaths.

"Hank, let's get to your place and then we can discuss this," Nina cut him off. She didn't want him to say the words. As though mentioning aloud that they should call the police might cause three squad cars to turn the corner, sirens blaring.

Heeding her caution, Hank remained silent for the rest of the walk. Nina could sense that Hank was exploding with questions to ask. *Did he suspect?* Could he tell that she wasn't who he thought she was? And what would happen when the police did discover the body? They would question the people who knew her and swear that they saw her that morning. Would Nina be a suspect? An identical stranger whose blood tests would surely throw all of the machine instruments out of whack with her other-dimensional microbes. And what if it wasn't Parker who had killed her? Nina's Parker in her home universe was never violent. A prick at times, arrogant and self-serving, but never violent. But in a reality where every possibility does occur, perhaps this Parker's insecurities manifested in violence.

When they arrived at Hank's apartment, Nina began to feel the reality of the conversation they were about to have weighing down on her. Calling the police and having the other Nina's murderer put away were only the first of many chasms to cross. She knew this dream where she was reunited with Hank would become a reality soon, the messy edges of this decision and ones the other Nina had made in the past would bubble up. It had only been a few hours, but she felt that she had lived another lifetime. It had only been hours earlier that in the fog of her worry and concern that she ran to Parker, and now she was about to abandon him. But she had Hank back, and Parker had a lot of explaining to do.

Once they were inside with the front door closed behind them, Hank had his phone in his hand. "I'm calling the police now!" It was the final definitive statement in an argument he had inside his mind during their silent walk. She nodded, accepting that he was indeed making the right choice. Taking the bags from his hands, she headed down the hallway. Nina didn't want to hear what he said to the police, if he announced his suspicions of her true identity. She would lose him again soon; she could feel it. The meek and bewildered younger version of herself, trapped deep inside, was mourning him all over again, deep in the throes of denial.

Nina dropped her bags down on the bed in Hank's room. Their room now. Her face flashed hot for a moment, other more physical thoughts flooded her mind. She willed her cheeks to cool and her color to return before he could walk in. Nina began to unpack the shoes and place them in ordered pairs along the floor of the closet when she heard metered buzzing.

She turned and saw her purse vibrating in time. "Thurston" flashed in stark white letters across the lock screen. Worried that she had been found out and was about to be ordered back to the lab and sent home, Nina pictured herself grabbing the already packed bags and ordering Hank to live a life on the run with her. A fugitive from the scientists who brought her here. But instead, she answered the call.

"Nina?" she heard Thurston bark into the phone before he began to cough.

"Yes, Professor Thurston?" she tried to keep her voice steady and calm. Perhaps a little worried, certainly there could be no good reason for Parker's boss to call her in the middle of the day. *Play dumb*, she instructed herself.

"Nina, I've just had a troubling conversation with Parker. I'm sorry to call on you, but I need you to come down to the lab." Before she could begin to answer, he continued, as though anticipating her objections. "For multiple reasons, first of all, I need to contain this situation and secondly, after the conversation I just had with Parker, I am concerned that he may hurt someone. And also, goodness, you're the first person from another universe to visit us, I need to interview you and record your impressions of our world."

He sounded winded, as though he had spoken each word while trying to run a marathon in three hours flat. His request had disarmed her. Thurston knew. Now that she was aware of his inclusion in Parker's secret, she couldn't lie or play dumb. Nina also didn't want to be here when the police arrived. She was sure that she had broken no laws or violated any rules, but that didn't ease her worries. And if she didn't go, if she stayed with Hank, what would Thurston and Parker do to bring her back in.

"Okay," Nina whispered. "I'll be at the lab as soon as I can." She left a brief note for Hank:

"I can explain everything. I love you. I have to go to Parker's lab. – Your Nina"

Nina wished she could have heard him coming down the hallway, calling out from the kitchen. Some final trace of him for her to remember before she slipped out the bedroom window and down the fire escape. She wasn't sure if that would be it, but she was determined that it would not be the last time she saw Hank.

M

The front door of the building slammed closed behind her. The empty classrooms left more room for the sound to echo and reverberate. The clock in the hallway read 3:46 pm. Nina didn't want to go to the lab. It was too close to the exit, the Portal, the way back to a universe where Hank was dead. Back to the universe where she felt dead. Nina sensed that just being within 100 yards of the University was too close, that the gravity of the situation and the machine itself would pull her back to her sad little reality.

It was a precarious situation. She felt like an outsider, like an alien trapped on a strange planet. Yet this is where Hank lived on. The sights and sounds were familiar enough, but each second felt stolen, borrowed. Nina thought, *I shouldn't be here, but here I am.*

She was afraid for Dr. Thurston and their research. If Parker posed a threat, he might have already destroyed the Portal. She didn't have any intention of crossing the Plain again. She had Hank now, and even though she would have loved to find the universe where both he and their daughter were both alive, Nina could compromise with one miracle to last for the rest of her natural life. Even though her life there would never be natural.

Silently, Nina entered the lab, unsure of what she would find. Her footsteps were tentative, as though each one was asking for permission to land on the dated laminate flooring. Odd as it was, the lab appeared perfectly in order. Thurston sat on one of the stools, his hands worrying his hair. He appeared lost in thought, concern drawing deep lines across his brow.

Thurston looked up and spotted her, his train of thought distracted. "Nina! Thank you for coming back in. Have you heard from Parker?"

She shook her head, "I haven't seen him since you asked to speak with him earlier."

Thurston accepted her answer, barely hiding his disappointment, "Well, he will turn up soon enough. But first things first, we need to document our first visitor!" He offered a weak smile, Nina assumed this was to put her at ease. This Thurston seemed just as kind, but perhaps more fatherly. He had a softness about him that Nina either hadn't noticed in his alter-ego or that wasn't there to begin with.

Thurston set up a video camera, an audio recorder, and some other machines on the warehouse side of the lab. He explained that one of the machines would monitor her frequency. That was how he explained it. She emitted her own decay frequency, which left a signature that could be seen on the instruments. That was how anyone could be found in the multiverse, they just had to know where and when to look, and the person's frequency as well. Nina felt like a test mouse with wires attached to her arms and her head.

For all of the trial runs and anticipation of this moment, Thurston was unprepared for this opportunity. Although, he did have enough of a director's eye to frame the video with Nina sitting in front of the Portal. He didn't have a set of questions ready to go; he seemed to just wing it. He began the recording, standing behind the camera that was trained on Nina.

"This is Dr. Norman Thurston. Today's date is August 8, 2018. It is 4:02 pm Eastern Daylight Time," he confirmed as he glanced at his watch.

Nina fidgeted as she tried to sit up straight for the video recording, her voice and invisible decay signature would not be subject to the same level of scrutiny as a visual record would. At least, that was what she thought.

"Lab interview 000001. Feminina Marks. What was the date when you left?" Thurston began.

"August 8," Nina kept her voice smooth and clinical. She put off the vocal fray that was so rampant in her world.

"What year?" He had cautioned her to answer his questions with specific and direct answers. She was already failing a test that she didn't know how to take.

"2018."

Thurston nodded as he continued down his hasty checklist, one he had jotted down just moments before he began recording. "Where did you live?"

"The District of Columbia, United States of America, Earth." Nina had thought that last word would be a humorous answer. Apparently, it was the level of precision that Thurston expected from her.

"How many hours are in a day?" His hand slid down the page with smooth precision as he moved from one question to the next.

"24."

"How many days in a year?"

"365."

Thurston quickly scribbled a note. "Um, 365.25 actually," Nina clarified. "We have an extra day added to the calendar every 4th year. We call it: Leap Year."

"Very interesting," Thurston nodded as his eyes went wide.

"How many days are in your year?" Nina wasn't sure if she could ask questions herself, but she was so curious.

"365.33 to the infinite. We have an extra day every third year." Thurston looked up and smiled, happy to have found something a little different. "This is bonkers," Thurston shook his head as he made a note. His cheeks flushed; Nina could see the excitement return to his eyes. She could tell that he loved every moment of that interview, even if he was ill-prepared.

"Who was the first President of the United States?" the professor resumed his line of questioning.

"George Washington," Nina wanted to know if any more of her answers varied from the expected answer. If anything was unexpected, Thurston did not show it on his face again.

Nina wasn't the first person to cross the Plain, as they were calling it. Parker would forever hold that record, as far as they knew. But she was the first person from another universe to visit this one, so that was good enough. Thurston was fascinated by the things that were similar. Fumbling through the interview, Thurston seemed to catch his stride around current events.

"Who is the current President of the United States?" Thurston asked several moments later after having passed through a general world history survey.

Nina was about to answer when she thought the better of it. "You might not believe me," and she chuckled. An all-knowing, *you're not going to believe this*, laugh was all she could offer.

"Well, we have Penelope Whittle." Thurston looked up from his list finally, breaking the formal and official nature of the questioning and having a conversation with Nina.

"Who?" The name he offered sounded foreign to her, a stranger's name.

"She isn't a politician in your universe?" Thurston prompted, trying to trigger a memory that she didn't have.

"Not that I know of. I don't follow politics much, although in DC it can be hard to avoid. I don't recognize her name though."

"Curious," Thurston scribbled a note in his journal.

"And Eleanor Roosevelt was President in this reality?" Nina asked, still so unsure of what was real and what wasn't in this world.

"Yes, 33rd President. Took the oath after Franklin died in office. Did that not happen in your world?"

"No. There's never been a female President of the United States in my world." Saying it aloud sounded sad. This world that she had been stolen to had not one, but two female Presidents already and perhaps more. The streets were clean and pedestrian friendly. The advertisements weren't objectifying. Nina marveled at how these small and big differences could have happened without interrupting her birth, Hank or Parker or Thurston existing. Or Dean Winchester for that matter.

They continued for a bit longer, but it was clear that Thurston would have been content to carry on for an infinite amount of time, to try and capture everything.

"I should have been the one to go across first," he said with a sigh as he turned off the recording. "Then none of this would have happened." Nina didn't know what to say to comfort him, but she could tell that the man needed reassurance.

"Maybe there are just some things that have to happen a certain way," Nina offered.

"Like a predestination paradox?" Thurston clarified.

Not even knowing what that term meant, Nina agreed. "Sure, exactly." But she would learn the meaning of that phrase soon enough.

N

The cord snapped and flopped against the floor, the sound startled Nina, and then it zipped as Thurston wound it around his arms. Only one of the many cables that had been in use during the interview, Thurston rolled it up and packed it away with the monitoring equipment first. He unplugged and stored away the device that monitored Nina's brain waves during the interview, leaving her to peel off the leads from her forehead, forearms, and neck. She found a box of tissues nearby and used one to wipe off the stickum that left a residue on her skin.

With the camera and voice recorder off, Nina let her thoughts wander to Hank. *When would he find the note? How long would it take him to wait for and explain the odd series of events to the police? When would the sirens begin their march, screaming towards campus?* Nina glanced up at the clock, their interview had already taken close to an hour. *Where was Parker? Where was the cavalry?*

Nina offered to help Thurston as he put away the video gear. She broke down the tripod and asked Thurston about the genesis of the project. Without much prompting, Thurston explained the experimental process that he and Parker worked through. It would have been difficult to push objects across the Plain, how would they ever know if it even arrived? Mice, lab rats? It wouldn't work, how would they ever be able to get back without the help of someone who knew what was going on? And they couldn't presume that someone in that universe would know where the rodent came from. Sure, they would have to have a machine, but they might just think their lab had an infestation. Or maybe they would think that someone had dropped something, unless they were there the instant that the Portal activated.

They also had the problem of not activating too many of them. They figured out that they didn't need to find the power source. They just needed to advance the Portal to the exact time when the first person would activate theirs from another universe to travel to Thurston and Parker's reality.

"So, you just waited?" Nina asked as she stuffed the audio equipment into a foam-lined bin. She couldn't imagine the agony of having such a powerful machine and not being able to even test it for an unknown amount of time.

"No, not at all. You see the only vehicle that can grant access to the multiverse is a time machine, by definition. So, we didn't have to find the exact power source and plug it in. We needed to find the moment in time when the machine would be activated and plug into that." Thurston explained this plainly, and in spite of Nina's limited understanding of cosmology and physics, she actually understood what he meant. Or she thought she did; the words not really sinking in, she was unable to use this knowledge later when she really needed it.

"But someone, somewhere still had to invent the power source then, right?" Nina thought about how far into the future this invention might have been. She assumed it would have to be in the future. She didn't ask any technical questions about the power source, doubting her ability to follow in spite of her track record for understanding these concepts.

"Yes, and if I ever get to meet that person, I will buy him a drink. But, until we do..." Thurston let his thought trail off as he pressed his hand to the side of the Portal, stroking it affectionately. Nina bristled slightly at the implication, *why did Thurston assume it would be a man who invented the power source?*

"How do you know which universes have developed a Portal? Or that it is even the same design and that it works properly." The questions were slipping out now, each one fighting to be launched first.

Thurston rolled his chair over to another bank of monitors hooked up to a supercomputer. The screens looked like EKG readouts with horizontal lines of various colors humming across.

"We can identify the frequency that the machine emits, just like with people," Thurston explained, referencing back to his previous answers. "Once the Portal is complete and operational it emits a certain signature." He pointed to a light blue line that appeared on the top of the first screen, with a quick glance Nina could see that it also appeared on the other screens.

"We've found a dozen or so universes with it. Each time we find a new one we add a monitor and begin to look for other similarities." She noticed that most of the screens had a bright orange line, almost all had a neon green line. Their lines spiking and descending in specific patterns, the orange more aggressive, the green more mellow.

"And each of us emit a certain frequency. Think of it as your fingerprint in the multiverse. So, you exist here and now," he pointed to a yellow line in the middle screen. "And you used to also show up here," he pointed to another screen that had a dead space in the middle.

"That's my home?" It was hard to imagine that the entirety of the universe that she came from could be displayed visually on one tiny screen.

"Yes, your line was here up until the time that you crossed over." He rearranged the screen and now she could see two faint yellow lines running in parallel. One cut off abruptly halfway across the screen.

"See how this one gets fainter, and then," he snapped his fingers, "Now you are here with this line. It was actually a little softer, so that is something we will want to test. Does your proximity to the instrument cause your signature to change slightly?" He jotted a note on the corner of a report, haphazardly leaving his questions to sit idly until he could discover them again. Nina's mind thought back to the other Nina, suffocated and sealed in plastic in Parker's basement. She stepped back from the screen to compose herself. If she told Thurston outright, he might not believe her. If he figured it out himself, he might jump to the right conclusion and be willing to help her, or at least wouldn't be as shocked when the police finally arrived. She was always good at thinking on her feet, quickly directing the conversation: "Well, does your line match up?"

"Yes, but–" Thurston looked puzzled. "You know, in all of the excitement, I hadn't checked that Nina. You sure you aren't a physicist back home?"

Nina smiled at him, flattered by the idea. But then she realized that it wasn't a crazy idea after all and that she should just accept it for what it was and not assign any added sentiment to it.

"And come to think of it, I'm not in every one of these universes. So, either I did not ever exist in those, or my alter-egos are already traveling across the multiverse and having great adventures." Thurston crammed additional notes on the margins before finally flipping the page and using the back-side for his thoughts.

"How can you tell which universe is which?"

"Well we have given them very basic nicknames, but we are cataloging them with the Greek alphabet. Here, where we are now is Alpha. Your universe, our first stop, is Beta. And that is because we are here and this is our starting point. I'm sure once we connect with some other travelers that we will need to agree on a common nomenclature."

"But to me, this is Beta and my home is Alpha," Nina confirmed.

"Precisely," Thurston gave an approving nod.

"So, are you sad that you'll never get to meet your alter-ego?" She tried to steer the conversation back to the issue, engineering a way to get him to realize why the other Nina's signature started to fade.

"I'm not convinced that I won't be able to. That is Parker's hypothesis and just because he might not have seen his alter-ego doesn't mean anything. I didn't get to ask him much earlier," Thurston noted as he glanced at his watch, the time eliciting a frown. He let out a sigh and continued. "Maybe that Parker is a flake." Thurston might have been making a joke, or he could have been commenting on his colleague who was still missing.

"Well, Parker told me that my alter-ego couldn't exist at the same time and in the same space as me. I feel guilty that I've exiled her to the void while I'm here." Nina played up the emotion in her voice, she did feel horrible but not because of anything to do with this metaphysical conundrum. She felt horrible that her alter-ego was dead and as the minutes ticked by, she became more and more convinced that it was Parker who had killed her. *Come on Thurston. Put it together.*

"That's Parker's theory. He would need lots of evidence to validate that. But when you do go back home, we'll have to see what happens."

"When I go back?" Nina stepped back from him involuntarily. Her body pushing her away from the thing that she wanted the least.

"Well, you do want to go back, right?" Thurston looked up at Nina, puzzled by her response.

"I'm not sure that I do." Concerned that her true reason for staying would come across, that Thurston would somehow sense her connection with Hank, she scrambled for a reason, desperate to fill the silence. "I have a better job, a nicer house, and it seems like the society here is more advanced." She imagined what her routine had been back in her world. It was grey, she walked to and from work with her head down, her shoulders slouched. That life was dreary, that Nina was muted, a tragic and unengaged version of herself. She had been walking around like a blown-out balloon. Her form growing slack, her movements wobbly. She lost Hank and even though it was painful, the worst part now was knowing that she had easily accepted it. Why hadn't she considered that they could be reunited in a parallel universe? Where had this simple but impossible idea been all those years ago?

Thurston gestured for her to sit down next to him. "Nina, I don't think that is possible." He sighed as he began to speak. His tone sounded hushed and reserved, as though he was about to break some bad news to her. "For one, what if your alter ego is suspended between the universes? That would be horrible to force her to continue to endure."

Nina opened her mouth to interrupt him, to tell him the truth. Thurston held up a finger, silencing her as he continued. "But more acutely, and again this is conjecture that would require more testing, you aren't from here. Things look and feel the same, but this isn't your universe. It wasn't made for you. You can't stay here and expect to have the same health quality, life expectancy. You have antibodies for common illnesses in your universe that will have no chance against the viruses here, and vice versa. You could be infecting all of us with a super flu that we have no chance of combatting."

"What if this universe is better for me?" In spite of the mounting evidence against the Parker of this universe, Nina sensed that everything else really did appear to be improved.

"But what if it isn't? What if you cut your life short by decades because of some anomaly in our universe that we can all stand or that we all need, but that is toxic to you?"

"How can that be, we're all human? Yes, I want to live a long and healthy life, but I want to live it. And from what I've seen, staying here will give me a more fulfilled life than if I go back. Maybe I was always meant to be here."

∞

There was a time for grand romantic gestures and there was a time to be practical. Now it felt like both. Hank worried that he was caught in an elaborate and visceral dream that he couldn't wake up from, a nightmare of epic proportions. Had he really just found Nina dead in Parker's basement, or was it just someone who looked like her? He had been with Nina when they made the discovery, so this had to be a bad dream.

He read through the note twice before moving. The note was real enough. He felt the thin piece of paper with his fingertips, the indentations from her pen strokes still fresh. Hank put it in his pocket and started off towards the University.

It had been a dizzying day of back and forth. He set out again, this time he felt his feet moving faster. Unable to walk or stroll, he marched at a brisk pace, cutting past people on the sidewalk. He dialed the emergency line again, informing the operator that he was now going to the University because he feared that Nina was in danger.

"Sir, was this the woman that you called to report missing yesterday?" the operator's voice sounded very nasal.

"Yes, but I just saw her today and-" Hank tried to explain again.

"This same woman you saw earlier today, who was with you when you discovered her body in a basement?" the voice sounded skeptical.

"Yes! I can't explain it, but Parker Lovett has a dead body in his basement and I think he may hurt Nina now. Aren't you supposed to help save people?" Hank sensed that the people around him were starting to stare at the mad man speeding by and screaming horrible words into his phone.

"Sir, please remain calm. I'm here to help," the voice said in a trained and clinical tone. Her words sounded rehearsed.

"If you want to help, get to the University Sciences Building now to prevent Parker Lovett from killing someone else!" Hank disconnected the line, pressing his thumb to the off button as forcefully as he could. He wished for a second that he still had a flip-phone and could have slammed it shut to emphasize his growing frustration and panic.

As the crosswalk changed from orange to white, Hank took off running. Forget trying to look calm, forget trying to not alarm the people around him. He was alarmed! As he ran, he brushed by several strangers. Had they been intentionally barricading him? How could people walk so slow? How could no one else sense the danger that was around them?

He needed to get to Nina, needed to protect her. He wouldn't lose her again. He wouldn't lose another one of his girls that day. Hank had spent the past few days trying to find her and years trying to win her back. Maybe he wasn't thinking straight, maybe he would arrive at the lab to find no one there. He was too confused and hurt and exhausted to worry about that. He had to get their first, he had to get to Nina before it was too late.

Parker closed the final door behind him, taking extra care to not make a single sound. He had checked every classroom on the first floor. They were all empty for the day. Parker scanned the hallway once more, no one running back to fetch a forgotten item, no one loitering, no one to interrupt his work.

He had returned to the lab after taking a few turns around the campus. He had calmed down, or at least he wasn't as blind with anger as he had been when he stormed out. Some food in his stomach helped too. He was prepared to apologize to Thurston, his frustrations weren't with his mentor, but he had lashed out on him instead. Parker knew that the rational thing to do was to make good with his mentor. His plan would work, he just needed to be patient.

Parker had been on the edge of the lab when he heard her voice. And something in his blood started to boil once more. He loved her, but he remembered the pain she had inflicted on him. In his mind, he knew they were two separate people, but he couldn't disassociate the feelings. He hoped that this Nina would be different, that she would be appreciative of what he was able to give her. But she had all the same faults, the same weaknesses.

No, this current plan would not work. But he still had time. There was more than enough time in the day to take another trip and find another Nina. A better Nina. A perfect Nina who would never leave him.

He didn't like the idea of taking another trip, but what choice did he have? Like a hunter, he stalked back down the hallway, past the dark spot where the lights were always burning out, and towards the lab. His footsteps were light, feline in the way he stepped from toe to heel. He had the element of surprise on his side and he intended to leverage it.

0

W*as that a siren?* Nina thought, desperately hoping for the police to arrive. She should just tell Thurston about the body. He would at least understand the ramifications of what her discovery meant. Anyone else would think she was crazy. *"Oh, I found my body in Parker's basement."* But Thurston would know it wasn't a delusion.

Thurston stood and gathered the tripod and video equipment under his arms and hauled the clunky boxes that protected the audio and video gear in thick foam padding away from the Portal, through the thick plastic curtains, out of sight.

Tell him now, Nina thought. She took several timid steps to follow him. And then there was a definite whine in the distance, an elongated noise that could only be a siren. Her senses prickled, adrenaline starting to enhance her hearing. Nina could feel it; something was in the air other than the charged particles around the Portal.

Parker didn't want to hurt the man, but he could not be trusted. He needed to stop this mess from spreading. He felt like the bank robber with purple dye all over his face. One problem resolved and two more pop up. *Does Nina want to leave me?* No way. *I only wanted to make her stop and listen.* But then she tripped. Parker remembered seeing her back was at the wrong angle and her eyes glassed over. Her skin became so very cold. *So, I found another Nina. One who I thought was worthy, but she will just leave me too. And then Thurston has to go and get all noble. No. No more mess. I'll clean*

this one up for good. Building his confidence, and rage, Parker stormed into the lab. Thurston had his back to the entrance; he was fiddling with something on a computer. No sign of Nina, but Parker had just heard her. *She must be in the lab.* He needed to take action; Parker pawed the first loose object he could find.

Thurston plugged the camera into the computer and saw that the download had started automatically. He set down the camera gently, careful to not jiggle the cord and disrupt the process. "100% Complete" flashed across the screen. *This ought to earn me a Nobel Prize.* He pictured accolades and interviews; congratulations being sent in from the corners of the globe. First, he had to handle Parker. But this interview was solid gold.

Thurston clicked on the file and dragged it over to his cloud account. That progress bar started to jog as well, fast then slow then fast again. He heard a soft *click* behind him. Thurston turned in just enough time to see him. Hand raised above his head with a hefty object. Face mean, primal, channeling all of his rage. And then, nothing. Thurston was no longer Thurston.

There was a resolute thud out in the ante-room of the lab. Without even thinking it, Nina's feet moved her closer to the partition. From behind the thick curtains of butcher plastic, she watched as Parker folded Thurston's arms over his chest and dragged him by the feet out of the lab. She could feel every follicle on her arms prickle with goose flesh. Parker had just hit Thurston. Naively, she hoped that he was only knocked out. *What kind of man is this Parker?* The body in the basement, the attack on Thurston, and of course, Nina herself. She hadn't come to this reality freely. She was brought here against her will.

Her hands moved to her pocket, palming the cell phone. Each screen and step took painfully too long as she tried to rush and send a message to Hank.

"In the lab, Parker is dangerous. If I don't make it out."

She hit send before she knew what the next step would be.

Should she tell him to call the police? Again? What jurisdiction would the metro police have in multi-dimensional crimes? Should she tell him to avenge her? Or should she just say goodbye?

Before she could decide, Nina heard Parker coming back to the lab. Frozen with panic, she watched as he marched directly toward where she was hiding. He was headed straight for the machine.

Nina moved back from the partition and held her body flat against the closest wall. Nowhere to hide in a big concrete box, she tried to remain still. Maybe if she remained still as a statue, he couldn't see her. But unlike other predators, Parker's vision was perfect and she had nowhere to hide.

6

November 7, 2015

The first months were unreal. It was as though Nina had finally decided to join the rest of the world after years of isolation in space. She had built a cement room within her memory for all things Hank to go into, air-sealing all of her feelings for him and putting them into a plastic tub, never to be taken out again. It was a new mechanism for moving on. She assumed that her therapy had finally kicked into effect, after the six sessions that she attended, before she stopped going.

Parker was romantic, he had studied popular romantic movies and had executed on the leading-male plot points perfectly. Within the first two weeks of their courtship, Parker ordered a bouquet to her office. Instead of flowers, he had couriered over a dozen carefully crafted paper decahedron on green pipe-cleaners. It was perfectly nerdy and well executed. Carol listened intently as she shared each exciting detail of their regular calls and texts. As Parker and Nina settled into their relationship, she shared less with Carol, because by that point he was just being a good boyfriend and it didn't need much fanfare.

One weekend they took a trip up to the mountains with Woody and Priya (it turns out Woody was not into Carol, so Parker had arranged for a graduate student that Woody had blushed at to accompany them).

Lemon scented bug spray is what she recalled the most from that trip. And the freezing rain that started at dawn. Sure, the meteor shower was beautiful. Sharing it with Parker felt special, his excitement for the event had amplified her own. Mostly though, Nina was excited to have a weekend away with her boyfriend. She didn't care that she sounded like a silly girl to be so proud to have a boyfriend. She felt ready to be happy again. Nina was ready to let new love obliterate her old cracked and broken heart and replace it with a new self-sustaining cylinder that had been 3D printed in an advanced laboratory.

In the week leading up to the trip, Nina had rented a daily car-share and went out to the sporting goods store at the mall. She picked up wool socks and pants that had ties at the ankle to keep water and cold air out.

She dug out her boots that had gone long unused in the back of her closet. The last time she had worn them was on a trip to the Grand Canyon with Hank. Hank had insisted that she needed solid footwear and bought her the pair. Rust colored dirt still filled in the tread. Nina's mind flashed to a hot and sticky day, holding Hank's hand even after the sweat collected between their fingers. The sky above and the canyon below went on as far as either of them could see. But she had worked up a thirst and Hank was hungry. Neither of them had packed for the long trail and they both worried about getting a sunburn given the amount of sunscreen that must have sweat off. So, Nina and Hank took in the view quickly and hoofed it back up the canyon to their air-conditioned motel room.

Nina brushed the dirt from the bottom of the shoes as she brushed the memory away. Comparisons did her no good. And given the forecast for the weekend trip, it would only further set the two men as arch rivals in her heart. Hank was heat; he was a warm spring day and a home-cooked meal. Parker was cool and unemotional, the kind of person that Nina needed because she had become that way herself. The meteor shower was predicted for Saturday evening, after the sun set and the temperature sunk below 50 degrees Fahrenheit. Parker always specified that he was referring to temperature in Fahrenheit. It was a nerdy quirk that made Nina smile. *Of course, I wasn't thinking of things in Centigrade, Parker. So silly.*

The couples slept in tents with down sleeping bags, an activity Nina would never have considered at an earlier time in her life. They stayed up to watch the meteor shower and roasted s'mores. It was easy to forget who she had been before Parker. That Nina was an average girl who had a good run of bad luck. It didn't matter that she had never been outdoorsy, because now she was the type of girl who was fascinated by cosmic events and the minutia of Parker's research and all of the ancillary activities that went along with that. Like camping in the woods to watch a meteor shower.

P

The various machines that were deconstructed and repurposed for the Portal must have been shiny and new when they were first unpackaged and broken apart. The mismatched screws and casings left room between the different components, allowing for a jiggle as Parker pounded at the keyboard. The metal sheeting fit poorly to the console, like clothes that were one-size too big.

A hiss released as a cloud of freezing air descended from the exhaust pipe above the Portal, bringing the temperature of the room down. Nina tried to hold her teeth together, refusing to let them chatter.

Whatever was in that plume had a horrible chemical smell, she couldn't place it though. Was it noxious or poisonous? How was she to know?

Parker continued to work at the screen, his fingers moving over the keypad with purpose. He knew exactly what he needed to do. On the monitor she saw more yellow lines, more Nina frequencies. Her gaze shifted over to the Portal. No longer a frame in the middle of a room, it was now filled up. Between the edges of the Portal appeared a wall of – something. It looked like a liquid because of the diaphanous way it seemed to rise and fall and swell and recede. But if it was a liquid it would have fallen, right? It appeared pearlescent, foamy. Her ears wanted to catch a tidal sound, the churning of this small sea and crashing of its waves. But all she could hear was the crunch and squeak of the machine before a massive roar began to fill the warehouse.

Looking over at the console, Nina saw one monitor lit up with the words "OPEN" flashing in bright blood red with a timer below "0:60". The Portal was activated, it happened that quick. Nina's brain wrapped around this concept quickly, a lifetime of sci-fi movies and dating a theoretical physicist helped with that basic understanding. But she couldn't quite understand Parker's next move, or hers.

A body in the basement of her alter ego, potentially a second if Thurston was more than just knocked out. This Parker was a murderer, a criminal. And he had access to the most powerful machine that had ever been thought up. Was he about to escape to another dimension? Live his life on the run, never accountable for his crimes?

The timer now read "0:45."

Parker had been so focused on whatever he had planned, if he had a plan at all, that he still hadn't seen her. She could just run out, go as fast as her legs could carry her. Sprint until her legs felt like jelly and her lungs burned for air. Nina could feel her feet beginning to move, to shift, preparing for the flight response. But her mind kept interrupting. *What happens if he goes through and never comes back? Who will have to answer for the body in the basement? How will I answer any questions about my identity? How could I explain who I was and what I was doing here?* No, Parker needed to stay put.

Without a plan, without thinking, she lunged for Parker. Charging from behind, he didn't see her coming. She knocked something out of his hand. A syringe filled with an orange liquid shattered against the side of the console.

"Nina!" Parker howled as he gathered himself. She tried to stay on top of him, to keep him from getting away.

"I saw you! You killed him! You killed them both!" The adrenaline that had triggered the fight part of the fight-or-flight response didn't help her brain put together eloquent sentences. But as she shouted at him, she felt herself growing stronger, angrier. Something that had been locked away within her for a long time had sprung loose.

But her strength had only been a result of a chemical reaction, an adrenaline response. Parker was actually strong. Or this Parker was. Her Parker never went to the gym and often joked that his favorite form of bicep curl was lifting french fries to his mouth. He was tall and thin but somehow never needed to work out to maintain his trim frame. This Parker had muscular strength. Which he very clearly demonstrated as he flipped Nina over, crushing her to the ground beneath him. He pinned her down.

"No, you won't get away with this!" she struggled to kick and punch. But it was ineffective.

"You and me, Nina. We're two quarks. The harder they try to pull us apart, the stronger our bond will be. We are meant to be together. In this universe, in the next. In all of them!" Parker didn't blink the entire time he screamed the words at her, hollering to be heard over the mechanical noise of the console. The fans within the computers trying their best to keep the components cool. The energy that would not be ignored pumping into the Portal. There was so much noise, and it shouldn't have surprised her. Chaotic moments are never quiet.

"You're a murderer!" she tried to scream louder. She hoped that someone, anyone from the lab would hear. But it was already well past 5:00 pm. The day had flown by between the confusion in the morning, reuniting with Hank, moving bags of items to his place, the interview with Thurston. It just slips away when you're not paying attention to it. Time can be so unforgiving. And at that time of day, no one would hear her, especially over the machine.

"I tried to give you a better life here with me, Nina!" He shook his head, his features were all bright red, the blood surged to his head and swelled the blood vessels on his forehead.

"No, you just needed another Nina because you killed her! I saw the body!" But her words didn't stop him. He was unphased by the accusation, a sure sign of guilt to Nina. He shifted and kept her pinned down with one arm while he grabbed for something on the table above.

"Now we can't have you running around saying things like that, Nina," his tone was unbroken. The sudden calm in his voice terrified her. He pulled back his right hand and in it was another syringe, also filled with orange liquid.

"What are you doing? Stop! No! Help!" Nina screamed until her voice began to break, her throat raw from effort.

"If you can't play along then we'll just have to find someone else who will." Referring to himself as 'we', he had definitely turned the corner from impassioned lover who killed someone in a fit of jealousy to just flat out bonkers.

He stuck the syringe into Nina's arm and plunged the liquid into her bloodstream. She didn't even know what it was. *Would she die? Was the needle sterile?* And then, as though the tide had changed suddenly on the beach and the roar of the waves had died down, a calm quiet came over her.

"Nina!" she heard a voice calling for her, outside of the room. Beyond the plastic tarps. A voice that made her smile, but she couldn't place it.

"Time to go!" Parker said in a hushed voice as he pulled Nina up by the arms. She tried to keep her weight low to the ground. She had to resist him. *Why did she have to do that again?*

"Nina!" The same voice again, it sounded closer. *Was it Hank? Yes!* That was Hank's voice calling for her.

"Hank?" she muttered, her voice weak and gravely. The sound of her own speech sounded wounded and faint. Her lips felt numb and unfocused; she could barely get the name out.

Parker had positioned her in front of the Portal.

"Nina!" she heard Hank again and knew for sure that it was him this time. She tried to turn around so she could call out to him.

"Hank!" she tried with all of her effort, but it barely registered. Parker, standing in front of her smiled. The drugs he had pushed into her system must have made her start to see things. She could have sworn he sprouted horns. And was that Hank that she heard after all? Nina saw Hank push through the plastic, he looked panicked. But was he really there?

She glanced over at the countdown on the monitor. It read 0:08.

Eight, just like infinity, only sideways.

Nina felt like she was falling backwards. Parker's hands were outstretched. He had pushed her down. No, not down. Through. She fell through the Portal into another universe. *Was that Hank she saw rush at Parker? Was Parker squeezing his hand into a fist to fight Hank?* It all happened so quickly. And then she saw nothing.

PART 3

Their worst fears came true: women took positions of leadership and the emasculation of our society began in earnest. After years of writing policy and winning the necessary legal battles to enact these measures, the women were finally able to settle the score and right some long-standing wrongs.

"Women in power need to be prepared to be shot at."
– Eleanor Roosevelt

Alpha

Nina hit the ground with a resounding *slap*. Her hands and left cheek connecting with the smooth cement of the lab.

Only, this wasn't the lab she had just come from.

Only, it was.

The room filled with the same eerie light coming from the Portal. She turned her head, heavy with a squeezing pain, in time to see the Portal's light flicker and go dark. She wanted to cry out, to reach back, as though she could undo what had just happened. But that's not how these machines work, that's not how time works. Even a true time machine cannot make something un-happen. It only transports a person across the Plain to another reality where that event just hasn't happened yet. But it did happen somewhere. And somewhere Parker was about to hop to another reality to steal another version of Nina to replace the one that he had killed after he hurt (or potentially killed) Hank too.

The first person to travel across the Plain had been so severely warped by the power that he was now about to wreak havoc on multiple realities on a whim, and no one knew it but Nina.

The headache felt familiar; she realized that this was a side-effect of crossing the Plain. Nina fumbled to her feet, her hands pushing up against the slick concrete. As she steadied herself, she caught the glint of the thin band on her left hand. The ring that Hank had given back to her, physical proof that their reunion had been real.

There was no plastic partition in this lab, one side of it flowed right into the next. The lights were off, but the eerie glow of the computer monitors lit the path for Nina to follow. Still finding her balance, she wobbled to the first desk she could reach. To say that she hadn't yet found her sea-legs would be incorrect, her multiverse-legs would be more accurate. Nina reached for one of the nearby computers. She hastily moved the wireless mouse to rouse the computer from its manufactured sleep. It blinked to life and prompted her for a password.

Already she spotted a difference from her home universe and the one she had just left. None of the lab computers in those realities had passwords on them. The door to the lab was passcode protected and that was security enough for the team; even though the alarm was only enabled after hours, during the day anyone could come and go as they pleased. Everyone who could get into the lab was trusted, although it appeared that it had been grossly misplaced.

Nina stared at the screen trying to think through the pain in her head, her mental capacity in a vice grip as each cell in her body began the process of mitosis in this new reality. Apparently, her still and solid gaze, caused by her absent inability to think, was the required password. A facial scan with a matching iris detection encoder had processed her gaze and the screen unlocked.

How curious that her face was accepted to unlock this computer. She had seen computers and smartphones in her home activate with this feature, but what shocked her was that the computer was programed to respond to *her* exact face.

Nina scanned each of the icons on the bottom ribbon of the desktop, reading them left to right. Nothing looked familiar, the method of using the computer appeared to be the same and the output produced an interactive visual display. But she didn't know the names or visual cues for any of these programs.

Finally, she opened one that appeared to be an internet browser: The Mesh. A clever allusion to the Net perhaps, but it made her think that it was restricted as mesh was a finer material than general netting. When she typed in "News" the browser popped up several stories. An economic crisis under debate. A mass emigration problem. Some things are just inevitable.

The date was correct; it was nearly 6:00 pm on August 8, 2018. President Elena Johnson was cited in two of the articles that Nina clicked on. There wasn't anything that specifically told her this, but the current reality felt darker, sinister. Perhaps the fact that the lab was dark and abandoned gave her that spooky feeling. Or maybe it was something on a molecular level that she could sense.

She closed out of the screens and locked the computer. Nina assumed that the door to the lab would be locked as well, and while her face-scan had unlocked the computer, she didn't want to assume that it would also grant her entry to the lab. That Portal was her only way back to her own home reality, but most importantly, it was also her only way to where she had just been. She had to rescue Hank, stop Parker, and set things right. From the looks of things, she was going to need some help, and that meant taking a risk. She had failed him before, on that dark evening a decade earlier. Now, she couldn't fail him again, especially when she had seen the impossible: he was alive. She had never been a fighter, never one for confrontation, never one to speak up for herself. But something had sparked inside her and she knew that if there was ever a time to fight and ever a cause worth fighting for, this was it. Hank was it.

Nina stood inches from the door, willing her hand to grab the knob, coercing her wrist to make the requisite motions to take her out into this new universe.

She took a deep breath, closed her eyes and said, "Hank, I'm going to save you this time."

Beta

The same hallway as always greeted her. The same speckled linoleum tiles, the same cork board on the opposite wall featuring campus flyers and posters. She couldn't read the content on the notices because the hallway was dark, all of the lights extinguished except for two in the middle, an opposite image of the hallway she had seen earlier. The dull light coming from the lab behind her offered minimal illumination as she peered down the hall to her right. The only other light came from the doorway of a classroom at the far end of the hall.

Nina couldn't hear any voices, perhaps a professor forgot to turn off the light on their way out. She hesitantly exited the lab. *This could be a fatal mistake*, what if she could never gain access to the Portal again? She could be stuck in this time and place. But she couldn't stay put either, Parker could jump through after her at any moment and then she would really need to run.

The lab door closed with a resolute *thunk*. She pressed her palm against the pad next to the door, testing to see if her identity would unlock the lab. Sure enough, the lock *de-thunked* and she pushed the door back open. Nina felt a slight wave of relief; she could at least get back to the Portal if she needed to. Although she didn't know if the power source existed here yet, if it was hooked up, or any of the specifics of what would be needed anyways. Thurston had said something about having to wait for someone else to turn it on, but how long would that take?

Nina closed the door again, confirming it locked properly before she turned down the hall. Not running, but walking briskly, she knew she needed to act quickly. Nina passed the familiar pair of office doors. Something about them caught her eye.

Maybe five paces after she passed, Nina stopped and counted back her steps before she turned to face the door to Parker's office. Only this time the sign read Dr. Feminina Marks. And across the hall was Dr. Marie Winchester. Before she could contemplate the ramifications of these changes, she was interrupted.

"Hey," a voice called out, catching her in the dark hallway. Her eyes widened; her hands bunched into fists reflexively. She was on edge, on the run.

"Oh, Dr. Marks! I didn't mean to scare you," the thin man tried to retract his brusque greeting from behind his mop and bucket.

"I - " she couldn't come up with a response.

"I didn't recognize you in the dark. I thought you left to go home hours ago," he sounded timid and congenial. Effusive in his care and greeting. But, if he knew the version of her that existed in this reality, why shouldn't he be kind and helpful.

"No worries, I uh." *Time to lie*, Nina thought to herself.

"Is everything okay?" He had inched closed, his feet taking small steps in spite of his height and his mop bucket squeaking as it trailed him.

"Well, my car broke down and I thought I might catch someone here so I could get a lift home." Nina didn't know where that came from, but she trusted the deeply imbedded part of her psyche that pushed this excuse out to guide her. She had nothing else to go on. Perhaps the time-travel induced headache impaired her memory and cognitive function.

It was only after this man, the night janitor at the University, offered to give her a drive home that something about his voice began to register in her mind. *Where had she heard that voice before?* There was a specific way that he said things, how he drew out the vowels and over-articulated his "o"s. It wasn't an accent so much as a manner of speaking.

Nina followed him out to the parking lot after he stored away his cleaning supplies. He seemed ashamed of his vehicle. An unremarkable sedan, it sat alone in a vast parking lot, the only vehicle in sight. It wasn't a bad car, but certainly wasn't one of the luxury cars that she had seen in the administrative parking lot on her way in, although that parking lot was a universe away.

"I'm sorry for the mess," he uttered for the third time as they pulled out of the staff parking lot. The lights faded away behind them as he pulled onto the dark streets, the sidewalks bathed in black with a few shop signs perforating the night.

His eyes on the road and one hand on the steering wheel, the night janitor flung everything from the front seat into the back with speed. As they continued down the familiar streets, he cleared each of the items, the detritus of his life into the backseat. Out of sight, out of mind.

As he repeated this action, she spotted the orange band cutting across his right palm. An inch thick, it made Nina wince to look at it. It was clearly an older burn, scarred over, but nonetheless, it looked gruesome.

He saw her look at it and shoved his hand into his jacket pocket, maintaining the steering wheel with the other. Nina overcompensated and moved her head so that she only had the option to look out the car window. The streets were dark. The leaves that shaded the walkways during the day were now casting amorphous darkness in the thin light that the moon produced, the edges of the shadows blurry.

"So, uh" Nina heard the man grasp at words to make small talk.

"Thank you for giving me a lift, I appreciate it." Polite, not overly gracious, not rude. Until she knew where she had landed, she would need to be careful. Her thoughts were quickly going into survive and evade mode. Her headache reached a new level of skull-cracking pain. Nina wanted to find an ice pack and lay with it on her eyes and doze, give her brain and her body a chance to recuperate. Perhaps if she fell asleep, she might wake up in her home reality, but she knew this wasn't a dream. And going to her home reality wouldn't help her save Hank. She needed a good long period of silence to sort out all that had just happened and what the desired outcome would be. Go home? Go back? Could she ever really go back now? How could she even get there?

"Of course, I was surprised to see you in the lab without Marie." His eyes were glued to the road. The way he said her name, Nina could tell it was someone that he was focused on. He didn't know what to do with his mouth after he said her name, she could see him fidget between a half smile and pursed lips, giving him the impression of gnawing at his own mouth. Maybe he was her boyfriend, maybe he just longed for her from afar.

"Oh, yes. Well, I'm not always with her." Nina was doing the mental algebra to confirm who she was. Marie. Marie, who? The only Marie she could think of who she knew to have any connection with the University was Dean Winchester. Her name had been on the door to Dr. Thurston's office. Or what Nina knew to be Dr. Thurston's office.

"Huh, right," he responded, giving a slight nod. Nina could see from his profile that he had just rolled his eyes at her comment. *Did he think she couldn't see? Had she somehow offended him?* Nina suddenly became very aware of the fact that she was in a confined space with this man and she didn't know where they were going. How would she ever be able to tell if they were going the wrong way? How could she plan to open the door and roll out of a moving car if she never saw a false destination coming? And why did his voice give her the chills? *This was a mistake.* She could feel her left leg start to bounce up and down, an uncontrollable tick.

"Why were you working so late?" Nina asked, trying to show an interest in his work. That was always the safe thing to do. People really only just want to talk about themselves. And while he appeared rail-thin, Nina didn't want to assume that he wouldn't have the upper-hand in a fist fight. *Or a knife fight,* she corrected herself. But why would she think such a thing?

"Just making my usual rounds," he turned his head for the first time to address her as he spoke. A sly half smile pulled at the right side of his face. His eyes were watery and tired looking, as though he hadn't slept in a month. His tall frame hunched over the steering wheel; his shoulders were jutting up so high they practically touched the lower lobes of his ears. Everything about him in that moment made her think of a vulture, stooped and preying on the leftovers.

He looked down at her thighs, Nina's hands resting folded, covering the crease where her legs crashed together. His leer made her squirm. He took his right hand from his pocket and gestured in her direction. In the direction of her lap. "You're not from around here, are you?"

While it sounded like a question, the way he said it conveyed that he already knew the answer. Nina half expected him to reach over and grab her wrist, try to scare her, take possession of some part of her body to assert his power. Instead he smiled and emitted a weak laugh. *What an odd thing to ask someone that you supposedly work with.*

Nina wanted the ride to be over. She wanted to get out of his dingy car. She spotted a stop-sign on the corner.

"Uh, I can walk from here," she blurted out as the car began to slow to a stop. *Smile, look like a nice lady who is just trying to make this favor easier on him. Smile, think pretty, and maybe he won't hurt you.*

He narrowed his eyes at her and did a micro-shake of his head. "Well yeah, of course you can. But I was going to just drop you off in front of your door."

"Oh, right. Thank you." Her smile didn't falter but her knee continued to pump up and down, faster and faster.

He pulled through the intersection and then navigated the car over just slightly to the curb. A neon sign flashed "OPEN" in the window of the laundromat on the corner. Nina spotted the glass door with the mechanized lock just off to the side, the residential entrance.

"Here you are," he sounded slightly annoyed. But Nina was more than happy to end this interaction. That suspicious feeling had landed and flourished in her gut. But out on the street things didn't look much better. The blurry shadows from the trees were menacing, warning her off. This was still D.C., the city that she knew like the back of her hand, but in another way, this was no place she wanted to know.

Nina unbuckled her seat belt and exited the car. Before she closed the door, she leaned down to say, "thank you," the pressure shifting to her frontal cortex and causing her to wince.

"Yeah, no problem Dr. Marks." He reached over to grab the door as she started to swing it closed. And that was when she saw the patch on the left breast pocket of his work-shirt. He took off and was down the street before she could gasp, or scream, or yell, or anything. She was finally able to place his voice. Identify her unease. She had seen him once before. But only in profile. The rest of her encounter with him back in her home universe she had only seen the back of his head, heard his voice as she stared down at her hands.

The name on the work shirt explained it all. His name: *Gus.*

Gamma

The car peeled away from the curb, accelerating loudly down the street. Nina felt her hands start to shake. *I'm actually losing my mind*, was all that she could think. The words played in her head like a headline ticker at the bottom of a cable-news channel.

Dumped in a new universe where she had no idea what was going on, what was safe, or what was dangerous. She had lost the love of her life for the second time and the pain of it was stunted by the fact that she was just in very close quarters with his murderer who thoroughly creeped her out.

Nina took a few deep breaths to calm herself down. She stood in front of a door that could be hers, or given the janitor's identity, it could be a trap. Nina was tired and hungry. But more to the point, more to the root of her humanity, superseding those needs, she felt scared. *I don't think Maslow was ever shoved into foreign universes so his theories are shot,* Nina thought as she rolled her eyes and gathered herself.

Nina turned to deal with her next challenge: getting inside the building (assuming that it really was her building, or rather, the Nina who lived in that reality's building.) She was on edge, worried that Gus Blanity, the man who robbed her of the best thing in her life in a senseless crime, knew this location. Even if it was a different Gus, she wasn't comfortable.

Nina looked at the names on the register next to the doorframe. She hunched slightly, stooping to bring the words closer to her face so that she could read them. As her eyes fell on "FEMININA MARKS," she heard a latch unlock.

Facial recognition locks on a dingy walk-up over a laundromat? Nina rolled her eyes and let the question go unanswered in her mind. Too exhausted to think on the advanced technology, she went through the door. The number on the sign next to her name had read "8".

She climbed the stairs, lined in a thin blue carpet, the white walls marred with scuffs and scrapes, likely from the furniture that had been moved in and out over the years. On the first landing there were three apartment doors. She kept going up until she found the corresponding door, once a bright red, but now faded from years of dim lighting and careless movers. Only the number was tilted on its side, slightly off of its fastener.

It looked like an infinity symbol: ∞

Luck had gotten her here, the ride from Gus, the entry into the building. She was lost in an unknown universe, but it still seemed made for her, adapted to her needs, or at least programmed for her likeness. These random events had led her to believe that she was going to be able to walk right into that apartment. That somehow the spring and the cylinder would take pity on her, the woman lost in the multiverse. Even though this wasn't her reality, it was a reality, and of course the door wasn't unlocked. Nina tried to turn the knob and it stuck. She tried it again and no luck. *How do the computers and labs and the front door have advanced security and this door still requires a key? Oh, it's actually pretty secure to have two methods.*

And because she existed in this universe, according to Parker, the Nina who lived there couldn't exist while she was there, so she was stuck on the other side of the door. Nina turned away from the door and let the weight of her exhaustion carry her to the floor. She tapped her head against it, hoping that it would will her brain to think of a solution, a way to get inside the apartment so she could rest and think of a way to get out of this situation.

After a moment, she heard a cascade of clicks and motions. The slide of a chain, the release of a bolt, the swish of a rotor. Nina realized that the sound was coming from directly above her. Someone was inside the apartment after all. *Was it yet another version of Parker? Was it a roommate who would recognize her, but she would have no clue who they were? What if it were Hank?* Nina got to her feet effortlessly, all traces of exhaustion gone from her bones, *what if Hank did open this door?*

The door couldn't open fast enough, she willed it to be Hank. She needed it to be him behind that door.

But it wasn't his earnest and perpetually tired eyes that greeted her. No, she saw a thin woman whose skin looked eerily pale, as though her natural coloring had been drained from her after years of staying cooped up inside. Her long black hair perfectly framed her face with long bangs that threatened to pin-prick her eyes at any moment. She stood at a medium height and she looked lean and not in the least bit intimidating at first glance, but she had a look in her eyes that hinted at her genius. The look of shock that she was trying to suppress was admirable, and there was a hint of a nervous smile, debating whether or not it should make a break for it, forming at the corner of her mouth.

"Nina?" she said in a voice that was at once familiar and foreign.

"Nina?" was all the weary traveler could echo back to her alter-ego.

Delta

She pulled Nina into the apartment by the wrist and slammed the door shut in one motion.

"We did it!" she beamed at Nina. Her hand moved to her head, as though she had to hold it still from all the moving pieces that were sliding into place. "We did it!" She had the exasperated relief on her face that Nina had witnessed when Carol had finished a marathon the previous year. The joy of finishing an arduous journey, the pride of accomplishment, the euphoria from a dopamine surge.

Nina examined her features, trying to study one part of her in detail every second. Unable to focus, she tried to catch her movements mid-progress for any sign that this couldn't possibly be her alter-ego. A freckle out of place, a different angle to her nose, a different shade to her eyes. But with each inspection it only confirmed what she once thought impossible. She was alive in the same place and time as her alter-ego. Seeing her alter-ego dead in the last reality had been a shock, but seeing this woman now, alive and dancing around an apartment crowded with too much furniture and the overwhelming smell of incense was almost too much for Nina to handle.

This shouldn't have shocked her, given what she had already discovered in Parker's basement, but it did. And she should have learned to not be shocked anymore, the journey so far had been nothing but a lesson in letting go of assumptions.

Her alter-ego moved quickly into the kitchen and began to take down two short glasses.

"Nina?" Nina asked, having trouble finding her voice, her throat tightened as emotions overwhelmed her. Nina scanned the apartment for signs of recognition. None of the furniture matched anything in her own apartment or the one she had woken to that morning. This place looked darker; all of the wood surfaces a deep dark brown that appeared black. The soft surfaces were only moderately welcoming with just enough cushion to be more relaxing than sitting on the floor. There were no stylistic touches to the space, most everything looked clean and clear and void of pattern or color. The only exception was a row of pictures on the far bookshelf. Some images she recognized. Mainly of Nina and her father on family trips or posing for a picture in front of a Christmas tree. The one image of her mother that had served as a reminder that she was once real.

"I can't believe that we did it! I want to hear everything! You'll need to retell it all to Marie, but I need to hear it all right now." Her alter-ego's words continued to spill out as she grabbed an open bottle of white wine and began to pour two glasses.

"Nina," she repeated as she moved closer, trying to catch her alter-ego's attention. Nina maintained her balance as she moved past the gray and utilitarian couch that had a lumpy blanket piled on one end and a thick notebook laid open on the other. She must have interrupted her latest entry, the pen acting as a placeholder in the crease.

She moved closer to Nina; a glass outstretched for her to take. This Nina, the other-other Nina, or the correct Nina for this universe was ready to celebrate. *Why was she not more shocked to see her alter-ego? Why was Nina the only one of them who was having trouble processing this? And how could they celebrate with Hank in danger? How could they toast when there was a madman in possession of a time machine and no one knew about it except Nina?*

"Cheers to being the first person to travel through the multiverse," she put the glass in Nina's hands as she began to sip on her own drink, not waiting for Nina to join her. The tremor in Nina's hand, that had been a secret that only her fingers and palm knew, was announced to both of them. A small portion of wine sloshed and crested in the small glass as she couldn't hold her hand still. Nina recognized the pattern etched into the vessel, a repeating spiral of diamonds, squares, and oblong shapes. She focused on the design and it seemed to calm her nerves, just long enough to give her the strength to get her alter-ego to focus.

"Feminina!" she heard her own voice shout. The shock of the noise interrupted the memory that she had of her grandmother sipping quietly from one of those glasses at her grandfather's wake and the sadness that she felt years later when she packed them in newspaper and moved them into her own house after she passed as well. The glass dropped onto the floor with a heavy thud. The white wine, freed from its vessel, started to spread across the lacquered hardwood floor. The glass, thankfully, didn't shatter. But her fear that it had took a few moments to abate. Nina ducked down to the ground, scrounging for shards that didn't exist. Her final defenses relented, allowing the dam of tears to finally give way.

Feminina's arms were around her quickly. She rubbed her back and made soothing sounds with her mouth, "there there," and "there's no need to be upset," and "you made it, you really did it!" and "tell me what's going through your mind."

Nina waited for the rhythm of her tears to die down, to get out the strongest and most pained thoughts first. When she could speak without her words getting drowned in tears, Nina told her everything. How Parker was the first person to cross the Plain, not her. How he brought her to his universe. How she found Hank again. How it had all fallen apart so quickly and ultimately how she was thrust through the Portal and across the Plain into this reality.

Feminina had cleaned up the spilled wine and listened intently. Nina could see that with each word she let her alter-ego down. She had gone from thinking she had been the first to cross the multiverse, an accolade for both of them, something that she could still relish in, to realizing that Nina had just been a bystander in this whole mess. Nina had just explained that she was a victim of the Portal, thrown across the cosmos by a criminal, even though no law proscribed his actions, it was still the worst kind of violation.

"So, you're not even a physicist?" was the first thing Feminina could manage to say to her.

Nina shook her head slowly.

"And you got here how?" Feminina sank to the floor, sitting inches from Nina.

She explained the setup of the machine in the lab, and the nearly identical configuration she saw when she crossed through. "I need to go back and stop him. We need to get back to the lab and activate the Portal."

"Wait the lab? You mean the University lab where we have the prototype?" Feminina confirmed that she had heard her correctly.

"It's not a prototype, it works," Nina asserted.

"But the University has been shut down for years," Feminina explained.

Nina shook her head. "What are you talking about? The computers in the lab were all on. It was definitely empty because it was night-time. But the janitor is the one who gave me a ride here."

"Marie and I still go back every week to continue our work," Feminina had started to talk over Nina when she very abruptly stopped. "What janitor?"

"His name is Gus," Nina said with more weight than was probably necessary.

Feminina's face shifted, the skin at her temples tightened as her ears pulled back, perked up, like an animal sensing danger on the savannah. "What?" she said in a flat tone, steadying herself as she tried to mask the ire that seethed from her nostrils, her breathing more deliberate and metered in the seconds since Nina said his name.

"Gus Blanity, do you know his name?" She must have recognized the frustration in her own voice.

"Seems we both do. He's been stalking me and Dr. Winchester for the past six months." Feminina responded and crossed her arms. "You too?"

"No," Nina crossed the air with her arms, ninja chopping that idea to pieces.

Feminina stared at her, waiting for a response, raising one eyebrow after a pause. This version of Nina, this other-Feminina, was much quicker to the chase. She had no patience for Nina's nerves.

"He attacked me and Hank almost a decade ago. He's the guy who killed Hank." Nina looked down at her hands as she spoke the words.

"Oh my God." Feminina's lip curled up in a snarl, she tensed, moving back from Nina almost imperceptibly. "That's so horrible."

"Yeah," Nina nodded.

"Wait, who is Hank?" Feminina demanded. Her manner of questioning was brusque and to the point.

She doesn't know Hank? Nina's mind couldn't make sense of that. How did she ever become a fully formed adult human in any universe without the joy of knowing Hank to get her through the invariably angsty early years of her independence?

"He was-" Nina's voice failed her. How could she explain him to someone else? She never could find the words even in her own reality, it made it easy for her to hide him so well. But how could she explain him with a splitting headache and absolutely no sense of what was right-side-up and what was up-side-down? "He was-" Nina began again.

"And why would you get into the car with someone that attacked you?" Nina didn't get the chance to continue. Feminina dismissed herself and walked into the other room. Clearly, Nina was the one who disgusted her, the one she couldn't bear to be in the same room with, not Gus. *How could she not be on her own side right now?*

Following her into the other room, Nina gave her explanation, although she doubted Feminina heard it. "I didn't recognize him until I got out of the car. I never saw his face the night of the attack. And at the trial I mainly saw the back of his head."

The room Nina had followed her into would have been a small dining area, opening up into a yellow and cramped kitchen. Feminina rummaged under a table covered with sheets of grid paper in disarray, the flat pieces each turned out at a different angle. Nina worried that Feminina would try to stand up too quickly, hit her head on the underside of the table and send the disordered papers all over the floor. More mess, more disorganization, more things to sort out and clean up.

"Hey, I need some answers here." The other-other Nina ignored her demand. Feminina continued to crawl on the floor; Nina ducked her head down to see what she was doing. Feminina found a shoe beneath a litter of crumpled pieces of paper, some in tight balls, but most in lopsided and disfigured fractal shapes. Quickly, Feminina put it on as she looked around, finding the other shoe close by. Perhaps she was upset with Nina for ruining her evening.

Nina was never one to raise her voice in frustration. It had been ingrained into her that a lady never raises her voice, never shows her anger. It was rude, it was impolite. Well this other version of Nina had never learned much about manners it seemed. She swept out of that tiny room and back past the entryway down a narrow hallway.

"Hello!?" Nina pursued her into a cramped bedroom. The bed had the pink patterned sheets that Nina remembered from her childhood home.

Feminina started digging in the closet for something. No reaction to Nina's latest sounds. *This was rude.* This had to be the most annoying and juvenile actions Nina had ever experienced.

"HEY!" Nina could have sworn she heard her voice travel out the poorly insulated windows with the echo carrying down into the brick lined alley between this building and the next.

Feminina turned slowly to face her. "Keep it down, I've got neighbors."

"Stop ignoring me. If this guy is stalking you, how did he get into the lab?"

"He was in the lab?" Feminina stood up straight, again she was on alert.

"He's the janitor. He was cleaning up one of the classrooms nearby."

"And when he saw you, he offered to take you home?" Feminina sounded incredulous. She folded her arms across her chest and pursed her lips.

"No, he was shocked to see me there so late. I asked for a ride because I had no clue where I lived and he did," Nina tried to explain, she was on the defensive.

"And you think it's normal for a random janitor at the University to know where you live?" Feminina cocked her head to one side as she asked this.

Nina hadn't stopped to think about that very much. It was a little weird, but she had tried to convince herself that the Nina in this universe was nice to everyone and friendly and there could be no harm done. Clearly, she had been wrong on both counts.

Feminina must have taken her silence as confirmation that Nina had been foolish with her own safety, their own safety, by not considering this earlier.

"Look, this guy is bad news. Ever since the University shut down, Marie and I have been meeting there secretly to finish our work. But we have to be careful. The prototype pulls a lot of energy, and this Blanity guy noticed the spikes in the energy usage and tracked us down. I told her we should have varied our schedule, but she insisted on every Sunday from 4:00 am to 7:00 am. So, a few months ago, this guy finds us there. He tried to blackmail us to keep our secret. Said if we didn't pay, we'll get arrested." Feminina let out a deep sigh as she finished. Something wasn't adding up for Nina, but she wasn't quite sure yet. Maybe the explanation was plausible for that reality, but something felt off about it. If Nina learned anything on her stop in that universe, it was to start trusting her gut and stop ignoring her doubts.

"What happened?" Nina asked her to continue.

"Marie boxed him of course," Feminina said as she brushed past Nina, as if she was bored with her own explanation and Nina's follow-up question.

What? Nina thought to herself as she spun around to follow her alter-ego. "What does that mean? She fought him in a ring?"

"What? No!" Feminina stopped to answer. "She reported him for stalking us. He got that little insidious pink box on his doorstep and reported for branding." Feminina took off again, heading back out of the room, no time for further explanation.

Branding? The bright orange stripe crossing his palm. That had to be it.

"Branding? What in the world?" Nina continued to follow Feminina down the hallway and saw her standing at the entryway, the door open.

"You coming?" she asked before slipping out. Nina followed in a rush, she didn't bother to shut off the lights or lock the door. Feminina was already down the stairs by the time Nina heard the apartment door latch behind her. Apparently, they were on their way somewhere, heading out into the night, to parts unknown.

Nina's sense of adventure had been expended in her last stop and this Feminina had no patience for explanations, so she followed blindly. Or so she thought. Traveling the multiverse was starting to teach Nina that she should never assume that just because she was behind someone that she was following them. As it turns out, Nina was the one who was leading in this case. Leading Dr. Feminina Marks and Dr. Marie Winchester to the biggest breakthrough of their careers.

Epsilon

The two women cut through the dark night, walking in step. Their identical bone structure and leg length made that an inevitability.

"Can I ask where we are going?" Nina finally mustered the courage to ask. She found her alter-ego, Feminina, intimidating. Nina worried that she would snap at her or tell her to beg off if she annoyed her. Nina felt as though she was back in middle school trying to impress the cool girls in her class and failing sorely.

"We're going to see Marie," Feminina muttered as they crossed another shaded street, devoid of illumination. Nina tried to look both ways before stepping into the road, but her alter-ego already stood on the other side, waiting impatiently. She was fearless or just bold beyond belief.

Nina expected that they would continue in this manner for blocks, but they had only just completed the first crosswalk and Feminina abruptly stopped at a door not dissimilar from the one she had found at the other apartment. Feminina pressed the innocuous white button once and the door unlocked. The two women were inside less than five minutes after they departed.

There were no stairs to ascend, only two doors on opposite ends of a long hallway. The bright white walls and doors were illuminated from one light in the center on the ceiling. Nina had an odd feeling of déjà vu, had she been in this cramped hallway before? Or was she just starting to see things as the night wore on and her adrenaline dissipated. Feminina knocked on the door to their right.

"It's so late, Nina" she heard Dr. Marie Winchester's familiar voice complain as soon as the door began to move open.

"Trust us, it's worth it," her alter-ego said with a weighted tone. She had a flare for the dramatic, clearly. The way she delivered that sentence. The hasty exit from her apartment without any notice. Even the way she wore her hair, their hair. This was a version of herself that Nina had never imagined, but she started to feel impressed.

After Marie finished rubbing her eyes, she must have been half asleep despite the early hour, she sighed and glared at Feminina. Then her eyes moved slowly to assess Nina, the stranger in the hallway, the interloper who looked all too familiar.

"Did you say us?" Her eyebrows moved together, forming a bulwark to fend off the improbable information being relayed to her brain by what was visible to her eyes.

"Yes, Marie. Us!" Feminina smiled and her recent frustration and panic seemed to have subsided for the moment. The moment that she and Marie had been working towards.

Marie opened her mouth to ask another question but stopped herself. She turned her body towards Nina, as though that would help her better investigate what was before her. After a moment of visual inspection, she muttered, "Nina, I have to admit that I had a few drinks and smoked a joint about an hour ago. Is this for real?"

Feminina nodded as Marie assessed Nina; she joined in confirming that she was in fact there.

Marie's eyes began to dart back and forth between them quickly. "So, this means-"

"It works, Marie!" Feminina couldn't hold it in any longer.

Excitement flashed across Marie's face, but she quickly erased it with a grim seriousness. "Get in here," she hissed as she pulled both of them through the door. The apartment looked clean and organized in an "I have way too much stuff, but it all fits neatly somewhere, so let's not call it hoarding" manner. There were figurines and plaques dotting the tops of each bookshelf. Neatly ordered series of books flowed across each shelf like lines of code, the book spines changing design or color abruptly as one series ended and the next began. Back issues of "Science" magazine towered in one corner by an oversized fish tank.

Feminina and Marie were conversing as though they had their own language. Nina only caught a few words that made sense to her, but she got the main points. Feminina explained what had happened, her alter ego from another universe arrived at her door, she quickly found out that the circumstances were less than ideal and they proceeded immediately to Winchester's abode. The discussion of frequencies, quantum foam, jitters, and other advanced terms might as well have been another language to Nina.

She continued her scan of the apartment as the two physicists talked fluent 'nerd'. They caught her attention again when she heard Feminina say, "Gus Blanity" as though she had just sneezed, ejecting the vial name from her system.

"We should call the police," Marie interrupted Feminina as soon as the words were out of her mouth.

"And say what? That we are consistently breaking and entering onto University property to continue our life's mission of developing inter-universe travel?" The two were absorbed in their conversation. Nina moved closer to them as they began to discuss next steps. This interested her, maybe if this had been her first stop in the multiverse, she would have been happy for them to make a plan and just tell her what to do. But she didn't like being out of control and that was exactly how she had felt for the past however many hours she'd been lost.

Just as Feminina and Marie were beginning to bicker over what to do next, there was a rapid knock at the door to the apartment. All three of them turned quickly. Nina half expected to see the door knob turning slowly, ominously. Her mind immediately flashed on Gus, creeping in, cornering the three of them, demanding some ransom, or perhaps just snapping and stabbing each of them. The police would surely be confused when they discovered two Femininas. *Feminini? Femininae?* Nina needed to think of a clear way to identify her and her alter-ego.

As Nina pondered the gory scene that could play out, Marie checked the peep-hole. "It's Sonali," she hissed at Feminina.

Without a word to Nina or any further instruction, Feminina disappeared behind the second door at the end of the hallway.

A short and curvy woman stepped through the door; her face streaked with tears. Marie reached out to hold her right away. The woman was none other than Sonali. The same Sonali that Nina worked with in her reality. Of course, it made sense for her to exist in this reality as well, but Nina was just surprised to see her at that moment, especially given the fact that the version of herself in that reality would have never worked at an agency.

"Sonali, honey. What's wrong? What happened?" Marie switched from panicked about the Portal situation to comforting effortlessly. The way her personality danced from one dynamic to the next, Nina regretted believing all the things that she heard Parker and Thurston say about her before.

Apparently, Marie's apartment was crisis central that evening. A pair of dark and large eyes looked at Nina from over Marie's shoulder as she embraced Sonali.

Those eyes quickly adjusted and she recognized the look that Sonali shot at Marie. The 'why the hell is she here?' look. Nina had seen it often enough and used it once or twice herself. "Well if it isn't Nel and Hick," Sonali muttered as she backed away a step, closer to the exit.

"We had a research emergency come up," Marie tried to explain.

"You told me that the research was done." Sonali's troubles were forgotten for a moment, while she debated the thing that they weren't directly saying. Nina was in Marie's apartment and that was a problem for Sonali.

"Sonali, if I've told you once, I've told you a thousand times," she hazarded a glance in Nina's direction before continuing in a whisper. The apartment was small enough so that Nina heard everything while she stared at her feet. "I thought we were past this? You know how I feel about you; I love you. Feminina has told you multiple times that she has no feelings for me. You have to trust me if this is going to work." She spoke with such softness, it reminded Nina of the tenderness in Hank's voice as he held her earlier that day. She could still feel his hand on her shoulder as she listened to Marie calm Sonali.

"I'm sorry. I'm just- I'm so upset right now. I'm not thinking right," Sonali rubbed her forehead with her hand. Nina could hear their intimate silence between them now.

"Sorry Nina," Sonali looked up as she addressed her. *How could she respond?* These women were somewhat familiar yet completely unknown to her. She was an intruder in the truest sense of the word. Just passing through on her way back to her own world and intervening in their own narratives.

Sonali slumped down onto Marie's couch; this was not going to be a quick visit. Her shoulders were hunched over, her breathing began to quicken as she relayed her troubles. Nina found a corner of Marie's desk to perch upon, wanting to sit and rest, but also wanting to stay mobile, ready to run if needed. The pace of the evening had slowed significantly. Nina had to be patient if she was going to enlist the help of both Marie and her alter-ego, but she knew that nothing this woman could be worried about could compare to her own inter-dimensional crisis.

"Ayush called me this evening, I could barely hear him through his own tears," Sonali's voice sounded thick with emotion. Marie listened patiently as she braced for the news. "He got one today, just sitting on his doorstep when he got home from work."

"Oh my gosh," Marie tried to conceal a look of disgust as she maintained a steady hand on Sonali's arm.

"Yeah, it was a small one too. I went over to see him right away. I don't know if I'll be able to look at him after tomorrow." Marie handed Sonali a tissue and let her cry out all of her emotions. As Sonali buried her head into Marie's shoulder, Nina saw Marie tilt her head, signaling her to go down the hallway. Nina took her cue to reconvene with the other Feminina.

Nina slipped behind the door that Feminina disappeared behind. Her alter-ego sat perched on a closed toilet, staring at the dirt beneath her fingernails, her lips pursed. She didn't even glance over when Nina entered. "I thought you would have followed me," was all that she offered without any emotion.

"I didn't know to," Nina shook her head as though her ignorance would somehow act as an apology. She felt that she should be sorry for something. Intruding, being involved in this mess, interrupting her evening. But she also seemed a little annoyed. *Is this what it would have been like to have a sister?*

"You don't know Marie and Sonali in your reality?" Feminina looked over at Nina with pity in her eyes.

"I know them. Just not very well." Nina explained her interactions with both of them in her world. Feminina shook her head, the word 'what?' circling her mouth silently.

"So, they don't even know each other?" She finally asked aloud, the mute questions Nina didn't acknowledge.

"Not that I am aware," again Nina shrugged. She noticed how inconsistent that motion, the action of shrugging, seemed with the woman before her. Her uncertain nature, her constant self-doubt was incongruous with Feminina's personality. She seemed to grow uninterested quickly, already back to inspecting her cuticles.

"Did you hear what Sonali said about her brother? Do you know what all that was about?" Nina squeezed by so she could sit on the ledge of the bathtub, the edge of the sink pushed against her rear-end as she tried her best to not trip over Feminina.

"Sounds like he is a filthy criminal who is going to pay his debt to society," her words may have at one time been ingrained into her for all of the emotion she put behind them, but Nina could sense that she had irritated her alter-ego. Something in her voice gave it away. Whether that irritation was targeted at Sonali for interrupting, her brother for committing a crime, or Nina for asking about it, she couldn't quite tell.

"Maybe he is innocent," Nina offered, trying to pacify her attitude. While her alter-ego appeared more assertive and self-assured than herself, Feminina was certainly more mercurial.

"You would doubt the word of another woman?" Her eyes were accusing Nina when she looked up, stunned at the harsh tone to her voice.

"I- I, I don't know," Nina stammered.

"That's right, you don't know. You don't know the circumstances, but if he received one of those insidious little boxes, you can bet that he did something wrong. Something against a woman. We're the superior gender, we've proven it time and time again. When they try to attack us, we have to respond without any hesitation. I trust in the system, don't you?" She used her index finger to punctuate each sentence. For a moment Nina worried that she might have been heard by Marie and Sonali.

"What system?" was all that Nina could give her in response.

"The box system," she paused as though she were waiting for this identical stranger to recognize her words.

"After the gender wars of the 1940s, there was a brief peace. But the males couldn't accept it and their attacks against women escalated. They were subdued after the mass riots of the '50s and we installed Winnifred Redford as President. The box system was implemented then, but it wasn't perfected until the early 1980s when the technology advances allowed for better tracking and surveillance. We've had a succession of strong female leaders ever since."

The words were like square pegs trying to fit into the holes in Nina's understanding. "What gender wars?" She couldn't help but catch the indignation in her own voice, the last reality had been so eerily similar to her own, but nothing in this new reality made any sense.

"After Roosevelt was assassinated all hell broke out-" she started, explaining her version of history.

"Teddy or Franklin?" Nina asked reflexively.

"Eleanor," Feminina said as she rolled her eyes. "After she was assassinated, the women in the factories took up arms-"

"Eleanor Roosevelt was assassinated? When?"

"Right when she was being sworn in," she snapped. "Right after FDR died, secret service alerted her and had an emergency meeting. She convened with Truman and other members of his cabinet and they verbally agreed that it should be Eleanor to take his place in the short term. She had already been doing many of the state-visits on his behalf because of his polio. So, they bring in a Bible and have her start reciting the oaths and some woman-hating rogue secret service agent shoots her in the back." Her eyes squeezed together, as though she were staring down the shooter at that very moment. "And then those sloppy bastards tried to cover it up. But the truth came out. Hick made sure of it. And we gave 'em hell for it."

As Nina watched a wicked half-smile cross Feminina's face, she thought on how the victors in war get to tell the story. Her alter-ego believed the facts, but the emotion behind her accounting of it was remarkable. It was like Feminina was right there, as though the rage and fury from that single event had been drilled into her for her entire life.

"Is that not what happened in your reality?" Feminina's gaze reached to Nina's eyes, looking for some validation.

"No, nothing even close," was all that she could whisper. Her mind tried to playback through all of the ramifications of those historical changes. *How did World War II end? Did the US ever go to war in Vietnam? Just how different was this reality?* This was certainly a much more pronounced deviation from her own standard than she could have ever imagined. But as she ran through the scenarios in her own mind, she knew that Feminina would do her own mental calculus as well. She was, after all, inside her mind too.

The door to the bathroom budged slightly and then swung open after a slight force knocked it loose. The ends of the doorframe were sticking and the jostling on the other side caught their attention.

Marie Winchester stood in the hallway, her face grave. "Come on, let's go," she said and then walked away before either of them moved a muscle.

"Let's get to the lab now," Feminina heard her voice coming from another woman's mouth. In the course of an hour it hadn't become any more normal. *I cannot sound like that,* she thought. The three of them were headed back to Feminina's place.

"It's the middle of the night, I think we should all get some rest before we head down there," Marie became the voice of reason. This Nina chick seemed impatient, but Feminina didn't blame her. It sounded like a bad situation. Feminina couldn't imagine what it must have been like to wake up in a strange universe.

"No, we need to get to work now," Nina raised her voice as she said it, her echoes reverberating off the buildings. She stood still in the street. Feminina and Marie turned around to face her, they had already walked a few steps ahead of her.

Feminina tried to imagine what it would feel like if she didn't understand theoretical physics. It was hard for her to imagine un-knowing something that she had studied her whole life. But she tried so that she wouldn't sound condescending in her response. "Nina, if it works, it's a time machine. We have all the time we could possibly need to get you back. And if it doesn't work then whether we get there now or when we are rested won't impact the outcome."

"But you don't understand. If he can kidnap me from one universe into another, and then shove me into yet another without any remorse, what else do you think he could do while we are sleeping?" Nina pleaded with them. Feminina had to admit she had a fair point. Before she could respond, Nina pressed on. "Also, it's today or we have to wait a year."

"What do you mean a year?" Marie asked her.

"The quantum jitters. Thurston told me that today is the most reliable activity for them," Nina explained, her words sounding less confident as she finished.

"But they can come on other days," Marie pointed out.

"But not with any reliability," Feminina finally stepped in. Nina was right. It had to be today. The potential damage to every version of reality began to spin in her mind. Every possibility had so many ramifications. What if they could never get Nina back and stop this Parker guy? What else could happen that they would have no control over? "She has a point. We only ever imagined that this would be a positive discovery. But it seems that this power has fallen into the wrong hands. What if this violent man comes here? What damage could he do here before we can stop him?" Marie gave Feminina a look, one she had seen often. It was her, "why can't you be on my side?" look. But it quickly faded and it became clear that she would acquiesce. It was two to one, after all.

"Okay, we'll head over there now, but we should pick up some liquid caffeine first," Marie sighed and the three headed back in the opposite direction.

I tried to regain my calm as I waited with Nina, with myself, we waited, she and I waited. There is no grammatical rule for how to refer to you and your alter-ego succinctly. How can you conjugate a verb to speak to that? I'll add that to my list of things I haven't solved for in the multiverse.

Zeta

A bottle shattered somewhere in the distance, invisibly covering some alleyway with glittering shards of glass. The wind rustled through the trees, causing the leaves to whisper in the dark as the three women walked towards the University. There wasn't anyone else around, no other pedestrians, no cars driving through. No one else. It was eerie, Nina felt a shiver run up her spine as she followed Feminina and Marie.

"What happened with Sonali?" Feminina asked as they walked back down the street.

"I told her to take an anxiety pill and I would come over tomorrow," Marie responded. Nina could barely hear her words; they were no louder than a murmur.

"How is her family going to feel about that?" Feminina retorted, as though she could anticipate the reaction. Sonali, or the Sonali that Nina knew, was a second generation American. Her family came from the Bengali region of India and her grandparents worked hard to afford her parents a good life, who in turn were devoted to their daughter's prospects. From their brief conversations at the agency, Nina could tell that Sonali's parents had high expectations for her. Good education, good job, good husband.

"I doubt they'll be in much of a position to object to their daughter's girlfriend when their own son is having his eye cut out," Marie seemed to let that comment roll off as well, unphased by it. The casual tone of the brutal punishment made Nina's own eyes pop out a bit.

"Wait, what?!" Her voice sounded too loud, even for being outside.

"If your right eye causes you to sin, cut it out and throw it away. Matthew 5:29." Feminina recited the verse ingrained in the flat tone of someone who was pulling from past memorization.

"So, he was accused of a crime and he is going to have his eye cut out?" The cruelty of the punishment seemed so profound. "What if he is innocent?" Nina dared to ask again.

The two women ahead of her stopped and turned to face her at the exact same time. Their identical reactions added to their retort. "You're saying the woman who he attacked is lying?" Marie chided. Nina could tell in Marie's tone that she had offended her.

"No, but shouldn't there be due process? A jury of his peers?" Nina wondered at the various crimes she may have unknowingly committed in this society. In an hour she may have jay-walked, or broken noise ordinances, and technically she trespassed in the lab. *What would be her draconian punishment? Would her hand be cut off?*

"Where was due process getting us? Men getting away with crimes against women. This way is more efficient." Marie dismissed the questions Nina had spoken aloud.

Nina opened her mouth to ask more, but Feminina shook her head ever so slightly. Her fringe bangs gave the subtle motion more emphasis. She held back further inquiries on the topic. Marie started walking again, leaving Nina and her alter-ego to walk side by side behind her, the sidewalk too narrow to allow them to walk three-abreast.

"It's so spooky out here with no street lights," Nina didn't realize she had spoken this observation until Feminina responded.

"What's a street light?"

Nina almost wanted to laugh at her question. "A light on the top of a pole to illuminate the street at night," explaining the concept felt like trying to explain what the alphabet was. How could Feminina not know this basic thing, or at least infer its purpose?

"That sounds horrible," Marie blurted out.

"Horrible? It's safer. For pedestrians, for cars." Nina felt thoroughly foreign in that moment. But her mind started to turn, how did these big changes in history result in such a vastly different present?

"Yeah, but it probably interferes with everyone's sleep patterns. Not very healthy." Feminina continued to criticize this thing that she didn't even know about. Nina tried to scan her brain for the first introduction of electric street lights. She had seen history books referencing them in the late 1800s. These two women should certainly know about them.

"Okay, but if you don't make it home then it doesn't matter if you can't sleep," Nina hadn't ever spent this much time talking about street lights before in her existence.

"Why wouldn't you make it home?" Marie asked, suddenly concerned. The woman who seemed so complacent about a man being enucleated over one accusation was confused about why a woman in a city may not make it home at night.

"Because you could be attacked, no one would think to attack someone if they could be seen in the light." Nina had never enunciated the reason before, but there it was. Street lights were synonymous with safety.

"What kind of universe are you from? Is there a war going on or something? Why so much concern about safety or being attacked?" Feminina's eyebrows were moving close together again, her confusion and concern fighting for which emotion would win out.

Nina almost didn't know how to answer. Of course, she was worried about being attacked. She and Hank had been attacked at night on their way home. If a person was walking at night, they would want to feel safe, that's just common sense. But perhaps it was not common here. "I'm a woman, I would never think to walk at night without taking precautions."

"That sounds barbaric!" Feminina scoffed. And for the first time, Nina realized that it was. "I can't imagine not being able to walk where I wanted to or having to worry about my safety all the time."

"I mean it's not all the time," Nina tried to explain. She pictured the last few moments she had with Hank, her Hank. Hands together, talking about something she couldn't even remember. No graceful last words. And then, bam. Right under the glow of the street lights, stabbed to death by Gus Blanity.

"I mean, you seem pretty agitated right now, and you said it was a man who kidnapped you from your reality. Sounds like your home reality doesn't offer much protection," Feminina continued.

Nina didn't even realize it; she didn't even catch it. She had no response to try to explain her home reality better; maybe it didn't deserve more of an explanation. "True, but the latest issue was a result of a megalomaniac having access to a Portal to other dimensions, which is pretty rare."

Both Feminina and Marie nodded their heads in agreement. They had been working toward multiverse travel for years; this wasn't something they had to wrap their minds around.

The trio stopped in front of a convenience store. "We'll need some provisions," Marie explained as she swung open the glass door and entered the store.

"Provisions?" Nina asked as they followed her into the den of packaged goodies.

"We need to get you back home and I can't think on an empty stomach," Marie nodded in Nina's direction as she made for the large refrigerators on the far wall.

For the first time in several hours, hours that felt like long and excruciating lifetimes, Nina smiled.

Eta

The tires were rolling slowly enough over the pavement that Gus could hear the crackle of dry leaves and tiny rocks beneath the tread. He guided the car into an open parking spot across the street from the laundromat. All of the windows on the upper floors were dark, only the brilliant fluorescent lights spilling out of the storefront gave any indication that the building was in use. But he knew they were there. He had dropped off Dr. Marks, or someone who looked like Dr. Marks, only an hour earlier. In that time, he'd gone home, paced the floors of his apartment debating his next move. The man had told him that she was dangerous and not to be trusted, had ensured him that he needed Gus' help. He couldn't let this man down, his brother in science, in arms against the oppression.

He thought that maybe the woman he had found in the lab might be different, might be a nicer version of Dr. Marks. But she was stuck-up, barely talking to him, so ungrateful for his help. Just like Dr. Marks.

After hemming and hawing, he got back into his car and sped back into the heart of the city. He knew the route like the back of his hand, muscle memory from the year before when he had been keeping tabs on the rogue scientists. He knew they were up to no good, and he had been branded a criminal for it, literally. Gus released his grip from the steering wheel; he hadn't even realized how tightly he had been holding onto it. His gaze fell to his right palm. Even in the dark interior of the car, he could still see the scar. He closed his fist, hiding the brand from his vision, feeling his anger surge.

He shut off the car, grabbed the keys from the ignition, and slammed the car door shut in one swift motion. Gus crossed the street without bothering to check for any cars that might be driving along. It's a thought that never would have occurred to him, no one really drove around past sunset in his world.

He bypassed the front entrance and made for the alleyway next to the building. With the agility of a person long trained to be silent, to stay in the shadows, he maneuvered himself on top of a dumpster, standing precariously on the edge. Gus reached up, his fingers aiming for the last rung on the fire escape ladder. He missed and nearly lost his balance. A fall to either side (hard against the concrete or face first into the empty metal dumpster) would be incredibly painful, if not life threatening. Gus took a moment to regain his balance and his composure.

It felt like everything depended on him being able to stop them. Stop Dr. Marks and Dr. Winchester from activating that machine, stop them from using someone else and then throwing them away like garbage, stop any more people from coming through that device. Once Gus felt ready for another attempt, he lifted his hands straight up, his eyes closed. He was certain that he must succeed. His fingertips grazed the cool metal, rough and rusted to the touch. He paused, lifted his feet up higher, now balancing only on the tips of his toes.

His hand closed around the rung and he pulled down quickly with all the strength that he could muster from his anemic arms. The ladder roared as it lowered down to meet him.

Within moments Gus had climbed up to the second-floor fire landing and then took the stairs up to the third floor. He tried to be as quiet as he could, but he knew that anyone inside the building would have heard the ladder for sure.

He reached the third-floor landing and sure enough the lights were out. It was just 8:00 pm, he doubted that Dr. Marks and her visitor were asleep. He had to find them right away.

Where could they be?

The three women scoured the shelves quickly and grabbed the snacks that would give them just enough of a sugar rush to get the work done quickly. Nina anticipated that she could help in some way, even though a nagging voice in the back of her mind told her she couldn't. Nina wasn't smart like these women, her internal critic said. *One of them is me*, Nina clapped back at that voice in her mind.

She picked up the same candies and energy drinks that Marie and Feminina selected, following their motions. She had no money on her. Not any from that universe, not from any other. Nina assumed they knew, hoping they would offer to cover her before she had to admit that she was penniless.

And then, as she prepared to be mortified like a third grader in the school yard with no lunch money, she noticed something. Nina probably wouldn't have noticed it if she had been trying to spot the changes. But the aisle of chips and crunchy-salty things was oddly colorless. Where were the nacho cheese and cool ranch chips that had accompanied all of her late-night study sessions as a teenager? Where were the crinkle cut potato chips with the French onion flavor in their bold green packaging? "Do you guys want any Doritos?" Socially, Nina didn't want to push her luck with them spotting her even $10 worth of junk food, but she was curious to see their reaction.

"What's a Dorito?" Marie answered without so much as looking back at Nina, her gaze fixed on the ingredient list of two seemingly identical candy packs.

"Never mind," she brushed off the comment, making a mental note to figure out what in the world Frito-Lay had to do with her universe. Just because Eleanor Roosevelt was sworn in and assassinated, Doritos were never invented? That seemed silly at first, until she realized the potential consequences; the ripple effect Eleanor Roosevelt's story had created in this world. And it would surely affect more than just who was or was not President. It would impact who was born or not, who met and married, what companies were founded or sunk. In that moment, Nina realized the miracle of finding another Feminina in the multiverse at all. How fantastic was it to know that all of the elements came together so splendidly?

Thankfully, Feminina had purchased snacks for Nina and they continued towards the lab. She noticed that she paid with brightly colored notes, each denomination a different color. On the front of the blue $1 bill Nina spotted the face of Eleanor Roosevelt, stoic and unsmiling. On the yellow $5 was a likeness of Harriet Tubman. Nina smiled as they exited the convenience store, their haul of snacks in hand.

The two scientists walked confidently, discussing the repercussions of inter-dimensional travel and calibrations to make on the machine. Nina followed with timid footsteps, afraid that some non-entity boogeyman would snatch her from the sidewalk and prove all of her fears to be completely founded and correct.

As Feminina and Marie discussed the best method for breaking in and sealing off their route from Gus, Nina pondered all of the snacks that they would never get to savor. Thoroughly hungry and growing impatient at the idea of waiting until they were in the lab to eat, Nina's mind hovered on the topic of food. How many times had she blithely uttered, "I would never want to live in a world without chocolate!" How true it had seemed in that moment. But having glimpsed a second chance with Hank, she knew that she absolutely did not want to live in a world without him. But knowing that she could very well be stuck in that reality forever, she genuinely hoped that they had chocolate, oh and Nutella. *Please let them have Nutella.*

Theta

Marie snapped a padlock through two links in a metal chain that she had wound between the handle of the front door. The chain had been left in a pile on the floor of the first classroom on the right. "Guess we got too complacent about these," she muttered as she pulled against the chain and checked that it was secure.

Now that they were all inside the building, Nina could sense the growing tension between the three of them; it was time to get to work. Marie and Feminina set themselves into motion quickly, turning on monitors, grabbing extra wires, pulling out their notes. Nina stood awkwardly in the corner. She thought they had already assessed that she wouldn't be much help with the science portion. Feminina already knew that Nina wasn't a physicist or any other type of scientist. Bad enough she had to tell her that she didn't even finish her college degree after losing Hank. She wasn't just one decision tree branch away from this Feminina, she was another species of tree altogether.

One thing Nina saw from the multiverse was that the term "anything is possible" barely scratches the surface. Everything is actually possible and has happened. Just find the right universe and sure enough, it would be there. For some reason, the timeline that forked back on April 12, 1945 and caused Eleanor Roosevelt to succeed her husband in two realities, still led to Nina's parents meeting in that reality, in her home reality, and in the reality that Parker kidnapped her. And all three of them, the collective Feminina, still lost their mothers before they could even remember her. All three of them raised by their father, and from what Nina can tell, they all lost him too. But one of them was a scientist, one was a creative director, and then there was Nina. Just enthused enough by the promise of a paycheck to show up at work, but not going anywhere quickly.

Was she destined to be great in her career of choice? *Am I not living up to my potential, our potential?* Nina wondered as she watched her alter-ego move about the lab effortlessly.

Marie flicked on the lights by the Portal, a switch that Nina had missed when she had been in the lab earlier. The computer monitors still shone their dull blue light, waiting, ready for someone to use them. "Hey, if the University was abandoned, then why is the power still on?" Nina wondered aloud.

"What do you mean, why is the power still on? Does the power go off in your Universe?" Marie asked, her tone concerned.

"Well, it can shut off if the grid is overloaded or you don't pay your bill," Nina started to explain.

"Pay?! For power?!" Feminina spun to face her alter-ego. "What kind of messed up society charges people for electricity?"

"Um, it's expensive to generate…" Nina offered as an explanation. The idea of free electricity never occurred to her.

"Wait, you don't have solar or wind power?" Marie asked Nina, trying to understand the problem. Feminina made for the large console by the Portal, unlocking the home screen with her face and opening several windows across the multi-panel display.

"No, we have those kinds of energy-" Nina started to respond to Marie.

"But you don't use them?" Feminina barked back, her attention still focused on the systems she was initiating for the Portal.

Nina opened her mouth to speak, but Marie beat her to it. "Nina, all of our power is run from renewable resources. Sun, water, wind. Everyone here has access to it. So, even though the University is closed, the power stays on. Unless we're talking about quantum power needed to get this machine working, then that's on us to discover." Marie's kind explanation was a welcome relief from the incredulous responses Nina had been getting all evening. She smiled back at the Dean, or not the Dean here, but that was how Nina thought of her.

"I'll need to run some regressions on the quant comp to see if we can figure out the power source for the Portal." Marie called out to Feminina as she approached the bank of computers. While Parker's machine had clearly been patched together, Feminina and Marie's device looked like it was held together with bubble gum and duct tape. Nina's heart started to beat just a fraction too fast for her liking. Her breathing grew shallow. The attack hit her before the anxious thoughts did. She would be stuck here.

The terms Feminina and Marie were throwing around were the same ones Nina had heard for years. Frequencies, probabilities, permutations, quantum computers. All a universal language among the variables of the multiverse. The constants that make such travel possible. The Portal had opened to get her here, but she didn't have much confidence in the ability of two part-time physicists being able to open it up again with a device that looked like it was a decade away from being operational.

Feminina riffled through some papers on the far end of the lab near a whiteboard covered with eccentric symbols and equations. "Anything I can help with?" Nina inquired with little expectation of a real task. She knew she needed to help them, they were going to need more than just some caffeine and sugar to get this done.

"Yes, there was a thumb drive on the table when we left this past Sunday. It isn't here now. Can you help me look for it?" Feminina described the drive as thick and metallic, very utilitarian. It was apparently a custom device that Marie had fashioned. The quantum computer was a necessary component for calculating all of the possibilities and finding the correct frequency signature. This part Thurston had briefly explained earlier, so Nina was able to keep up. But the computer had to do too much processing to have much storage. They developed the quantum drive to act as an expanded storage device that held more than most high-end computers and external drives. It had their saved coordinates from the frequencies that they had been able to find. Nina remembered Parker explaining this as well. She could picture the device that she had seen earlier that day. Nina set about looking for it.

"So, you know it can work?" she tried to not sound hopeless as she looked under the back desk for the thumb drive.

"Oh, it for sure works. You wouldn't be here without it." Feminina continued to look under piles of folders that appeared as though they hadn't been touched in months. The likelihood of a thumb drive being hidden beneath it seemed laughably small, but she was desperate for the device. Nina began to search in earnest as her spirits rebounded. If the

Portal needed the quantum drive to point her in the right direction, then she would most certainly make sure it was found.

Nina scrambled onto her hands and knees, moving between the various wires below the desks that hooked up each of the monitors. As she slid along, she looked for anything shiny that might catch her eye. She was meticulous. Feminina had already doubled back and started re-examining the same area again. Nina had a question on her mind that begged for attention like a bug-bite in need of an itch.

She tried to be discrete. It was a significant date for her, but perhaps it was troublesome here, or perhaps it would mean nothing and that might crush her. Or it could be a repeat of when she had asked Hank and she could really offend Feminina.

"Does August 8th mean anything to you?" Nina asked, her voice wavering a bit.

"Today is August 8th, so I guess from here on out it will be the day that someone from another universe came to visit. Though, I'm not sure anyone else will ever know about it." Feminina moved some papers that had been in disarray from one lumpy pile on the main table to another.

"Oh, right. That is significant." Nina turned her face away, hiding her disappointment.

"And, now that I think of it, Marie and I finished the schematics for the Portal three years ago today." The speed of her speech started to accelerate, the cadence of her words picking up. "Yeah, it was August 8th that we completed the plans. I remember because we went out for a drink to toast and of course, I didn't say cheers, not on that day, I said-"

"Here's to the infinite-infinite" Nina finished her sentence. Memories of summers gone by flashed in her mind. Star gazing in the backyard with her father, museum lectures on cosmology, failed at-home experiments with baking soda and food coloring. He always had something special planned for that day, and he always called it "the infinite-infinite". As Nina grew older, he would sneak a glass of wine and offer a toast to the advancement of humanity and the extent of their knowledge. He loved little things like that. Twisting the eights to look like infinity symbols. Catching every date in the new millennium that offered a play on numbers, 1/1/11 and 12/12/12 and the like. But August 8th, 8/8, the infinite-infinite, was always their special day.

"I miss him too," Nina heard Feminina's voice break through her thoughts. She didn't know what to say in that moment. They both knew the loss, both felt it. Perhaps there was nothing to say. Thankfully, Feminina started to speak, sparing Nina the awkward task of trying to find words.

"He was the reason I became a scientist. That's why I was so surprised that you weren't. He struggled as a lab assistant for years, unable to move up to fulfill his dream of being a chemist and a teacher because of his gender." This didn't mesh with Nina's memory. Her father had been an amazing chemistry teacher, he won teacher of the year twice. He loved what he did. Nina told her as much, she figured it would give her some closure to know that somewhere in the cosmos he had been living his dream. She smiled.

"Was it?" Feminina asked without having to finish the question.

"Yeah, cancer," Nina confirmed.

"Damn, same here," she could hear the disappointment in her voice.

Thinking her previous technique had been helpful, she went for it again, "maybe in another universe we're an oncologist." Thinking multi-dimensionally had started to ease some of her sadness on the topic, but exacerbated her anxiety in other ways.

"No way we catch it soon enough though," she reminded Nina. Her memory flashed on his rough cough that turned out to be small-cell lung cancer. It was too far developed. The chemo and radiation were hopeless from the start, but he tortured himself through it anyways.

"Yeah, probably not," Nina agreed, defeated.

Naturally, the moment that their attentions were turned elsewhere and they genuinely stopped looking, they found the thumb drive. More like a palm drive, the shiny stick of data was sitting idly on one of the lab benches. Bold as it was, unhiding, always been there, never left. They both rejoiced in this small victory, although they felt idiotic for having upended the rest of the lab to find something so plainly available.

Nina and her alter-ego joined Marie by the Portal. Without any ceremony she took the drive and inserted it into the computer. The screens lit up, perfectly clear and quick in spite of their dated appearance. The glow mesmerized Nina. Much like the futuristic films that she had seen in her own reality, things had a soft glow of white and blue. Marie navigated through the programs; the files and systems responding as rapidly as her fingers could move.

Within one minute, her screens were all displaying the frequency lines that Nina had seen on Parker's device, the formatting looked different, but the frequencies were the same. Marie did a frequency search and found a bold yellow line. "That's us. Double the Feminina," her alter-ego remarked. With a few keystrokes Marie labeled the top screen "HOME."

As Marie started to move onto the next display Nina stopped her. "Wait Marie, this is home for you and Feminina. But not for me or any other person traveling the multiverse."

Marie turned slightly, her expression daring Nina to offer an alternative. Anytime someone intentionally tilted their head down so they can get a better look at her above the rim of their glasses, Nina expected that she was about to meet their disapproval.

"So, the universe that I came from was the first to have a visitor from the multiverse. That's Alpha." Nina pulled what she could from her conversation with Thurston. "The one that I was in earlier today was the second to have a visitor from the multiverse. That's Beta. And that makes this the third, so Gamma."

Nina looked at both of them, hoping that she hadn't just said something so infinitely stupid that they would forbid her from speaking again.

"That's true, I just don't like the idea that we weren't the first." Marie made the edit.

"I don't like that it was a man who did it first," Feminina muttered beside Nina. The blatant anti-masculine sentiment shocked her system yet again. It was like a large gulp of water after days dehydrating in the desert or the first painful prickles of heat in her fingertips after walking around in freezing weather without gloves. It wasn't refreshing or welcome, but it marked a massive change in the way Nina thought. "Also, how do you know the Greek alphabet?" Feminina asked of her alter-ego.

Chafed at the implication that she was somehow a dullard just because she wasn't a physicist, Nina retorted, "I'm not stupid, Feminina."

"I was impressed, that's all." Feminina put her hands up, a sign that there was no ill will intended. Nina rolled her eyes.

With the changes made, they created a map to get back to Universe Beta. The one where Nina had just come from, where Hank was in danger of attack from Parker. Perhaps he was already hurt, or worse. They pinpointed the exact location in that universe, on that planet, in that city, in that lab.

Now they just needed the power source to get them there. The problem that they hadn't been able to solve for three years, they now had to solve it before the day ended. The frequency of the quantum jitters on August 8th made it a necessity. If they took too long, they would have to wait a year to try again. With a Portal to the multiverse in front of them, a functional time machine, a year seemed like an impossibly long amount of time to sit and wait.

"Where did we leave off with the calculations?" Feminina asked Marie, as if reading Nina's mind. Marie stood and walked over to a rolling chalkboard on the far end of the warehouse portion of the lab. What looked like mathematical gibberish to Nina, in spite of her study on the topic, must have made sense to Feminina. She nodded as she reviewed the equations.

Then Marie flipped the board on its hinges, showing the opposite side. It appeared to be much more chaotic. Without having to ask for explanation, Feminina began.

"So, on one side we have our equation for what makes all of that work," she gestured to the screens. Nina sat down at the controls as she listened. "But the other side is where we are with the power source."

"That's doesn't look good." Stating the obvious earned her an eyebrow raise from Marie.

"Yeah, that's the trouble right there. This one unsolved equation. We figure this out, then we can get this thing to work," she said as she turned to assess the board again. All three of them looked at the board, each daunted and confounded. It was as though they had trekked for miles to get home, only to find that they had no key and no other way to get inside.

"So, we now know that the Portal works and that it has been used to travel here, which means that we can use it to travel as well. All we need to do is pinpoint the moment of arrival and reverse engineer the amount of power required." Feminina explained in what she must have thought were layman's terms.

"Then we have to source it," Marie reminded her.

"That sounds relatively simple, am I missing something?" Nina asked, hoping that they already had an answer.

Marie shook her head and she looked at the board. "That's the thing about science, if it sounds simple it has a lot of brain power behind it. We're going to need some caffeine and a lot of math."

Iota

Marie popped the tab on her energy drink, some of the fizzy liquid spilled over and dripped onto her shoes. Feminina followed and wiped up the liquid, glaring at her lab partner. Nina could see the clear lines of who was the mess and who was the neat freak, where their strengths and weaknesses complimented each other.

Nina watched them as they went to work. The minutes sped by with abandon. Each of them wasted, frittered away with Marie and Feminina circling the mental path that led them back to the same result. Every second skipped ahead, gleefully taunting Nina, laughing at her misery as time carried her further and further away from Hank again.

On the walk to the University, Nina tried to recite a list in her mind of everything that she wanted to write down from this experience. The questions bubbling up in her mind. All of the fine historical details that she had been too lazy to ever look-up. Of the universes she had seen, two had Eleanor Roosevelt rising to power as the first female President of the United States. That hadn't happened in her reality, no woman had done that yet. It seemed like a notable benchmark. But then she thought about the technology here. The facial recognition on the outermost apartment door, but the standard lock and deadbolt on the inner doors. The palm and fingerprint recognition on the lab door, but no street lights. This place was awash with conundrums. *How had all of these changes, big and small, manifested to this? Was there a nearly identical version of this reality that had streetlights, but where Nina and Marie had not built the Portal? How could one event or non-event have such far-reaching implications?* Just how many realities existed that were almost imperceptibly similar to this one, but where one small detail was out of place. Parker had described the Quantum

Multiverse to Nina before, but the magnitude of it only started to sink in. She had experienced two other universes in an infinite string of them.

Nina felt as though she was hanging on to a life raft in the Indian Ocean, lost and surrounded by miles of water around and beneath her. This was what being lost truly felt like. She felt lost in the multiverse. For all of her whining and moaning and refusing to let her grief for Hank abate, she had no concept of feeling profoundly alone until that moment.

All of the past and present changes, all the things that were out of Nina's control scared her. But it also made her think of all that she could control, should have controlled. She could have been a genius scientist like Feminina. She could have at least finished her degree. She could have done a lot of things. But she let her past dictate her future, two concepts that were quickly losing meaning for her.

In the hours Nina spent waiting for a solution, she busied herself as best as she could. Nina gave herself permission to do a little searching on The Mesh to learn more about the universe she found herself in. If she wasn't going to be any help with the physics of it all, she could at least be a curious traveler and learn something.

She learned about the nuances of the parallel universe she found herself in. She found history books online and devoured them with her eyes. She found one lone textbook in the corner of the lab, likely abandoned by a student years earlier when the University was still operational. She desecrated its body by taking a page to keep, but paid homage to their corporeal sacrifice by folding it penitently to put in her pocket. A printed page with the timeline of events in American history made the perfect souvenir.

Eleanor Roosevelt's assassination had been a major inflection point. With women in control of government and industry by the early 1960s, there had been a surge in economic and technological advances. Progress was made, people were helped, but in spite of all these big changes, so much stayed the same. 9/11 still happened there as well. It seemed improbable, but in a multiverse where anything could happen, there seemed to be a specific recipe in the three that she had experienced. Some things just had to happen and maybe they had nothing to do with the invention of the Portal, but maybe they did.

In her online searches she also discovered that there was no Parker Lovett, not as a physicist, not as a person who could be found online. Nina did find Hank though; he taught English Literature at a University abroad. She wrote down his information and slipped it into her pocket as well. Feminina had been right, his family expatriated from the country. She caught a few references to the United States as the Vestal Kingdom; how different the world had become with women in charge.

Marie and Feminina started to squabble over some point that they were hung up on. It distracted Nina from the listing she found on her favorite boy-band crush, he had become a salesman in Memphis.

"This is hopeless!" Marie threw her hands up in the air.

"Don't say that, we can do this. It's been done before; it can be done again." Feminina played the calm and collected counterpart to Marie's hopeless frustrations. They seemed to ebb and flow between the two states, working in a balanced system.

"Let's run through the process again," Feminina prompted Marie.

"Right," Winchester nodded her head accepting that this was the next step in their mental exercises. "Turn on the quant. comp. Identify the frequencies for other universes that have an active Portal. Isolate one frequency and call it up on the system. Power on the machine." She added that last directive with a sarcastic tone.

"Which, we will figure out," Feminina highlighted as Marie continued.

"Inject the supercybin. Watch the Portal transform before our eyes. Walk through." Marie finished the list.

Nina turned to face them from across the lab. "What did you say you injected?" She pushed herself back from the table and let the chair roll a few inches before stopping it with her feet. She didn't ask it as much as demanded to know.

"Supercybin. It's an enhanced derivative of psilocybin," Feminina explained as though she were answering a toddler who had demanded the answer to yet another trite question.

Nina wracked her brain for the word, she knew she had heard of it before. "The psychedelic?"

"Yeah, why do you think you're not freaking out right now?" Feminina said with a shrug of her shoulders, as though Nina should have known this. "Without it your brain would have too much trouble comprehending what was going on. Your brain would scramble in the membrane between realities."

"You told us that Parker injected you before he pushed you here, right?" Marie jumped in as she finished her third cup of coffee in as many hours.

Nina reached for the tender spot on her arm. And then she remembered drinks the previous night, the night that felt like it had been a lifetime earlier. Had he drugged her with it to get her to Universe Beta?

"So, which one of you developed that one?" Nina walked over to join them.

"What do you mean?" Feminina asked. She did a micro-shake of her head, wriggling her long bangs like tassels, motioning them out of her eyes. Not the expected response from a scientist, they often feel underappreciated and unrecognized for their work. Neither of them should have shied away from taking credit.

"Well you both developed the Portal and the quantum computer together. So: physics and computer science," Nina gestured to each of them accordingly based on their areas of expertise in this reality. Nina had already made the mistake of asking Marie if she was still a chemist in that reality. Marie had responded with a stern 'no' and that she was one of the foremost experts in computer science and engineering. Another odd switch up from her own reality.

"So, who was your chemist?" Nina wasn't sure what had led her to this line of questioning or the suspicion she could hear in her own voice. Maybe it was that thread of a thought that she just couldn't place, a loose string that she needed to rethread and mend.

"Our chemist is no longer with the team," Marie said in an overly placid tone, as though trying to pacify Nina and keep her calm. "But not to worry, we have more than enough supercybin to get you home and then some."

"I told you I'm not going home; I'm going to stay in Beta with Hank. Who was your chemist?" The point-blank nature of her words shocked even Nina herself. She could feel the threads coming together, twining like embroidery floss.

"It was Blanity, okay!" Feminina blurted out.

"Femi!" Marie chided her.

"What, she might as well know. We had some creative differences on the project. He had a sinister sense of humor and we weren't sure that he could be trusted with a key to the multiverse." Her face twisted, like a towel being wrung out, all the water dripping out. Only this wasn't water, it was the truth, both equally difficult to hold.

"And we were right," Marie jumped in. "He went crazy, started stalking us."

Nina nodded her head slowly. The details seemed to appear in her mind exactly as they spoke them. Had she been here before? Was this the déjà vu feeling that came with traveling the multiverse that she had read about in popular fiction? Or were each of these truths so obvious, so evident that there was a level of precognition associated with them.

"So, do you think that's why I found him here tonight when I arrived? To access the Portal?"

Both Feminina and Marie looked at Nina, they were starting to puzzle over it as well. "Can we see a log of all visits to this universe? Does that exist?" Nina's mind focused in on these details; distracted from their mission of finding the power source. For some reason the questions she asked them seemed like they would eventually take them back around, like a long, winding road.

"Um, I don't know. You're the first one to visit," Feminina trailed from one thought to the next. Marie moved quickly over to the console; the board of equations forgotten for the moment.

"But I can look," she finished her sentence and with a few keystrokes, Marie had the input on the screens flash backward. The small red light on the massive thumb drive blinked as the data passed through it, processing all the information in the known multiverse.

"Here!" Marie pointed at the screen.

They each looked at the center screen in the panorama. There were large spikes, three of them.

"I zoomed out so we can see all of the activity over the past month." About halfway through the screen she saw the first large spike, a bright flash twinkling in the middle of a plain grid. Then another one shortly after. And then the third, way on the far-right edge of the screen.

"So about two weeks ago it looks like someone came through that Portal, and then again a few days later." Marie gestured at the screen. The two lines both terminated early on the morning of August 8th.

"Who could have done that?" Nina asked.

"Who else? Parker!" Feminina scolded her, displeased. Perhaps Feminina didn't like being the smartest version of them, Nina thought. All of the flaws that Feminina knew so well must have led her to believe that there was a perfect version of her out there somewhere. But this Nina, her existence refuted that very belief with her mediocre life, lack of post graduate degree, and overall air of failure.

"But why?" Marie asked as she eyed the reports on the screen.

"To get more of the supercybin. He had access to a limited amount, I saw the container back in Beta. The University would have only given him enough for his test trip, not enough for his little detour." Maybe Nina wasn't that mediocre after all. Maybe spending time with Feminina and Marie, even just a few hours, had a positive effect. Their genius somehow rubbing off on her, allowing her to tap into this unused section of her brain.

"But how would he know to come here to get it?" Feminina asked, calling attention to the obvious. In all the potential universes that Parker could have selected, why would he pick this one?

"Does the supercybin give off a frequency?" Nina asked, worried her question would show that her understanding of the concepts was superficial at best. Marie and Feminina looked at her blankly. "I mean each of us gives off a frequency, so does the Portal. Why wouldn't the supercybin? If he could see a large concentration here that might tempt him into making a visit to steal it."

"Are you sure you weren't a scientist in your home universe?" Marie crossed her arms as she appraised Nina.

"I'm sure I wasn't. I just dated one for three years, I picked up a few things." Nina shrugged off what was clearly intended to be a compliment to her intelligence.

"Okay, so Parker came here to get the extra supercybin, but why come back?" Feminina reminded them of the second line appearing on the screen.

"It has to be Gus!" Nina called out. While they weren't making progress on the power source, they were solving some mystery. Figuring this out seemed important, Nina felt compelled to follow it through. She simply had to do it; she couldn't explain it any better. Some loops just have to be closed.

"So what? Gus caught Parker lifting the supercybin and he demands payment?" Marie suggested.

"Or they make some arrangement to create more." Feminina continued.

"Then Parker comes back to get more, and then what?" Marie asked.

"And then Gus waited for him to come back. It explains why he was here when I arrived," Nina cast her glance from one set of eyes to the next.

"And why he didn't start yelling at you. He realized you weren't me." Feminina explained one of the odd events from earlier that evening. Nina thought back to her encounter with Gus. He had been kind at first, perhaps he was in shock. Perhaps he wanted to believe that something good had come out of the machine. Perhaps he was curious to see what would happen next. Nina couldn't figure that part out.

"So, Parker came and *went*." Marie emphasized the final word clearly. She spun around in the desk chair to face the screens again. "Which means we can get out of here too!"

Kappa

A wayward brick served as the perfect instrument for his plan. Gus found it lying near the entryway to the Sciences building, probably upended from some sidewalk or left over from some construction project on campus that would never be completed. He found a first-floor window near the front of the building, he hoped it would be far enough from the lab that it wouldn't alert the women to his presence.

As he approached, the building appeared just as deserted as everything else on campus, the only light coming from the parking lot. When Gus inched closer to the Sciences building, he peeked through the cut-out windows on the front door. He glanced down the corridor, every light extinguished except for that one patch of light in the middle. A thin stream of light slid out onto the floor, slipping underneath the lab doors. *Gotcha.*

Gus moved around to the side of the building and found a pane of glass just wide enough to allow him through, not too far off the ground either, perfect for getting in. He tapped the corner of the glass with the brick, trying to hit the exact point necessary for it to shatter. *Tap tap tap.* He tried again, pushing harder this time.

Tap tap. Crack.

Gus smiled a bit and pushed a few pieces of glass through with his fingertips. Once he created enough of a hole, he wrapped the bottom of his t-shirt around his forearm and pushed the rest of the glass in. He could hear the glass falling onto the floor, but he doubted that anyone else would have heard it.

Carefully, he climbed through the empty window pane, cognizant not to slip on the glass at his feet once inside. He crept past the desks that had gathered a fine layer of dust and peered out of the classroom and into the hall. He could hear their voices, but only slightly. He stepped out of the classroom and started to inch closer to the lab at the end of the hallway, their voices becoming clearer with each step.

Feminina and Marie resumed their sophisticated calculations, a new burst of energy hitting them as they realized that there was a way to operate the Portal. Nina watched them move in silent awe. They were speaking a different language, one that was – literally- universal. These calculations would apply across the multiverse to allow for travel across it, but it was still lost on her. And she observed Feminina in wonder. Perhaps for this all to happen, there had to be a reality where she didn't know Hank. Where no sweeping romantic destiny distracted her from her true destiny, her real purpose. Because with Hank in Nina's life, she would never feel discontent, she would never strive for the external validation of greater possibilities, galaxy shattering discoveries. With Hank, Nina already had everything she needed, he was the proton to her electron. Together they were a complete system.

But that can't be right either, this theory doesn't hold true in Universe Beta, the reality Parker kidnapped Nina into. Because there her alter-ego had Hank and a family and they lost their little girl. Perhaps there were no universal laws regarding how horrible things are represented and retold, only a temporal anomaly mandating that she and Hank find each other but then break apart. Clearly, the version of Nina in Universe Beta had been longing for him, the bond between them too strong to ever allow them to be apart forever. Nina felt like a satellite, circling back around in orbit and he was catching her again with his gravity.

And even in Nina's own home reality, she had settled. She settled for her job. She had tried for a promotion, but even she had to admit to herself that it was a half-hearted attempt. She settled for a boyfriend who wasn't great for her, but she stayed. The loss of Hank was so damaging and permanent that she felt like an imploded star, the weight of the pain too heavy for all of her atoms in her body to hold. So perhaps it was that Nina could have been great, could have been a multiverse pioneer in any of these realities, but she accepted the losses without rebounding. She allowed that force to be pushed upon her and she never pushed back, she had no equal and opposite reaction. She did nothing.

Nina watched as her own alter-ego, this brainier Feminina, moved quickly from one symbol to the next, her hand moving fast, almost smearing the marker on the whiteboard. Her motions became frenzied, as though her body appeared to resist the speed at which her brain was operating. Her hands shook from the sheer force of thought that she needed to push through them.

Until she abruptly stopped.

"Marie!" she shouted while staring at her work. Nina sprung up from her seat as Dr. Winchester approached from the other side of the lab.

Marie brushed the errant hairs that had escaped her bun from her eyes, she stood with her fists on her hips as she followed the equation. Her mouth silently moved as she read through what Feminina had written. Her eyes found the edge of the board and then quickly moved to Nina's face. Nina noticed that Feminina had already turned to face her head-on as well.

"What is it?" she asked, anxious to have both of them looking at her.

Marie started to laugh, "Oh this is too funny. We've been working at this for years and it was so simple."

Feminina chuckled behind her hand, a coy gesture.

"I don't get it," Nina looked to them for some kind of clarification.

Marie continued to laugh as she stumbled to the Portal. Feminina stood closely behind her alter-ego as Marie set to work. She stooped down and released the clamps at the bottom of the Portal. Each let out a soft hiss as the air that had been locked beneath them released.

"Based on the original equations from the schematics, we knew we had to have the Portal on a thick riser that would span 12 feet in each direction. The math just didn't make sense without it." Feminina began before Marie cut in, continuing the explanation.

"Our thinking had been that it would be a stabilizer, that the sheer force of the required energy would blow the portal away if it wasn't grounded." The last word required a heavy effort from Marie as the final clamp released.

"But I never thought of it as a track before," Feminina finished her partner's thought.

"A track?" Nina asked as the answer dawned on her. Yes, she had seen this in the lab before, in the other lab. What had Thurston said? *We needed to find the moment in time when the machine would be activated and plug into that.*

"So, what we have here isn't really a Portal," Marie began

"It's a time machine," Nina and her alter-ego said in unison.

"We do need to find the power source," Marie let out with an exasperated sigh as she pushed herself back up to standing. Her face flushed from the physical exertion. "But we don't need to discover it. We need to find when it first appeared." She smiled and gave the frame a light nudge and it slid slowly down the track about five inches. Gliding silently, she demonstrated her point easy enough that even a paper-pusher like Nina could understand.

The frame rested to a stop, the gravity of its weight acting as a downward force. Feminina and Nina moved quickly over to the console to pull up a regression of what that five inches equated to in terms of time travel. They had only just reached the screens, silently jockeying for the seat in the lone desk chair, when they heard Marie cry out.

"No!" she shouted in just enough time to warn them. A deranged man lunged towards them with a red brick in hand. Whether he sought to harm them or the machinery, he looked crazy enough to do either. His eyes blood-shot and his hair matted to his forehead with sweat, he was a scary sight. If it hadn't been for the embroidered name on his work-shirt, Nina wouldn't have realized that this man was Gus Blanity. The same mild-mannered guy who had helped her earlier in the evening. Her mind flashed on that horrible night from a decade earlier when he had attacked her before.

Marie had caught up to him and jumped up to grab the brick as Gus raised it above his head. Feminina kicked at his legs. Nina stood in brief shock as she saw the two women launch a coordinated counterattack. They did work in sync together, not the best time for her to admire their efforts, but she benefited from their protection in that moment. Nina tried to think of what she could do to help, and that was just the problem. She should have been acting off pure adrenaline, but she was stuck. Nina's hands and arms were locked in place as she leaned back into the table holding up the computer displays. *Move, move!* She commanded her arms, but she stood stock still.

Can someone feel their eyes bulge out of their head? Can they feel their own body freeze up on them? Nina witnessed it all without moving, and the most terrifying part was yet to come.

Lambda

Nina saw who she could have been, who she could have become, if she had been born into a world where men had to fear women, and not the other way around.

What if she hadn't learned to be quiet, to make herself small? What if no one had to encourage her greatness because it had been assumed? If that subtle undercurrent of misogyny hadn't been put upon her, would she have been this modern warrior-slash-scientist? A small and persistent force can knock a person off course, and the impact of the male-dominated society Nina lived in was apparent when she interacted with her alter ego. Even in Universe Beta, Parker still felt the need to kill her. Only in a world where men feel the same fear that she had always lived with, would women be free from male violence.

But even in that reality, the one where Nina watched Marie and Feminina pummel Gus Blanity into submission, there was violence against women. Although, perhaps Blanity's motives weren't fueled by a hatred for all women, but merely a hatred for those two specific women.

He spat out horrible vitriol as they pinned him to the ground. Feminina blew the hair out of her face as she looked over at Nina and asked, "you okay?"

"Yeah," she nodded.

"You okay?" she asked again, this time raising her voice. Nina could see the wild look in her eyes, the adrenaline still keeping her charged up. She must have answered in her mind only, or maybe she just hadn't been sure of her words, so she kept them as silent as possible.

"Yes!" Nina responded, a little too brusque, almost yelling the answer at her.

"Good, move the Portal until the device activates!" she called out. Blanity had tried to move the arm Feminina had pinned down. She redoubled her efforts to keep him restrained as he whined in pain.

"Give me the drive!" Blanity's words gargled out of him like hateful lava bubbling from an unstable volcano, his words were wet and thick. He sounded as evil as he was, as he had been made to be under the influence of Parker and the society he grew up in. Feminina sucker punched him in the gut, quickly returning her hand to its place on his thigh, pinning him down.

"Go slow Nina, slow and deliberate," Marie called out as she dug her elbow into the man's neck. Nina approached the Portal and pressed her palm to it gently, she could feel it loose on the track and ready for motion. Nina gave it a slight push and it slid quickly down the track another few inches.

"Too fast, Nina! Walk it down the line slowly." Marie instructed. Nina could see that both women were struggling and sweating. Their effort might give out soon. She needed to find the exact position on the track, the exact position in time.

Nina felt as though she was walking on a high-wire, placing each foot in front of the next with deliberate precision. But she wasn't suspended in the air, she was in the lab, moving a very rare and powerful machine into place. Is this how the men who built the atomic bomb felt as they loaded it onto the Enola Gay? Did they feel the power and potential destruction in their hands?

What seemed like feet to Nina was really only a few inches, but it took what felt like a long time to move the Portal frame slowly, slowly down the track. Nina saw the top screen on the computer console light up and she felt the metal of the frame begin to vibrate ever so slightly in her hand. It wasn't a pulsing sensation, but more of a faint buzz, like the alloy had come to life.

"Secure the clamps!" Marie tried to scream out, but her voice strained against the effort it took to restrain Gus. Feminina had moved her left arm to pin down his shoulder, she pressed down further each time he tried to make a sound. Nina crouched down to lock the clamps. They gave another hydraulic hiss when they were secured.

"Is that good?" Nina called out to Marie.

"Yes, go to the console!" She ran as the words hit her. Nina saw the blinking message counting down on the screens. 0:48. The next quantum jitter was about to occur, the Portal was powered up, it was all coming together so seamlessly.

"Lower right drawer, the key is in the lock already," Feminina turned to say this to Nina, her grip on Blanity loosening for just a second. She didn't see, but Nina could hear from behind her as her fingers tried to work as quickly as possible. Both women grunted and Nina heard Blanity cry out, he had been tamed, for the moment. With all of the raw anger and power in the room, Nina felt as though the atmosphere had changed. Was she breathing in this toxic aggression, or was it something spewing from the Portal, shining and alive? The room filled with a thunderous noise as the Portal prepared to open into another dimension.

Nina grabbed the box at the bottom of the drawer and slid it over to Feminina, it wasn't as smooth as the Portal had been on the track, but it got to her just the same, the faint whooshing noise of cardboard against concrete drowned out by the sound created by the open Portal. Nina collapsed on the ground in front on the console as she watched the rest unfold.

The screen continued to flash. 0:26

Feminina grabbed a vial from the box, these were the same neon orange color that Parker had in his possession in Universe Beta. Only these were ready to use, ready to go. Feminina popped the plastic lid off and stabbed the vial into Blanity's leg.

His face contorted and then calmed.

0:15

Marie, with an agility Nina hadn't thought possible for a woman of her height and size, leaned across Blanity for the box and grabbed a second vial. She stabbed it into his neck, the liquid draining out and into his bloodstream instantly.

0:12

"That's too much, he'll lose his damn mind with that dosage," Feminina knocked the vial from her hand, but it was useless. The damage was done, the supercybin coursed through his system.

"Good" Marie said, a sneer forming on her upper lip. The universal sign of disgust. Of contempt. Of hatred.

Both women pulled him up, each taking one of his elbows.

0:09

His legs were limp. No longer fighting back, the two women were able to drag him across to the Portal. The pearlescent sheen of the non-fluid filled in its borders, just as Nina had seen in Universe Beta. Gus' weak attempts at resistance only evident by a faint twitch in his ankle. Feminina's face showed all the signs of strain and muscular agony that accompanied the heavy load. Marie must have been handling the bulk of his weight.

0:03

With a final synchronized grunt, they shoved him through the Portal, head first. His legs stuck out of the Portal for a second before being sucked through.

0:01

0:00

The light that the Portal emitted shut off abruptly, casting a dark shadow across each of them. The roar of the machine cut off, abruptly thrusting the room into near silence. Marie and Feminina were slouched on the floor, panting for air. Their deep gasps for oxygen were the only noise in a room that had once been full of sound: loud, pounding, cosmic sound.

And then, without realizing what her mind had put together, Nina shot up from the floor and spun to examine the screens on the console.

"Where did you send him?" Nina asked, worried that she already knew the answer to this question.

Mu

"When did we send him?" Marie asked with a slight laugh to her voice. The metaphysical humor was not Nina's priority at the moment.

"Back to the first time this machine was ever used anywhere in the multiverse. Most likely somewhere that doesn't have a machine yet though, we didn't plug in any coordinates." Marie closed her eyes as she continued to regain her regular breathing. Feminina looked up at her alter-ego, concern spreading down from her forehead. Nina could barely read the expression in her eyes, hidden behind a curtain of fringe. But she could see Feminina purse her lips tight with worry.

"I think I know where you sent him," Nina whispered. On the first screen that they had labelled Universe Alpha, her home universe, she watched as a new frequency, erratic and unpredictable, just like its human counterpart, appeared. In the late evening hours of August 8, 2008, not too long before midnight, this entity had appeared in Universe Alpha. The prototype that Thurston had built long before Parker ever joined his project was the gateway. Nina could only watch in horror as Gus arrived at the exact time that the machine was first powered on, ever, but in the wrong place. He arrived in Universe Alpha just in time to stumble out of the University, through off-campus alleyways, and continue his fight with the only Feminina he could find in that reality.

Nina winced as she pictured it all again, happening once more. The attack, the sharp edge slicing through the air, darkness. A compulsion to ask all those questions, a lack of movement to stop Feminina and Marie from sending him anywhere. Her inability to jump in and help, it all made sense now. This had to happen first. This was the temporal loop that had to be closed, the predestination paradox at work. They had to send him back, so he could commit his crime, and change the trajectory of Nina's life forever.

Nina could picture him, crawling through the vacant lot, guided by the streetlights along the sidewalk. A spotlight on Hank and his date, Nina. A bulls-eye for this mad man. And then, violence.

Nina did the only thing she could do in that moment; she let out a scream of futility. "No!" she bellowed from somewhere deep in her gut. The worst thing that had ever happened to her had been preventable; she just couldn't see it until it was too late. She could have stopped it, but she felt powerless against it. There was no formula on any of the boards surrounding her that factored in fate, no symbol for this pervasive constant that stole Hank from her at that very moment, back in time.

Feminina's arms were around Nina, comforting her. She fell back into her alter-ego and they both crashed to the ground.

Nu

"Hey, we only have a little over an hour left," Marie reminded Feminina and Nina, the Femininae. The clock on the wall approached 11:00 pm, time was running out. Nina sat cross-legged on the concrete floor, aware of all the thick and scratchy dirt clumps that must have been tracked in over time. In a different universe, Nina might have stood up immediately and wiped off her bottom, but a little dirt was the least of her concerns.

"Nina, we have only a few more minutes before the next jitter," Feminina whispered as she rubbed her shoulders. The timer on the console had started to count down again, sensing the impending disturbance in the veil of space-time.

For all of the things that were different in Universe Gamma, the civic structures, the societal expectations on men and women, the advanced technologies, there was one thing that appeared to be constant: time. The way it moved, the way it was measured and communicated. It was just math really, and it was universal, multiversal. It was going by quickly. The quantum jitters would become less predictable, there might not be any more for a year. They had to act quickly.

But all Nina wanted to do at the next jitter was to undo what had just been done. She wanted a do-over. She wanted to follow after Gus and take him out before he could kill Hank. Or better yet, go back before she stumbled into Universe Gamma and be better prepared to take on Parker. She felt a heat down in her stomach, a flame ignited.

"So, where do we slide this thing to?" Nina walked over to the Portal, ready to push or pull it as needed.

"I don't think we move it at all," Marie muttered, her eyes moving left to right quickly, as though she were reading something written in the air, processing some new equation.

"That would send us back ten years, we need at maximum four hours to get Nina back to Beta," Feminina walked past Marie, dismissing her.

"No, that just gets her back to Beta. We need to make sure she can get back to Alpha," Marie corrected.

"No, I want to stay in Beta with Hank! But first we have to save him," Nina protested, but the two were starting to dialog in their science-speak.

"You're right, Marie. We need the power source, then we can move through the multiverse easier," Feminina stepped away from the track and back over to the computer console.

"But we have a power source, we just need to move this to the exact moment that I came through," Nina knew she had caught on at least that much.

"Okay, Nina," Marie said. Nina turned to face her. Marie stood over by the board; she had a piece of chalk in her hand. "Why don't you work out the exact algebra for us then, and it has to be absolutely exact. Not even a pico-meter off, or else it won't work."

Nina's felt her ego chafe at the suggestion. She could do basic algebra; she had studied math in college before she dropped out. She knew how to do the math, even if she wasn't some fancy professional physicist. But she started to feel the weight of Marie's request. Nina's days were filled with basic analytics on marketing campaigns, applied mathematics in its most basic form. *Could she do the full calculation and then move the Portal into the exact spot necessary in just a few moments?* Nina's confidence waned. It must have shown on her face, she lowered her gaze from Marie's, breaking eye contact, accepting defeat.

"Okay then, Feminina, do you have the coordinates?" Marie brushed past Nina. She didn't like that Marie thought she was stupid, or at least not as smart as her or Feminina. But Nina didn't have time to worry about her opinions.

"Yes, I have time, space, and location for the very first use of the Portal." Feminina's hands were moving quickly over the keys. Nina saw the timer already near the end of its countdown. A new window appeared, Feminina had already labeled it as "Delta." The machine started to fill the room with sound once more, their ears still ringing from the last use. "X marks the spot," Feminina said with a smile, she winked at Nina.

Feminina and Marie each grabbed a vial of the supercybin from the bin and injected themselves. "Should we lock it up before we leave?" Nina asked as Marie handed one to her.

"No, it's coming with us," Feminina added the remaining 7 vials to a bubble wrapped envelope. Nina uncapped the vial in her hand and plunged the needle into her arm.

"Okay, so we go there, we confirm that we can copy the power-source," Marie said as Feminina handed her the large thumb drive, "and then we get Nina back home."

The pearlescent glow appeared through the frame of the Portal. It was time to go.

PART 4

8/8: *The Infinite-Infinite.*
Universe Alpha (my home reality)

∞   *The day when Galileo's telescope was inspected by the Venetian Senate.*

∞   *The day Smith & Wesson filed their patent for metal bullet cartridges.*

∞   *The day the Tempel comet passed close to Earth, just missing us.*

∞   *The day Harry Truman signed the UN Charter.*

∞   *The day there was a race riot in Miami, FL as Richard Nixon was nominated by the Republican Convention. Oddly enough, the day he announced his resignation several years later.*

∞   *A day when we discovered a distant galaxy, fittingly an infinity away on 8/8/88.*

"Someone once told me the definition of hell; on your last day on earth, the person you could have become will meet the person you became."
— Anonymous (statistically speaking, probably a woman)

01000001

The three women spilled onto the floor, collapsing onto each other. They grunted and groaned at the uncomfortable feeling of being pinned beneath a heavy body. Their ankles twisted together as they all fumbled to stand up. Feminina checked the packet of vials, all still safe and intact, in spite of their hard landing. She fell against Nina's back, her rear-end cushioning the precious package. In all of the sciences, Nina would be known for having the butt that saved the multiverse.

This room didn't belong in any University laboratory. It appeared far too clean, professional. The University lab they came from was part warehouse, part museum for ancient computers. This room looked sleek and shiny. The surfaces were smooth and clean, a faint shine to the cream walls. And the room was empty of extraneous boxes or desks. The floor seemed to shimmer, it felt so clean and cool. The Portal closed and the room fell quiet except for the gentle hum of the quantum computer running in front of them. The track extended out to their left and curved in an arc that followed the edge of the room.

Behind the control panel a young woman with side swept bangs and her hair pinned back in a low bun stood up, her motions shaky and her breathing panicked.

Before Marie, Feminina, or Nina could begin to talk, this woman began to stammer. Her gaze darted quickly to a clock on the wall. It was crooked, hanging cockeyed. It wasn't just a small misalignment. The 11 was practically to the apex. But it still kept the beat. *Tick. Tock. Tick. Tock.* Time is a funny construct when you think about it too much. Which is probably why most people don't. They let it slip away, they squander it on status updates and selfies, they pour it into endeavors that will never reward them. It is the one thing people can never get back. Except –

"Nina," She heard Feminina finally speak. But she wasn't addressing the woman she had just jumped the multiverse with. She spoke to the young woman behind the compact and uniform control panel.

Her face appeared young and fresh even though her eyes belied the exhaustion of unending work. It was them; it was her. Another part of the "we" they were collecting across the multiverse. Another Nina. To herself, she was the original, but to Nina, the young woman standing before her was Nina-3. The third one she'd encountered on her journey.

"This isn't possible," the younger version of herself mumbled.

"Nina, it is possible." Nina dared to take a step forward. She felt odd to speak in the first person and third person at the same time.

"We only just turned the machine on." Nina-3's hands clamped down on either side of her forehead. She closed her eyes and subtly shook her head. Nina couldn't help but notice how much younger she appeared. Where Feminina looked like a near replica of Nina, down to the fine lines forming around the mouth, this Nina looked as she had almost a decade ago. Then Nina remembered, they went back in time ten years. *How had she developed this powerful machine at such a young age?*

"That's the funny thing about these Portals," Marie tried to add some humor to the situation. Both Feminina and Nina glared at her. Not the time for temporal jokes.

"No, this doesn't make any sense. We only just solved for the power source." Nina-3 nearly fainted back into her chair.

"You found the power source?!" Feminina and Nina asked in unison.

"Where is this building?" Marie asked above the din of their questions. She sauntered over to the glass windows that looked out into an inky black night sky. Inspecting the glass, Marie must have been curious about the strength of the material to withstand the power of the Portal. Nina felt curious about it too, but she had many other questions to try to answer.

"Nina?" Feminina tried to catch Nina-3's attention. The phrase, *this town is not big enough for the two of us*, rang in Nina's mind.

"Are all three of you me?" she looked up at them with her mouth agape.

"No," Marie clarified. "Don't worry, you won't end up looking like me. Just them."

"Where are you from? When are you from?" Nina-3 began to pace in front of the console.

"I'm from Universe Alpha. The first multiverse to have a visitor. That we know of," Nina began to walk closer to her, her need to comfort Nina-3 stronger than her safety instinct. This younger alter-ego looked confused and scared, she could lash out, but Nina had an innate feeling that she wouldn't.

"I'm from Universe Gamma. The third multiverse to have a visitor." Feminina said, the word 'third' sounding bitter even as she spoke it.

"Are you from Beta?" Nina-3 directed at Marie.

"No, I'm from Gamma. I work with Feminina. We built the Portal together. We had everything we needed, except the power source."

"Well then someone has to be from Universe Beta," Nina-3 began to piece some items together in her mind. Feminina and Nina both recognized her expression. The one that takes over when her mind is too busy processing information to be worried about looking composed. "Wait," Nina-3 sat up straight. "Did you just say that you had everything needed to operate the machine? You can plug in coordinates to another universe?"

"Yes," Marie answered, gesturing to the room around her. "Yes, we do." She pulled the chunky metal drive from her pocket and held it up for Nina-3 to see before returning it to its hiding place.

"You had everything but the power source. And all we have is the power source." It finally clicked for her too.

They had traveled back to the first time the Portal had ever been powered up and used anywhere in the multiverse. It only seemed fitting that Universe Delta, the 4th to ever experience a visitor, would now function as their change station to get to other points in the multiverse.

Nina, from Universe Alpha, explained the long tale of events that had brought all three of them to Universe Delta. Nina-3 listened in horrified silence.

"He'll be crushed to know that his machine was used for something so nefarious." Nina-3 leaned back in her chair in horrified awe.

"Yes, we need to get back to Beta to stop Parker from doing more damage," Feminina used her no-nonsense tone as though she were speaking to a child. Seeing that Feminina's methods had no impact on the younger version of herself, Nina tried a more emotional tactic.

"He is going to hurt Hank," Nina poured all of the emotion that she felt into her words.

"Who is Hank?" Nina-3 asked.

"You don't know Hank either?" Nina felt genuinely surprised again. Perhaps their love hadn't been as universal as she had hoped. Nina sunk down into the spare rolling chair at the console.

"You don't recognize Parker's name either?" Feminina asked with an air of suspicion to her voice.

"So, you built this machine with who then? Not me, or a version of me. Not Parker. Not Hank," Marie started to rattle through the options that she knew of.

"Hank was never a scientist." Nina cut in.

"Neither were you," Feminina reminded her.

"What about Thurston?" Nina asked.

Nina-3 shook her head to all of them. Her face awash with confusion and delight, happy to finally be able to relay some new information to these travelers. "I can't believe you don't know. It's been his life's work."

Feminina gasped audibly, catching onto the answer much faster than Nina or Marie did. Just as Feminina seemed to have made the connection, Nina felt a breeze push against her. A noise that sounded like the distant, but powerful, hum of a jet engine filled the room. Nina turned and saw that the Portal had activated. Someone or something was about to come through it again. Fearing the worst, Nina braced to come face-to-face with Parker or Gus Blanity. But it was neither of them.

No, the person who stepped through was a much more powerful and important man.

01000010

His hair was combed nicely to the side, steely silver locks with strands of pure white weaved throughout. His skin looked pallid, fitting given the hours he would have spent tinkering in the lab, working with unique and fixed focus on this problem. His eyes were aquamarine, a piercing blue that could cut into you. His expression was a mixture of exhaustion (Nina could see that in the wrinkles beneath his eyes) and elation (his smile was that of a child on Christmas morning).

It was him. In her wildest dreams, Nina may have hoped to have Hank back, but she never allowed herself to question seeing *him* again. It would require too much pain and suffering to experience it. And yet, after the past day of agony and violence, there he stood.

"Dad?" the three Feminina asked at once with varying levels of incredulity, awe, and surprise.

"Oh my, what do we have here?" he asked in amazement. It was as though he had perhaps expected to come back and see them all there. Had he realized that if he was the very first, his machine might be used as an anchor for other travelers of the multiverse? Or did he just know everything because he always knew everything. Every inane question, every broken rule in the house, every white lie to cover for a friend. He had always known.

And how had they failed to figure it out, to not intuit that he would be the guide at the end of their long journey? The Wizard in the Emerald City? Feminina had said it herself. Had it been a premonition, or just a happy coincidence? X. Marks the spot.

01000011

On August 8, 2008 in multiverse reality Delta, the first activation of the Portal occurred. Dr. Xander Marks was the first person in all of history to use the Portal. He transported himself from his laboratory in Washington, D.C. to a sister facility in Tokyo, Japan within the same reality. The test was a proof of concept that the machine was functional. His team had pioneered the new energy source that would power the machine, but they had yet to crack the code on pinpointing the exact coordinates for other machines in the multiverse. Knowing the exact location of the machine in Tokyo, Marks was able to successfully walk from one room to the next. Wait for the next quantum jitter, and pass back through.

While in Tokyo, Dr. Marks had his photograph taken with the local team and had his bio-metrics quickly assessed. His heart rate, blood pressure, mental function were all clear. The next jitter occurred, the Portal reopened, and he expected to walk back through to the same room that he had left ten minutes earlier.

At least, that is how he relayed it to the four women upon his return. Instead of another candid photograph with his daughter / lab assistant, a trio of multiverse travelers greeted him.

Not only had the machine worked, but it continued to work, and thus resulted in the scene that he discovered.

It was 11:11 pm on 8/8/08. The frequency of the jitters would continue to intensify for the next 49 minutes and then dissipate over the next few days.

There was something about that date that aligned perfectly. And the timer for the next jitter had already started. 12 minutes.

Nina wasted precious moments in shock that her father, the man who she most admired, was alive. Feminina had already run over to embrace him, repeating the words, "I can't believe it" over and over again. Marie quickly wrote down a diagram of who was who and from which universe so that they could get moving. Nina-3 sat still next to Nina, observing her reaction and Feminina's as well. Nina felt something tickle her cheek. She realized that it was an errant tear and brushed it aside.

"You're both from 2018 you said?" Nina-3 whispered to her.

"Yes," Nina nodded, refusing to take her eyes off the scene before her. Feminina gushed, effusive in her excitement to see their father. Her stolid demeanor banished for this reunion.

"And you both lost him?" Nina could hear the pain in her younger alter-ego's voice as she dared to ask the question. Nina forced herself to turn and look at her. She recognized that young face, the scared look in her eyes. Their reactions must have been enough to confirm it, but she wanted verification.

"Yes," Nina said. She couldn't embellish or soften the blow.

"When? How?" Nina-3 demanded quickly. Time was the most valuable asset that they had to work with. The idea of spending any of those 49 minutes trying to rewrite what was yet to unfold, or may never unfold, in Universe Delta seemed pointless.

"It may be different here Nina. But tell him you love him. Don't ignore his emails, even the dumb jokes that he forwards to ten people because it says that you have to. Ask him to show you how to make his favorite dishes, and humor him when he makes odd requests. My only regret is that I spent so much time being afraid of losing him after his diagnosis, that I avoided him. It was too painful to talk to him, knowing it could be one of the last times. So, I just stopped calling. I was stupid. Don't squander this time with him-"

Nina's words were cut off by the very man she was talking about. "How glorious. Three of my daughters all in one place. All of you travelers of the multiverse. I'm so proud of each of you!"

Nina turned to face him; his arm draped around Feminina's shoulders. His fatherly glow of affectionate pride evident to all in the room. Nina could feel the heat rising on her cheeks, the prickle beneath her eyelids.

She didn't want to cry. She didn't want to lament over what was lost; how much she had lost compared to her alter-egos. She didn't-

"I hate to break up the family reunion Mister- er Doctor Marks, but we have to get back to Universe Beta now!" Marie implored him to review the hasty diagram in her hands.

"What's the rush, we've got time on our hands, right?" Dad turned to face her and gestured towards the Portal, his voice slightly more affected, a different lilt to it than Nina remembered. *Was that what joy sounded like when he spoke?* He had always been the hardest working man she knew, but this success surely must have eclipsed anything he ever experienced in her reality. Nina's mind flashed on those final days in the hospital, his final words barely audible through the pain of his body shutting down. To see him so alive, so carefree, so unencumbered by mortality, was almost enough to make her cry out "Daddy!" But Marie was right, she didn't have time for that.

"No, we don't have time. We have less than an hour to get back to Beta, stop Parker, save Hank, and get everyone back to where they are supposed to be."

He spun around, his arm leaving Feminina's shoulders. It hadn't been Marie or Nina-3 or Feminina whose shouted words had echoed in the minimalist room, reverberating off of the pearlescent walls. It was Nina. She was the one who had caused the raucous.

"Then let's get to work," he said, nodding at her with a twinkle of admiration in his eye.

Something finally clicked for Feminina. She had spent the past few hours learning that her alter-ego was a love sick hopeless romantic, blathering on about getting back to Hank. Her back-from-the-dead, alive-in-a-parallel-universe love seemed so silly to Feminina. This other version of her had thrown her whole heart into believing that she could have him back after a decade of living without him. How could she buy into that so quickly? Now Feminina understood. One look at her father and something inside her mind snapped. She wanted to stay, forever. Abandon her research, leave

Marie to continue their work on her own, forget about paying her rent. Feminina wanted to stay with him.

She remembered just how horrible his illness had been. Feminina hadn't asked Nina for the details, she had seen the same look on her face the moment that they briefly discussed him. She still looked shell-shocked, like a war veteran having seen mass atrocities. And losing her father had been an atrocity. To Feminina, it was the worst thing that had ever happened. She remembered when the radiation and chemotherapy tore apart his body. When he coughed up blood. When she would wake him up in the morning only to smell that he hadn't made it to the bathroom in time. Her idol, her hero, had been reduced so far because of his illness.

Feminina had cursed herself over and over for not having enough foresight to study biology and chemistry. That she had worked her whole life to accomplish the things that were out of his reach, and ultimately none of it helped him survive even a minute longer.

She saw her father, younger than she remembered, moving across this foreign and advanced lab. He had all the resources he could imagine. He had everything he wanted in that universe, and Feminina wanted to be part of it. She needed to be part of it. She had lost a part of her when he got sick, when she failed to keep him healthy, when she watched him die.

Feminina looked over at Nina, she saw the look on her face. *Was she thinking the same thing? Could they both get him back? Could they set right all the wrongs that had been made against them?* Feminina turned her gaze over to the Portal. She wasn't sure if she could fix everything, but she knew she was going to try.

01000100

The scientists started to hash out the details. Feminina explained how they came to the decision to go there and copy the power source equation.

"Well done, Feminina," her father, or at least her father's alter-ego appraised her.

"And I'm guessing Parker can get through as well," Marie added. "Or he will soon," she nodded her head back towards the Portal.

"He definitely hasn't come through yet, you are the first visitors," Nina-3 responded as she began to tap some commands into the keyboard.

"Well, based on what you've explained, it would seem that he knows how to calculate the exact location of other universes, something we are probably years away from doing," Dr. Xander Marks began.

"Unless we share some notes," Nina-3 chimed in.

"So, all he had to do was figure out when someone from here, Delta, would eventually travel to Beta. Then he could slide the machine to that exact moment in time, power up the machine, and go where he would like to," their father carried on as though he hadn't heard his daughter's suggestion.

"Oh, that's really smart." Feminina said with a slight nod of her head, clearly impressed.

"So, we didn't need to come here after all?" Nina asked.

"No, but I'm glad you did," he added.

"Dammit, I hate it that he outsmarted us," Marie shook her head.

"I'm not, I'm glad I got to see you all. And given your time constraint, it was the most logical choice at the time." His approval warmed Nina's heart.

Feminina relayed the most pertinent information on pin-pointing the exact location to their Dad as Marie worked with Nina-3 to reconfigure the program for multi-dimensional travel. Feeling inept in the company of the scientists, Nina made herself busy by examining the Portal. It looked well put together with seamless edges. The metallic parts gleamed as though they had never been touched or smudged by human hands. The sterile feeling of the room, of the lab, gave the device more significance to her. She felt so enraptured by the wonderful machine, the cleanest of its kind so far, that she didn't notice when he approached her.

"So, you're not a cosmologist or physicist?" he asked with his hands behind his back, the right holding his left elbow.

"No, I'm not," Nina shook her head. Unsure if he would be disappointed or not.

"You studied mathematics in college then?" he asked as though calling out the answer to a logic problem.

"Yes, I did. Did Feminina tell you that?" She wondered at how he might have known that information.

"No, but your mother studied mathematics, applied mathematics. So, I figured that if you didn't follow in my footsteps that it might have been hers." He offered a kind smile with his answer.

"I did," Nina smiled back and nodded her head. *Should she tell him that she didn't finish her degree? Should she tell him that she was an entry level marketing analyst, unable to motivate herself to reach for more, a waste of potential? Should she tell him she picked math because Mom died when she was so young? Was she still alive here?* But it wasn't the right moment for that conversation, and knowing that she may never get back to this reality to be able to see him, she just appreciated the silence. Nina felt his hand land on her shoulder as he pulled her in for a hug.

"And, you mentioned the name Hank. Is that your husband?" She could hear the nervous tone in his voice, she thumbed the ring circling her finger. Was this a name he needed to keep in mind? Should he ban Nina-3 from dating anyone by another name?

"No, he was murdered in my universe before we could get to that point. But he is alive and well in Universe Beta, that's why I have to get back there. To save him and stay there with him," Nina explained.

And then she saw a face that she hadn't seen for a long time, the 'young-lady-I'm-about-to-lecture-you-face.'

"You absolutely cannot do that, Nina. You're out of place there, you're out of order. It's more than the subtle differences in the atmosphere that will slowly and painfully kill you long before your natural expiration. It's the aura around you. Something isn't right in the multiverse because you are here, but you are from Universe Alpha. The order of things will be out of place if you stay there. How many times in your life have you thought, 'hmm well isn't that lucky?' You hit every green light on your way to work and cut your commute by 5 minutes. You're in the right place at the right time and happen to win something. All those bits of luck and chance happened in your universe, a place where you belonged. You will never have any manner of luck in Universe Beta, and inevitably, violently, that reality will try to chew you up and spit you out."

"But, he's worth it Dad," she wanted to explain to him that if only he had seen what Hank's death did to her, how it crushed her, that he would understand. Could he somehow channel the thoughts and memories of the Dad she knew? The man who had to hold her hand in the hospital after the attack, the one who had to help her move back home after leaving college. Couldn't he understand that love was worth it? She wanted to ask him, *what if it was Mom?*, but bit her tongue. He pulled her in for another hug. Could he sense that she needed him more than ever?

"My fierce Feminina, don't be so sad," he whispered into her ear. She tried to breathe in every bit of that hug, but the longer she held on the more she felt that she might fall apart.

"I'm just tired, it's been a long day. And I have a splitting headache," Nina realized that it had been her persistent companion on that trip and she had started to get used to it.

"Ah yes," he said as he released her. "My head is starting to feel a little tight as well. But what an ironic choice of words. A splitting headache." He laughed to himself. Nina didn't get the joke and he must have seen that in her expression.

"Oh right," he gestured to her as if he needed to remind himself that she didn't know all of the intricacies of the machine. "In all of the theoretical models that discussed travel to alternate universes the device has been debated. Some theorists proposed a machine that would clone the existing universe, others, one that would *split* an existing universe into two versions, forking at the moment that the machine was used. But I consulted with my colleagues in New York and we agreed that this should be a probability wave evolution machine. And bam!" he clapped his hands together. "That's what worked!"

"That's why the machine will power on if you slide it to the exact moment on the track when it was powered on previously," Feminina called out from behind the console.

"She finally remembered that bit back in the lab after we spent three years trying to solve the power equation," Marie shook her head as she looked over to Feminina.

"Okay, I'm ready to plug in the coordinates," Nina-3 interjected as she stared at something on the console.

Marie handed her the drive. "It's not just one set of coordinates. You need this entire drive to run through your quantum computer. All of the universes and the planets within them are moving. This helps you find the exact moment in space and time."

"Wow," Nina-3 said, clearly impressed by the simplicity of the solution.

"And there is room left on the drive for you to include your math on the power source," Marie added.

Dad spun on his heels quickly. "Absolutely not! After everything that you've described so far there is no way that I could ever allow this technology to leave this laboratory."

Marie opened her mouth to object, but Feminina shot her a sharp look. Nina joined them at the console, wanting to see the machine at work for herself. The interface looked much cleaner than the screens back in Gamma or even Beta, but it appeared to function the same way. Multiple wave-lengths displayed on the top screen. A thick yellow line showing for the Femininas and single lines for Marie and Xander. Nina-3 slid the drive into the USB port and the data started to display on the screen. Even with all of the possible configurations and sizing changes within the multiverse, the USB A input was still the same. Against all odds of different inputs and the variables that could have made the drives incompatible, it worked.

Feminina took over the controls and quickly keyed in the log of changes and found the exact moment that Nina was sent through the Portal from Universe Beta. She clicked "execute" and the Portal whirred into place on the curved track, moving about a foot to the right. The mechanized movement happened quickly, fluidly. It was so clean and silent, as though it had moved on its own instead of responding to a command. Marie and Nina both looked at Feminina with amazement.

"What? Was that not supposed to happen?" Nina-3 asked, her voice betraying an uneasiness and insecurity about the machine.

"No, we just had to move it manually. We only just realized that it could move at all." Feminina explained as she navigated to the quantum jitter timer. Another one was set to occur at 11:47 pm, in two minutes. Feminina saved the coordinates to the quantum computer and put the drive back in her pocket. The system was set now, it didn't need the drive to be in the computer in order to execute the command.

"Well, we knew that eventually the Portal would need to be mobile, so we built in the automation capability," Nina-3 smiled with pride at knowing that she had solved for something that her older and more experienced alter-ego had missed.

"It's time," Dad said as he came over to them and gave Feminina and Nina a hug, he offered Marie a polite and professional handshake. "I'll be here to monitor how things go over there for you all," pointing to the wave signatures on the screen. "And to record it for all of human history!"

Nina tried to commit that last hug to memory, the pressure of his arms around her, the smell of his hair. But she knew she couldn't overwrite her true last memory with him either, holding his hand in the hospital as his agonal breathing become more infrequent. She felt her hands start to shake as she pulled away.

Universe Delta had been a change station in more ways than one. It changed Nina's views on what loss really was, what it meant. Having already made peace with his passing, why was it so hard to say goodbye again? *I already said goodbye, I was done saying goodbye to him*, she thought. And now she had to do it again. To relive one of the worst moments. But she couldn't not say good-bye.

The clock had begun counting down: 0:88 seconds.

As Feminina had her final moment with their Dad, Nina looked over to Nina-3. She could see that this was an existential crisis for her too. Nina-3 watched her Dad give a final goodbye to his daughter, to her, but not her. Nina couldn't bear to leave her as helpless as she had been. It was a split-second decision, if it can be considered a decision at all.

"Nina," she whispered to her younger alter-ego whose neck snapped quickly at attention. "Change your main focus to oncology. Have him start getting screened now. Regular screenings every 6 months, without fail." Her eyes went wide, not with shock, but with absorption. Trying to take in every detail of that moment, trying to commit it to memory. Nina knew, because it was what she did when she tried to remember something. Nina moved across the room before Nina-3 could ask any more questions, already unsure if she had done the right thing.

The system took care of the work for them, the pearlescent glow started to materialize between the borders of the Portal.

Feminina finished her goodbye and joined Nina and Marie in front of the machine. Xander had left out three vials for injection, although theirs were clear. "Supercybin, but with a strong painkiller to help with the headache," he said with a wink.

0:37 seconds.

They stood on the threshold and injected themselves again, each of them developing a bruise in the crook of their arms.

0:19 seconds.

"Hey, who was the 33rd President of the US? Just curious." Nina asked as the roar of the machine began to intensify. She wasn't sure if her words were even audible to Nina-3 and her Dad, standing only a few feet away.

They looked at each other, brows furrowed in confusion. Nina looked on as Nina-3 counted back on her hands, trying to get to the right answer.

0:04 seconds.

"Eleanor Roosevelt!" she called out, her words almost lost in the sound of the machine, but perfectly enunciated so Nina could pair them with the motion of her mouth.

She smiled and looked over at Feminina and Marie. It was time. They stepped through the Portal as the quantum jitter was about to time-out.

PART 5

Space and time are curved, they are notoriously non-linear. So, I should have expected the bag of tricks that ensued upon our return. But my brain hadn't yet begun to think multidimensionally.

"How men hate women in a position of real power."
– Eleanor Roosevelt

Q

Nina heard Hank scream out in pain. It was a sound she would know anywhere, having replayed it in her head over and over again for the past decade. She heard it before she felt the linoleum floor and before she sensed that Marie and Feminina had come through with her. Her eyes were slow to open, to see what was in front of her. She had left that spot hours earlier, but it felt as though days or weeks had passed.

When Parker had pushed her through the Portal and into Universe Gamma, she felt defeated and scared. But now an anger built in her, welling up in her stomach. It fed her energy, pulsed through her muscles. And without realizing it, her body reacted. From flat on the floor, she pounced up and onto Parker, pelting him with her fists as best as she could to get him to stop his attack on Hank.

Hank lay on the concrete, turned on his side, his legs protecting his stomach and his ribs. Nina could see the purple-red swell starting to pucker his face. Suddenly, Nina found herself next to him on the ground. Parker had flipped her and dropped her hard onto the floor.

But was it really Parker? She had to stop thinking of him as her Parker. There was a Parker and an Anti-Parker, this had to be the Anti-Parker. Just like matter and antimatter. Everything looked the same, but he was negatively charged. *But if I exist*, Nina thought in that moment, *then surely there is an Anti-Nina, where could she be?* After meeting two of her alter-egos and seeing the lives that they built, perhaps she was the Anti-Nina. All of this passed through her mind as she crashed to the floor.

Her head smacked against the concrete, she could have sworn she felt her brain slosh back and forth in her skull. Still feeling the heat and rage that had filled her, she tried to snap back up again, but her limbs were slower to respond. Thankfully, Feminina and Marie were already on Parker, having pinned him to the ground. Nina looked over to the rows of metal shelving on the far wall of the lab. Surely there would be some kind of rope or wire.

Nina could hear the faint sound of sirens just beyond the building.

Oh, right. Dead body in the basement. Hank had probably called them before he had rushed over to the lab.

Nina could see a pile of bright colors on the third shelf, just above her eye level. She reached her right hand up, blindly groping for these items. Something sharp and pointed hit the flesh of her palm. *Nails.*

She reached again and felt a malleable bag of cool tiny orbs. She pulled it closer, spilling 2-centimeter ball bearings on the floor. They scattered like marbles.

Nina reached for a third time. Her fingertips grazed something that felt like twine, like braided polyester. Rope!

She pulled it down and sent a box of bright orange wire caps spilling onto the floor. Nina turned back, preparing to run toward Feminina and Marie, proud of her discovery. A cord of rope, at least fifty feet worth. More than enough to subdue Parker and keep him from hurting anyone else before the police arrived to arrest him.

She stood only twenty or so feet away from them. Nina lifted her knees, leaned forward and prepared to accelerate. But instead she found herself back on the ground. Her back slapped against the concrete again, her neck stiffened, keeping her head from taking another blow.

Nina assumed she must have slipped on the ball bearings. That was the only reasonable explanation. She pulled herself up onto her elbows. The fire in her stomach almost completely extinguished, she needed to get moving. Nina could see Feminina and Marie struggling to keep Parker down. Their tactics that had worked so well on Gus Blanity, were barely a match for Parker. And then a pair of legs in boot-cut jeans obscured her view. She saw the white rubber and black canvas of a Converse sneaker just as it lifted and swung forward to smack into her head.

R

"**N**ina!" She heard her own voice cry out. No, not her voice. Feminina's voice. *But I am Feminina. But I am also not Feminina.* Her thoughts were fuzzy and unfocused.

"Nina," she felt her throat groan out the syllables. Just as she felt another blow to her body, this time her right side. She heard something snap. One of her ribs, she knew for sure, was broken.

In the fog of pain and confusion, Nina looked up and saw Parker standing above her, wearing his typical novelty t-shirt. **NaBro** in bold letters across the front of his chest, an anti-emblem for the anti-hero. His face looked tight, pinched with hatred. *But how could Parker be here when he was also being held down by Marie and Feminina?*

As his leg lifted again to try for another kick, she realized the answer: *time machine, Nina. Duh.*

Nina reached out her arm to try and grab his ankle, a roaring pain in her right side slowed her reaction time. She closed her hand around air and felt the full force of his kick. Curling over onto her left side she balled herself up, guarding against another hit.

But it didn't come. Perhaps they had broken time with all of their mis-matched travels. Was it a second that she lay there or a minute or an hour? Perhaps death had come to her, disappointed that she had dared to come back and try to set things right. In the end doesn't death just feel like time coming to a stop?

But it wasn't any long period of time. Because Nina could still hear the sirens, their wailing now fixed, close by. No longer approaching, but arrived.

So where was the cavalry? And where was the next attack from the other Parker. Or was he another Parker? She needed a better way to keep them straight. And then she heard a low guttural grunt: heavy and powerful, coming from behind her.

S

By Nina's count they had maybe another 5 minutes before the police made it through the parking lot, into the building, and found the lab. Being the last lab on a long hallway was a blessing and a curse. Nina didn't want this violence to continue, someone had to stop Parker and perhaps the police could stun him and then lock him away for a very long time. But they would also have a lot of questions and she didn't have any answers that wouldn't land her in an asylum. She knew enough to realize that this all had to be kept very, very quiet.

But the room was anything but quiet at that moment. She could hear Feminina and Marie exerting themselves, pinning down a flailing Parker. And that growl, the animalistic sound that had been emitted into the warehouse, what could it have been? Nina rolled her head up, unsure of what she would see. The seconds were passing like molasses, slow and thick.

She saw Parker above her, his back to her now, bracing to attack his next target.

She strained her neck a bit and saw that it was Dr. Thurston. His cheeks were slack and his eyes appeared to be unfocused. To Nina, he had been so brutally clobbered by Parker hours ago, but in Universe Beta it had been only a few minutes. He had regained consciousness quickly and hobbled back into the lab to stop Parker.

"You'll never stop me, Thurston. You've held me back for too long. This is my machine and I will make a perfect world with it!" Just by the fire in his voice, she knew that this was the Parker she had dealt with last time. Parker-Beta. *So, who were Marie and Feminina wrestling with?* Nina would have to figure that out, but she felt too weak to stand, the painkiller in her Dad's supercybin wasn't strong enough to overpower the injuries she'd just sustained. Her mind still spinning from the hit to the head, the multi-dimensional conundrums, and the repeated travel through the Portal. She was in no shape to assist Thurston.

But he didn't seem to need any help. He didn't counter Parker's verbal barbs, he just pounced. In an uncoordinated but powerful run, he knocked Parker down, tripping him over Nina's outstretched legs. She crawled out from under them as they continued to brawl.

"Nina!" she heard Marie call out from the other side of the lab. Nina did her best to get back to her feet, careful to not slip on any more of the spilled items from the shelves or to get caught in Thurston and Parker's argument. Her feet pounded heavily on the floor as she made her way over to them, rope in hand. Marie and Feminina quickly bound Parker's feet and hands.

"Which Parker are you?" Nina asked, her words loud and unfocused.

"He just said that I had to come with him, that there was a man trying to destroy our machine. I've worked all my life to build it and I knew I could never let someone destroy it!" His eyes were lit with the flame of passion. In some other universe, this had been his life's work as well. His eyes passed over each of them quickly, focusing on each face for one second. There was no trace of recognition as he looked at Nina or Feminina. This was a Parker from a universe where he didn't know one of them.

"It's my life's work too!" Marie said as she grabbed one of supercybin vials from the pack and injected him. Once drugged they dragged the new Parker to the floor by the Portal. He mumbled as the drug took effect. Unable to move because of the restraints, they turned their focus to the next problem.

Feminina went back to the monitors immediately and pulled up the timer. The next quantum jitter would be in 6 minutes.

Nina expected half a dozen police officers to bust through the main doors to the lab and filter in through the opaque plastic barrier at any minute. They were going to have a lot of explaining to do and no time to get their stories straight.

As she tried to do the mental math on how much longer they would have, the fight between Thurston and Parker seemed to be swaying towards the latter. But Marie came to Thurston's aid and clocked Parker on the head with a heavy fist.

Parker wilted to the ground, his legs wobbling like jelly. Thurston, on his back and astonished that help arrived just in time, accepted Marie's hand as she helped him to stand back up. He leaned into her with all of his weight. Feminina pushed the desk chair over to Marie, the castors rolling smoothly across the floor. Thurston collapsed into the chair once it arrived at their feet.

Feminina then rushed to grab a knife from the toolbox on the far shelves. She cut the trail of extra rope that was left over from tying up one of the Parkers and quickly ran back to tie up the one that Thurston had just grappled with.

Feminina finished the knots just as he started to move and resist. Together, Feminina, Marie, and Nina (mostly Feminina and Marie) carried the second Parker over to the Portal.

"No, he has to stay here and answer for his crimes," Thurston called out to them. Nina turned to see him, slouching back in the rolling chair, his eyes only half open. He was in pain, on the edge of consciousness, and this was the one message that he had to get through to them.

"He's right," Nina said as she turned to Marie and Feminina.

"Oh shy, silent Nina, please speak up for me," she heard Parker's voice call out from behind her.

"Shut up!" Feminina yelled at him. Nina saw her leg start to arc back, ready to kick him while he was down.

"No!" she shouted. Feminina looked at her, confused, hurt, betrayed. How could Nina stop her from taking out her anger on this man? But they differed in many regards on this topic. Nina had no chance to explain herself before Parker started in.

"I did see him, Nina." His words were so charged, they seemed to suck all of the oxygen out of the room. "When I first crossed the Plain. I was at the lab working late, I couldn't stand to go home, to see your body there, lifeless. The dread and the grief immobilized me. I knew there wouldn't be a poltergeist waiting for me, you looking to enact revenge from beyond. I just knew I wouldn't be able to sleep or think or breathe knowing what I had done. And at least at the lab I could pretend to be busy, that I wasn't alone. But I was alone, and I had been scrolling through all of the frequencies and I found you. I found your frequency in a reality that didn't appear to be all that dissimilar, except for one big factor. You were still alive." His eyes were fixed on Nina's, his voice pleading for mercy.

"Because you hadn't murdered me in that reality," Nina tried to cut in, to call out his lunacy.

"You promised me. You said you would never leave, that things were so broken with Hank that you'd never go back. But you were lying!" Nina could see the pure hatred he felt in that moment, his disgust.

"I had to get you back, I had to make it right! And the procedures just happened. We had agonized over the order so many times, my hands adjusted the dials and plugged in the coordinates. The first quantum jitter was just opening up, it was so unexpected, the timing was perfect. So, I crossed over the Plain to find you."

"You have the most powerful tool in all of humanity at your disposal and you use it to cover up a murder?" Feminina finally cut in.

"I had to get you back!" Parker snapped at her, before looking back at Nina. "I had to get *you* back. You have no idea the strain I was under, the pressure, the responsibility for this device."

"Uh, actually we do. We built this ourselves and we didn't murder anyone," Marie said as she towered over him, arms folded against her chest. *But they had used Gus Blanity, both her and Feminina*, Nina thought.

"You said you saw him, my Parker?" Nina looked right at him as she asked the question.

"Yes," Parker muttered and cast his eyes to the ground.

Nina could hear a loud march of boots approaching, running down the hallway. She crouched down beside this imposter, this man who was nothing like the Parker that she knew. The Parker that she knew may have been arrogant and an inattentive boyfriend, but he was never violent, he would never harm anyone.

"And did you kill him too?" Nina said this right to his face, up close, where he couldn't avoid her.

"Yes, I sent him out on the next jitter. But I didn't plug in any coordinates. He just-," Parker struggled for the word. "He just went." Nina pictured her Parker floating in the vacuum of space, lost forever.

Without needing to know that she was okay with it, Feminina knelt beside them and plunged the next vial of subercybin into his arm. The drug took effect quickly.

The doors to the lab slammed open, it would take less than a minute for the police officers to come through the classroom portion of the lab into the warehouse. Nina stood up; her eyes flashed onto the timer on the computer. 2 minutes remained on the countdown. She turned so that she could face the officers when they came in; Feminina and Marie moved closer to her, their bodies forming a wall. They stood shoulder to shoulder and braced for the worst. Their arms were ready. This was it.

T

"Help!" Nina ran screaming through the thick flaps of opaque plastic. Her hands were above her head as a sign of surrender, she didn't want to be shot after all. But her voice called out in a persistent manner, loud, and full of all the emotion of the day.

"Help me, please!" She collapsed at the foot of the first officer, a tall female in an imposing black uniform. Nina reached for the hand of the second officer. Anything to stall them further.

"Ma'am, are you alright?" The second officer asked looking down at her.

"Please, you have to help!" She continued with her line of panicked pleas. Nina could hear the machine on the other side of the flaps powering up, the hum now turning into a roar. Could they see the shapes of Marie, Feminina, and the Parkers just beyond the anteroom?

"Officers, the lab continues through there!" Nina heard Dr. Winchester as she entered the room with two more police officers at her sides.

"Marie!" Nina called out as loud as she could, hoping that her alter-ego could hear this as a caution on the other side of the lab. Nina scrambled to her feet, using the arms of one of the new officers to steady herself. All five of them fixed on her, this hysterical woman in front of them.

"Feminina! Are you alright?" Dr. Winchester remained cool and professional; her tone concerned but suspicious.

"Dr. Winchester, it was Parker!" *How much longer could she hold them?* Nina heard the machine getting louder and the gentle rustle of the plastic flaps, the energy that the Portal created must have produced enough of a breeze to move them.

"Who's back there?" The first officer asked as she stepped out past Nina, inching closer to the warehouse. Nina could see her raise her weapon again, now alert and on guard.

"Parker! He attacked Dr. Thurston! He attacked me!" At this Nina called out as loud as she could, obnoxiously brash given the close proximity of the officers, but the machine was gaining power and noise as well. Nina raised her right arm to point to the warehouse, wincing in pain as she did so. That part required no dramatics, her ribs were definitely broken. She just hoped that Thurston could hear her too, in spite of his clear concussion and the noise in the warehouse portion of the lab.

"Parker?" Dr. Winchester asked for clarification.

"Yes, it was Parker!" Nina held out her arm to the Dean, needing to steady herself. The energy that she had expended to stall the officers had exhausted her within a minute. As she started to collapse into Dr. Winchester, the four officers proceeded into the warehouse portion of the lab. They walked deliberately, purposefully; their weapons drawn towards the plastic partition.

Had she given them enough time? The officers would certainly be confused if she hadn't.

"Feminina, here sit down," Dean Winchester positioned her towards one of the rolling chairs by the first row of desks. Nina slumped into it, the adrenaline in her system starting to recede, leaving her awash in exhaustion and pain. As though it was all perfectly synchronized, the impressive sound of the machine died down. Just as the police officers cleared the plastic flaps, the lab seemed unnaturally silent and still.

"He ran that way!" Nina could hear Thurston from the other room, but just barely. Then she heard footsteps scrambling and running and the thick metallic release on the back exit of the lab, the same one that she had used earlier in the day.

Dr. Winchester left Nina and proceeded into the warehouse. Nina wanted to join her, but she needed a moment to gather herself. *Could she run? Should she run?*

7

Nina went home. It wasn't really home; it hadn't felt that way for a long time. But it was where she came from, where she was supposed to be in the multiverse.

She collapsed back into the lab, leaving Universe Beta in the early evening of August 8th and arriving back to Alpha just before 12:30 am on the same day. She marveled at how empty and still the lab felt. As though it were just any other University lab, as if something terrible and remarkable hadn't just happened. As if an entire day where everything was on the brink of disaster hadn't just passed, even if the clock on the wall couldn't contain it.

The headache, fresh and relentless, became easier to handle knowing that it would be the last time she would ever feel that way. Nina had work to do, and it had to be completed before Dr. Thurston, the one who lived in Universe Alpha, arrived at 6:40 am to prepare for his daily lectures.

Nina had only just spoken with him an hour prior back in Universe Beta. After he sent the police on a wild-goose chase through campus, she joined him and Dr. Winchester in the warehouse portion of the lab. An officer squatted down attending to Hank, her attention focused on his pulse and breathing. Winchester approached Thurston, a torrent of questions on her lips.

"Marie, I will explain everything later," Nina heard him whisper, his words compressed under the weight of his breathing.

She looked around the warehouse, expecting to see some trace of Feminina or Marie. But all she found was the large silver drive sticking out from the computer console. On the monitor, she saw three frequencies: two regular, one heavy, flash on the screen in Universe Gamma. While everyone else was distracted, Nina pocketed the drive. They were gone now, with no way of coming back if they didn't have the drive. As much as Nina wanted to say good-bye and thank them for their help, she felt she would never see her alter-ego and her genius lab partner again.

Two ambulances arrived and the paramedics attended to her wounds quickly. Nina was given the option to ride with Hank or Thurston. It felt like the decision of a lifetime. She expected that her heart would pull her to Hank, but she knew that if she rode in that ambulance, if she held his hand, that she would never leave him. So, she opted to ride with Thurston.

The ride to the hospital felt bumpy, Nina winced at every jostle and brake. She could feel them in the fracture of her bones. The medics had navigated the small space within the back of the ambulance so easily, finding tubes and needles and leads, more devices coming out of cupboards than Nina would have imagined possible. During her last ambulance ride a decade earlier she had been unconscious, so it was fair to say that she hadn't seen any of this before. Thurston appeared to be the same way, unconscious, his eyes closed and his breath condensing in flashes against the plastic mask across his face.

Apparently, he should have considered teaching a course in acting as well as physics, because once the medics were distracted by paperwork to document the doses administered, Thurston reached for Nina's hand. He squeezed, she thought for support. But really, he had placed a key into her palm, the key to the lab, which was in the process of being locked and sealed off as a crime scene.

Once they arrived at the hospital, she followed as doctors led him to a room. Finally alone, Nina asked him how he felt.

Thurston pulled the oxygen mask down to his chin to speak. "I have always been more interested in science than anything else, I've spent years staring at the sky and then working out equations on a chalkboard. This was the most physical activity I've had in my entire life. How do you think I'm doing?"

Nina smiled at his humor. "Thank you for saving us," she tried to look directly into his eyes, to make her point clear, but his lids were heavy and his eyes were partially closed.

"I'm so sorry that this happened, Nina," Thurston uttered, a hint of moisture brimming at the corner of his eye. "He'll go to jail for the rest of his life for this murder," Dr. Thurston seemed vindicated when he said this. Perhaps for him it was difficult to distinguish between the Feminina he knew, the one whose body had been found in Parker's basement, and the one standing before him.

"I don't even know where he is and even if he makes it back, he'll get a decade at most," she tried to – she wasn't exactly sure what she was trying to do.

Reassure him that his mentee wouldn't rot away forever? Make herself feel slightly less guilty, knowing that her presence was necessitated by her alter-ego's death, that her presence in Universe Beta would make the case more confusing and potentially increase the chances of an acquittal?

"What are you talking about? This is murder. The only sentencing option is life imprisonment." Thurston pulled the oxygen mask back to his mouth for a moment, his chest rising and falling heavily.

"Huh," was all that she could muster. It was interesting to her that the penal codes were so standardized in this enlightened universe, this more-just version of American society. Wasn't there room for gray area? Wasn't there room for accidents and self-defense? Perhaps those justifications weren't needed in a society where men and women were equal. All she could manage to do to explain herself in that moment was to draw a comparison. "Maybe that is the case here. Where I come from if a woman killed a man, she would spend the rest of her natural life in prison. If a man killed a woman, he would likely get a sentence of a decade or two which would be commuted within a few years."

"Well, that is not the situation here, Feminina. We value all life equally. A life for a life, the debt to society can never truly be repaid, so the sentence is always life imprisonment," Thurston's voice turned hard and focused. "It can never be repaid," he repeated himself.

"I can stop it from happening again," Nina offered, holding up the key to the lab that Thurston had handed her.

"It's inevitable Feminina, what has happened has happened. It can't be undone," Thurston tried to explain.

"Then I'll find a reality where it isn't," Nina insisted. She thought of all the horrible events that had transpired. A murder, a kidnapping, several attacks, so much suffering.

"You can't keep jumping from reality to reality in hopes of finding one that you can fix. Or one that is perfect for you. No reality is perfect. You're exactly where you're meant to be. You have to stand and face reality." Thurston said in his professorial tone, his words weighted with meaning. As someone who had never traveled the multiverse, he seemed to have a much better sense of it than she had. A lifetime of theorizing about it provided him with a wisdom that was hard for her to accept. "So, you know you can't stay here then, right?" He finally focused his gaze on her.

Tears brimming, her face hot and likely red from trying to hide the fear and emotion in this realization. *Dammit, I do know it,* Nina thought to herself as her mind flashed on Hank, of the joy she felt at seeing him earlier. She would never get to see him again. She would never get to hold him or kiss him. But she had a glimpse of what their life could have been. And it wasn't perfect, it wasn't a fairy tale ending. It was real and messy, and now he would change even more by having to mourn her. She thought of her father, so alive and excited to realize a dream of his, so proud of his daughters.

Nina nodded and dared to answer Thurston, "yes." She had to whisper it, because if she gave it any more force, she would be awash in tears. Nina held his hand again for a moment before sitting down at the chair in the corner of the hospital room. After she waited a respectable amount of time and the professor nodded off to sleep, Nina wandered outside of the room and asked a nurse where she could find a cup of coffee. The nurse pointed down one hallway and Nina took the first turn before doubling back and leaving through the side exit.

She found it easier than she had expected to get back home. The police had cleared out by then; she was surprised by how much time had actually passed on the drive over to the hospital and her pained jog back to the lab. She knew exactly what to do, having watched several excellent scientists already accomplish the task.

Nina had the drive, she knew where the vials of supercybin were kept, and she had time to slowly and precisely walk the Portal over to the correct space. And then she just had to wait for the next jitter. While she waited, Nina wrote out an explanation and precise instructions for Dean Winchester.

Take the Portal off of the track.

Wipe the records and frequency logs.

Dr. Thurston will now focus on introductory physics and will no longer conduct research on theoretical physics or cosmology.

She left no further explanation, but Nina knew that Thurston would fill the Dean in on the rest once he returned to work. And then she left.

Nina stood in front of the Portal back in Universe Alpha at 12:30 am, back in her home universe. She did exactly as she had instructed Dean Winchester. She unlatched the clamps and removed the Portal from the track. Heavy and cumbersome, she maneuvered it across to the far side of the warehouse and slid it behind the metal shelves. She left a similar note for Dean Winchester and Dr. Thurston so that they had an explanation as well. Finally, exhausted and unfeeling, she plodded out of the lab at 5:00 am. Nina passed by the twin offices, one for Thurston and one for Parker. She taped her notes and instructions on Thurston's door. Nina glanced over at Parker's door and then kept walking down that long hallway.

Nina slept away the rest of the day, a day that she had already lived several times over. She explained away her absence at work to a sudden head cold, but Carol seemed to think it had to do with her special day, August 8th. Carol was more right than she would ever know.

After Nina accepted that she would never get to see her alter-egos again and realized that it didn't leave any kind of hole in her, she felt able to take action.

She settled on the idea that Parker was gone. Before she had cleared the logs on the University quantum computer, she had reviewed all of the records. It seems that her Parker had been sent out into the void not long after evil Parker, Parker-Beta had arrived. While she knew that her Parker hadn't been the evil one, it was difficult to think of him otherwise. She mourned him in the months that followed and then cleared out his things, his memories.

Her depression rebounded briefly, the new-found confidence and zeal had faltered upon her return. Nina felt painfully alone, with no one to tell her story to. And when two detectives came asking about Dr. Parker Lovett's disappearance, she had to lie, convincingly.

Nina felt the weight of the responsibility to protect the multiverse on her shoulders. But also, the weight of knowledge. *Penelope Whittle, was she alive in this reality? Or Elena Johnson? Did she ever feel that she was meant for more, meant for something Presidential?*

When the Smithsonian opened an exhibit on Eleanor Roosevelt a few months later, Nina had to go. After her return, she spent months learning as much about her as possible. Nina felt close to her in a way, as though her life and her potential was wrapped up in her own.

Nina needed a creative outlet to process the pain. With each action that she took after a decade of swimming idly through life, her world felt more alive. It hadn't been waiting for her, but it was still there, ready for her to join in. Nina signed up for regular yoga classes and got a kitten. She started to leave work on time, in a rush to go home and start something new. A photo class, a trip to Japan, a volunteer project. Nina started living a life with so many more sounds and variables. More people to interact with, more micro-decisions to manage. *Red shirt or green? This bar or the other one that we liked? Do you want to get together some time for a drink?*

Afraid that she would forget all of the sounds, colors, and intricacies of her journey, she began to write it all down. She filled notebooks with furious lines of text, needing to get the words out as quickly as she could before the thought receded back into a dull memory. She debated putting the ring from Hank away, it was never hers. But it was her reminder that it had all happened, it was her reminder that she deserved to be happy. Nina locked the notebooks away with the quantum drive, keeping this cosmic secret to herself. Until now.

This story doesn't end. It is infinite, it is on an ever-playing loop. Just as all lives are lived that way. A memory triggers us to take action in the present, the hope for the future causes us to work harder today. It took a trip across four universes for Nina to realize it:

There is no end.

EPILOGUE

And the day came when the risk to remain tight in a bud was more painful than the risk it took to blossom.

–Anaïs Nin

Xi

A Few Months Later

The sounds of the airport were familiar, although when she focused in on any one conversation the language was foreign and the verbal noise was unintelligible to her. Feminina glided from the baggage claim to the line of waiting taxis effortlessly, her long black hair and loose trench coat flowing behind her.

She arrived at the train station just in time to catch the 8:37 am train to Ghent. Feminina had to fill out a bundle of paperwork to get permission to present her work at the University. All of her experiments with Marie were unconfirmed as of yet, but they were gaining traction. The international community had shunned any research coming out of the United States for decades, but it seemed that the tide was turning in their favor. The presentation in Ghent would go a long way to help build their reputation, not just for her and Marie, but for all scientists in the "Vestal Kingdom" as it had been nicknamed by the international press.

But the presentation wasn't the only reason she was looking forward to her journey. As the views of the Belgian exurbs and suburbs blurred by on the train from Antwerp to Ghent, Feminina thought about everything she had been told about him. Nina had been so confident in her assertion that they had been destined to be together in every reality. Feminina had tried to remind herself that her alter-ego wasn't a scientist; she was a romantic. But who said that a gut instinct, a feeling, couldn't be right every once in a while?

He had been easy to find, one of the many expats whose family had moved out of the United States as soon as the Pink Box Policy, as it was referred to colloquially, was instituted. What parent would want to raise a monster that would attack a woman? But, most of them were concerned that their sons would be maimed and they couldn't stomach that either, so they left. His biography on the University website listed two publications that he had written on the evolution of the American novel from a story of discovery to one of diaspora. She had read them as she weighed her decision to meet him in person.

Feminina had found several speeches he had given on the topic online as well. She tried to hear his voice in her mind as she reread the introduction to his first paper on the train. When she finally arrived outside his classroom, she felt her heart start to beat faster. She fussed with her hair and wondered at how silly she was to not check into her hotel and leave her bag there before attempting this introduction. She checked her watch and tried to figure out how she could get to the hotel, check in, clean up, re-rehearse her introduction, and make it back to that same classroom within two minutes. She had the solution, but the time machine was decommissioned and the pieces all sitting in meticulously cataloged boxes in Marie's storage unit.

The door to the lecture hall swung open and a stream of college students shuffled past, a heavy breeze of hair products and body spray inundating her as they all marched by. After the last student shuffled out, Feminina slipped in, tucking her luggage on the opposite side of the door. The topic on the white board from the lecture read "The American Diaspora: Literature from a Life in Exile."

The professor stuffed some papers into his leather satchel. A failed attempt at organization in the face of just wanting to get a move on. He looked handsome, very scholarly, but still very young.

"Hello," she stammered to get his attention.

He looked up at her quickly, regarding her as a student. "I have office hours on Wednesdays and Thursdays."

Stunned into silence, she expected something more akin to a chemical reaction to occur, eyes to lock, lips to sweat. That kind of thing.

"I'm not-" she began.

"I didn't recognize you as one of my students," he smiled as he started to climb the stairs to where she stood.

"Then why?" Already off guard and feeling foolish, she wanted to fly back to DC, reconstruct her machine, find Nina, and tell her this was all a big mistake and that she never should have infected her mind with such foolish notions.

"Why else would a pretty woman want to talk to a bookworm like me?" His self-deprecating question didn't fool Feminina. He approached her with a captivating smile and swagger of confidence.

Not knowing how to accept such a compliment, one that might have never been spoken in her home country for fear of reprisal, she extended her hand to initiate a formal introduction. "I'm Feminina Marks."

He didn't accept her hand right away, she dropped it. "The physicist who thinks we can travel to parallel universes in spite of the definition parallel meaning that the two can never touch?" He cocked his head to the side, his long hair shifting as he waited for her to respond.

"Ah, yes actually." Impressed that he knew her work, astounded by his blasé dismissal, she didn't know where to go next in the conversation. Especially since it was their repeated connection in parallel universes that she needed to address with him.

"Excellent, I'd love to pick your brain about it." He began to walk towards the classroom exit, expecting her to follow. "Coming along for coffee?"

He finally offered his hand in greeting and told her something that she already knew. "The kids all call me Dr. Jankowski, but you can call me Hank."

Maybe there had been a reaction after all. Feminina smiled and followed him through the door. Another portal crossed, another long hallway to follow.

The story continues…

Check out *The Alpha-Nina*, the next book in The Feminina Series:

Once you know something, you can't unknow it. And Nina Marks is still trying to sort all that she just learned. After her harrowing experience being kidnapped across the multiverse, she finds herself unmoored in her home reality. Her alter-egos aren't faring too well either. Picking up where *The Infinite-Infinite* left off, *The Alpha-Nina* is a sweeping adventure back through time and space.

Can Thurston and Nina really keep guard against future visitors from parallel universes? What happened to Femi, Marie, and Parker once they returned to Universe Gamma? Is Hank okay, and what about the body he found in Parker's basement? And who is driving that non-descript sedan that is trailing Nina all around Washington, D.C.?

The long-awaited sequel to the feminist science fiction masterpiece, *The Alpha-Nina* is the continuation of the time travel saga that makes us all question, "what if?"

Acknowledgements

As I finish getting this book ready for it to head out into the world, I have to marvel at the herculean effort that creating a book takes. This is my fourth published work. I keep expecting that it will get easier each time, but I have found that while the mechanics are the same (write, revise, edit, edit, publish) that the process always feels very distinct.

As I wrote *The Infinite-Infinite,* I meditated quite a bit on how each person is really a collection of all their past selves, all of their future potential selves, and who they are at present. In the years that it took me to write this book (yes, years) I went through my own transformation. From a part-time author with a dream, to a full-time author with a business. From someone sitting on the sidelines waiting to take action, to someone who decided waiting for someone else's permission was silly to begin with. I hope that as you have read this book that you have been able to reflect on how you have changed and dream of all of the possibilities ahead for you.

And, I hope that you will indulge me and take a moment to read through the long list of thank yous that will follow. This book and the world that you just visited would not have been possible without the following people:

Thank you to my amazing husband for his continued support and devotion to my creative pursuits. Thank you for always being my first reader and putting up with the weird things that I say as I consider plot points. Thank you for being the de facto President of my fan club and cheering me on. None if this would be possible without you my dear.

Thank you to my mother who instilled a love of reading in me from a young age.

Thank you to my amazing editorial team. Debbie and Jeff, this book would be riddled with plot holes and errant commas without you. Your work and time dedication to this story have shaped it into a readable book instead of just a pile of my crazy ideas.

Thank you to my wonderful launch team who helped to make this book a success. Each of them supported the book by reading it, providing honest feedback, and promoted it to their network. Thank you to Alexis LaRosa, CA Martin, Chelsea Brett, Jen Kern, Jen Smith, Joel LaRosa, Josh Overmyer, Linzy Anderson-Serby, Lisa Negron, Nikki Pirtle, Omar Negron, Susan Clayton-Goldner, Tori Katen-Narvell.

Thank you to Brian Greene for his lifetime of work in physics and cosmology and for condensing it into something that I could understand. Your recorded lectures and books were instrumental in the development of this book, especially *The Hidden Reality*.

As I started to shape this story, I realized that I needed a mechanism for our hero to realize that something was different, something was amiss. I had initially envisioned a very dark and serious literary novel. But with the recent cancellation of the only television show I had regularly watched in years, *Timeless*, I decided that what I needed most was a fun adventure. I dove into books with alternate timelines and histories. But within a month or so, I had exhausted what was available at my library. With these thoughts rolling around in my mind as I considered where this story would go, the two eventually smacked into each other and gave birth to this multiverse tale. Without those who pioneered this genre, including Michael Crichton, Philip K. Dick, and many others, I would not have been able to forge my own path into this topic. I also have to give a big shout out to all of my fellow *Timeless* fanatics, aka the Clockblockers. I know this story will never compare to the adventures of Lucy, Wyatt, Rufus, Flynn, and Gia; but I hope you find some of their spirit of adventure in these pages.

Thank you to those who have served as a mentor to me over the years. From those who encouraged my writing: Cordelia Biddle, to those who served as instructors from afar through the magic of the internet: Joanna Penn.

I also have to give a special note of thanks to two particular people who have given me the gift of their time. I was fortunate enough to have the opportunity to talk all things writing and author culture with Doug

Nordman. His advice and encouragement gave me the crazy idea that I should leave the fog of work and focus on my real passion: writing. And a big thank you to J.D. Roth who talked some sense into me and inspired me to refine my craft and keep learning new things.

I must end with the most important note of thanks, and that is to you! Thank you for supporting my work. Whether you purchased this book or checked it out from the library, I am extremely grateful that you spent your time with Nina, Hank, Marie, and Parker (and their alter-egos). I will always cherish the time that you have given to this story and I hope to continue to entertain, inspire, and thrill you all for years to come.

About the Author

M.K. Williams is the author of three novels, two self-publishing guides, and one collection of short stories. She has also co-authored a financial independence workbook. You can follow her for more in-depth information on these books at 1mkwilliams.com. To receive updates on upcoming books, please take a moment to subscribe.

If you enjoyed this story, please consider leaving a review for *The Infinite-Infinite*. Each review helps other readers discover this book. Thank you for your support.

www.ingramcontent.com/pod-product-compliance
Lightning Source LLC
Chambersburg PA
CBHW050259110726
47898CB00007B/2467